Dark Hollow Road

Book 3 in Taryn's Camera

Rebecca Patrick-Howard

https://www.facebook.com/rebeccaphowardwrites

www.rebeccaphoward.net

Rphwrites@gmail.com

@Rphwrites (Twitter)

In memory of those found...

Molly Bish (August 2, 1983 – c. June 27, 2000)

Holly Piirainen (January 19, 1983 – August 5, 1993)

Holly Bobo (October 12, 1990-April 13, 2011)

Pamela Jackson

Cheryl Miller

Mitrice Richardson

Hannah Graham (February 25, 1996 – September 13, 2014)

And those still missing...

Brookelyn Farthing

Brittanee Drexel

Rachel Cooke

Ashley Freeman

Lauria Bible

Lauren Spierer

Prologue

As the radio blared George Strait's "Check Yes Or No,"
Cheyenne stood in front of the full-length mirror, gazing at herself
as she adjusted her tank top and shorts. She was glad she'd used
the self-tanner from Bath & Body Works, even if it did make her a
little orange. Orange was better than white. She needed to get to
the tanning bed, and soon. She'd straightened her hair – it hung
down to her waist in a long sheet of molasses, not like the frizzy
mess it usually was. Her eyes, encircled with liner and dazzling
with glitter from Maybelline, stood out from her pale face. Still
watching herself, she sat down on the laminate bedroom floor
amid rejected piles of clothes, and tugged on her red leather
cowboy boots. She continued to hum as the song changed from
George to Jason Aldean.

School was out – for good, too. With graduation three days
past this would be her first official weekend as a free woman. Sure,
college was starting in the fall, but fall was months away. She had
the whole summer to hang out, enjoy herself, not have to listen to
anyone's rules. She didn't even have to go to college in the fall if
she wanted; she could take some time off and just earn herself
some money. She'd thought about that.

But tonight... tonight was what mattered.

There were three hundred people in Cheyenne's high
school, and every one of them would be at her uncle's farm for the
party of the year. Or, at least, everyone who *mattered*. Like Evan.

Nobody cared what they did out there. Some of the kids were even talking about skinny dipping, though the creek would be freezing. Then there was the booze. She had free clearance to stay out all night, if she wanted to. She didn't even have *that* at prom. But she was an adult now. Today was her birthday and eighteen couldn't have fallen at a better time.

A gaggle of giggles echoed down the hall and soon the bedroom door was filled with a handful of teenage girls, each one prettier and younger than the other. "Have you seen my straightener?" a leggy redhead demanded with a pout.

"It's in the bathroom," Cheyenne replied absently. She stood up, turned around, and looked at her backside in the mirror. It was important to make sure you looked good from all angles. She was almost ready.

Being May, it was still a little too cool for her top so she grabbed a jacket, just in case. Her blood was pumping, the anticipation of the night almost more than she could take.

In just about half an hour she'd be sipping on a Bud, dancing around a bonfire, talking to Evan. In just about half an hour she'd be starting her brand new life.

And, by the end of the night, she'd be dead.

Chapter 1

*A*re you sure this is it?" Matt asked, his brow creasing in worry.

Taryn held the sheet of directions in her hand and stared at it again. She was almost certain she'd read them correctly, but the gravel road they were bouncing over was washed out in several places, and they'd been on it for at least ten minutes. Walled by towering trees on both sides, there wasn't anywhere they could turn around; right place or not they'd have to keep moving.

"Yeah, I think so," she mumbled. "Can't back out, can't turn around. We may as well keep going."

"Okay," Matt replied, his voice lacking enthusiasm.

"It's supposed to be a cabin the director of the program owns. They She thought I'd like staying there instead of a hotel," Taryn explained to break the silence, although Matt already knew this.

"Well, it's private enough," Matt winked, casting a good-natured glance over at her, "in case you want to get frisky."

She laughed and batted him in the arm with the directions just as the road opened up before them. "See!" she pointed. "There it is!"

The cabin looked like a Swiss chalet with its gingerbread trim and decks overlooking the sweeping valley. Dense vegetation

3

and a thick forest grew around it, but the lawn was cleared and offered a gently sloping expanse of greenery landscaped with benches, shrubbery, and arbors. "Oh, and it's pretty, too!" she gushed.

A silver Camaro idled in the driveway and when they pulled up a short, plump, middle-aged woman in thick glasses got out and waved. "That must be Thelma," Taryn whispered, even though nobody could hear them. "Be prepared: she's a peppy kind of person."

"Hello!" Thelma called as Taryn and Matt got out. Taryn was eager to stretch her legs, and it felt fantastic, especially after being in the car for almost seven hours. Matt was the kind of person who, once on the road, didn't want to stop.

"This is beautiful," Taryn gushed, turning towards her. "Really. I love it."

"I'm so glad you like it," Thelma beamed, immediately engulfing Taryn into a tight embrace. She eyed Matt with curiosity but was too polite to ask. "We had it built several years ago and don't get to use it as much as we'd like. We *do* like to put guests up in it when they come." Taryn thought a shadow crossed over Thelma's face at this, but it disappeared as suddenly as it came.

Taryn automatically began running the logistics of the place in her head. The small liberal arts college was located half an hour away, but she wouldn't have to go every day. Her classes ran for two months and only took place on Tuesdays and Thursdays. She'd have the rest of the time to spend to herself, something she was greatly looking forward to. The classes were for the community so anyone could enroll; anyone, that is, who had an

4

appreciation for historical architecture and painting. So far there were already twenty students signed up and classes didn't start for another week.

"Well, come on in, and I'll show you around!" Thelma hollered, interrupting her thoughts.

Taryn felt grimy from the drive; her long, red curly hair was greasy and tangled. She yearned for a shower, a bath, anything that included running water and soap. She could also do with some junk food but figured that would have to wait.

The cabin boasted four bedrooms and two living areas. The "formal" living room contained a seating area, an antique chest filled with board games and playing cards, and a picture window that looked out onto the yard. The "family room" had a forty-six inch flat screen television, a computer with satellite Internet, two comfortable floral-print couches that also let out into beds, and a fish tank without any fish.

All four of the bedrooms were at the top of a spindly, winding staircase. While Taryn went up with Thelma to check them out, Matt got busy exploring the kitchen. She could hear his enthusiastic moans of excitement over a bread maker and a waffle iron even a floor away. "He loves to cook," she explained when one particular excited "whoop" echoed through the walls, causing Thelma to jump a little.

"Honey, if you have a man to cook for you, you've hit the jackpot." Thelma patted her arm.

Taryn wasn't sure how to respond, especially since she and Matt hadn't discussed the status of their relationship yet. Did they even have one? She just let the remark go.

The bedrooms were cozy and well-decorated in log cabin style: thick wooden bed posts, mountain landscapes on the walls, rag rugs on the hardwood floors, and patchwork quilts. She placed her suitcase in a room that didn't get the morning sunlight and decided she'd let Matt figure out his own sleeping arrangements.

Thelma continued walking her around, showing her where the thermostat and breaker box were, just in case, and the log pile if they wanted to build a fire. It was November now and getting cold. "Shouldn't be any snow for a long while yet," Thelma laughed. "But you never know. Don't worry, though. If you get stuck we'll come in and dig you out!"

"Good to know," Taryn agreed.

"Listen, I want to give you a day to get settled after your long ride, but tomorrow I'd like for you to come in to town, look around, have lunch with us, and see your classroom. Will that work?"

While Matt brought in the rest of the luggage Taryn got directions from Thelma and made plans for the next day. After she drove off Taryn stood on the front porch and let herself quieten down and just listen. The air was almost completely quiet with most of the birds having already migrated further south. There wasn't another house for miles and the main road was nowhere in sight. They really were out in the middle of nowhere.

"So, what do you think?" Matt asked as he came out and joined her. He stood a few feet away, hands in his pockets, as though unsure of what he was meant to be doing. His tall, lanky frame was a little awkward, and she found the fact that he bit his bottom lip comforting. He certainly didn't give off the vibe of someone who worked for NASA and made the money he did.

"It's nice," Taryn concluded. "Peaceful. So, do you think you're going to be able to stay away from your office for a month? Will they live without you?"

"I don't think so," he smiled. "What about you?"

"I know I couldn't," she laughed.

"So how do you feel? Do you think it's okay?"

Taryn took a deep breath, looked around, and exhaled. "I think so. Miss Dixie and I took some pictures and it all looks okay." She patted the Nikon that dangled at her side. "Not a ghost in sight."

Walking over to him she looped her arm through his and laid her head against his arm. Together, they watched the sun start sliding down behind the trees, the shadows creeping closer and closer.

Matt had built a fire in the living room fireplace and sitting before it was cozy, especially with a full tummy. But Taryn needed some air. And to be alone. It was too cold to stay outside for long, but she slipped on her old Carhartt jacket and pulled a wool cap down over her ears before letting herself out on the front porch.

That far out in the country, without any lights or haze from the city, it was almost pitch black. She'd never been to this part of Georgia before, not even to drive through it. The northeastern side was different in geography than the area around Atlanta she was used to.

Thanks to the moon she could just about make out the faint tree line that encircled the lawn, but the trees were hazy at best now. There were very few night sounds this time of year, but the sky was alive with stars and their brightness was dazzling against the darkness.

Taryn crossed her arms in front of her chest and stared into the night, an unsettled feeling sinking in. It wasn't unlike the feeling of being perched at the top of a roller coaster hill, getting ready to fall down. Matt's lasagna and garlic bread had been delicious, and the cheesecake she'd made for dessert (okay, so technically adding whipped cream wasn't making it, but still...) left her full to the point of bursting. The house was gorgeous, the long ride up not as uncomfortable as she'd thought it would be made it out to be. Thelma had been unquestionably pleasant. She was actually looking forward to the job. She'd never taught before but maybe it was time to try something new.

And yet, something picked at her...

The events over the past six months were enough to make anyone feel a little disconcerted. She'd gone from working in neglected, incredibly interesting old houses with few people for company, the excitement of seeing ghosts and becoming involved in mysteries she still wasn't sure she had all the pieces to. And her beloved camera, Miss Dixie, that had been her constant

8

companion for years, was now helping her lift the veil between this world and the next. Not to mention, of course, the grief of losing her husband. She still dealt with it on a daily basis, although the hard grief was becoming less and less biting these days; the time was passing by more quickly.

And yet...

Things *were* starting to go her way. Matt, her childhood friend of more than twenty years, came through for her at the last minute. He'd always been there for her as a friend but now they were starting down a new road together, one neither of them had a map for. They were both timid in this area, despite that their physical relationship had escalated quickly, but she felt they might be on the cusp of something great. Taryn was excited and stimulated in a way that was completely opposite to the one night stands she had suffered since Andrew's death.

It was no wonder she was confused.

This place, she thought, looking around, had potential. *Maybe this is where the rest of my life starts*, she thought. An owl hooted in the distance, as though in agreement.

And yet...

Miss Dixie hadn't caught any suspicious images in any of the pictures she'd taken around the property that afternoon. The house itself was rather new, built within the past ten years. She'd experienced no bad or unusual dreams since she'd been sleeping (and literally sleeping) with Matt. Call her paranoid, but something was in the air.

"Hello, Queen," Matt called shyly, softly closing the door behind him as he stepped out to join her.

She laughed at his pet name, one he'd given her as a kid when she'd made up a story about descending from Swedish royalty (like she even knew where Sweden was).

"Sorry," she apologized. "I just needed some air."

Matt didn't like to leave her alone for long. He had no problem being alone himself, actually preferred it, but now that she was with him he didn't like to be more than a short distance away. This both charmed and unsettled Taryn, who had gotten used to being by herself most of the time. In a moment of rare abandonment for him, as he was drifting off to sleep one night he'd whispered he was afraid of losing her, of waking up to find she was just a dream.

Still a little unsure what the boundaries were, Matt walked over to her and put his hands in his coat pocket. "It's a nice night. Quiet," he remarked.

"You forget how much background noise there is these days, even in the suburbs," she agreed. "Overhead planes, television sets blaring from next door, car engines, sirens... Of course, living in downtown Nashville with windows that haven't been updated in twenty years, I get it all."

"I like this. I don't get out in the country much. Mom's got about ten acres outside of Little Rock, but I haven't been there in years."

Taryn nodded, understanding. Her parents had been aloof and disinterested in her before their car crash, but they'd loved her and she felt it. And she'd certainly been loved by her grandmother, someone she'd lived with even before the death of her parents. But Matt had gotten a raw deal. He had never felt love

10

or acceptance from any of his family members and they were all still alive.

"I, uh, put my bags in your room. If that's okay," he added quickly, not meeting her eyes.

"It's fine."

"If you want me to sleep in another room I can. I just thought..."

Taryn laughed and stepped closer to him. "I would've gotten in bed with you no matter where you slept."

He smiled and reached out to her, brushing a stray strand of hair back out of her face. "You're just using me for the good night's sleep."

"It's true," she admitted. Taryn had suffered from nightmares her whole life. They only grew worse as she grew older. Sleeping with another body in the bed made things easier. Even as a teenager she'd still crawled into the bed with her grandmother, taking comfort in the skin that smelled like baby powder and Icy Hot.

"Something's bothering me, Matt," she confessed after a few minutes of companionable silence. "I don't know if it's my nerves from being on a new job or something else. I can't put my finger on it."

"What's the problem?" His nose was red and white puffs of air came from his mouth when he spoke. They'd have to go in soon but what she was feeling was better expressed outside, in the open.

"Dread, I guess. Like something bad's going to happen or maybe already has."

Matt studied her, his dark eyes shining through his thick lashes in the glow of the porch light. Cocking his head to one side, he considered. "I think I know what you mean. I am getting a little bit of a vibe myself but, like you, I just can't put my finger on it. . Not yet anyway."

"And you're supposed to be the rocket scientist," she teased.

"And you're the ghost whisperer. Fine pair we are!"

"What do you think it could be?" she began. "Do you think maybe we're—"

Taryn's words were cut off by a hollow, yet piercing, scream that cut through the night air and struck both of them, shaking Taryn to the core and sending Matt a step back from her. The sound echoed, seemingly coming from all directions at once, a thunderous sound that sent Taryn into a funnel of emotions. And then, as quickly as it had come, it faded into the darkness: a snowflake melting in a blaze of heat.

Gathering herself together, Taryn stared wildly out into the night. "Hello!" she called out in shock. "Hello, who's there?"

Thinking only that someone might be hurt, she forgot her fear and started off towards the edge of the porch, ready to jump off and follow the noise. Matt, right behind her, grabbed at her elbow and pulled her back. "Wait," he panted. "Just wait."

"Why?" she demanded, confused and heart racing. "If someone's hurt..."

"It wasn't real," he panted, just a hint of terror in his voice. "Whoever screamed, they're not here. Just stop. Can't you feel it?"

And she could. With Matt's hand on her arm and the warmth of his body so close, she *knew*. Like a bolt of lightning, the truth flashed through her mind: whoever had called out in the night was no longer alive and had been that way for a very long time.

Chapter 2

*T*aryn's workspace for the next two months was bright and

cheerful. The room was large and, with its position on a corner of
the building, was surrounded by two walls of huge windows that
poured in the sunlight. She was provided with oils, acrylics, and
watercolors, and all the brushes and canvases she could possibly
need. Of course, she'd brought her own as well.

Each student would have their own easel and as Taryn
stood in the middle of the room she envisioned setting the space
up so all the students were in a semi-circle around her rather than
in rows. It would feel more comfortable that way, like they were all
in it together.

"I hope this works," the woman who stood in front of her
declared. She was a tall, fiftyish woman with short black hair and
muscular arms that peeked out from her short sleeves. As the dean

of the Art Department, Taryn would be working directly with her, even though the class technically fell under the community education program and was offered to non-students as well as those enrolled in the college.

"It's great," Taryn replied. "Works fine. So tell me about the kinds of students who have signed up already? Are they art students, history students? Local folks who are looking for a hobby?"

"I can assure you," the woman (her name was June) began with pursed lips and a little defensively, "they're all very serious about the class. Even the non-official students."

"Oh, okay," Taryn stammered. "I just wanted to get a feel for who I'd be working with."

Thelma stepped up from behind June and took the reins. "Most of them are art students, although you have some history buffs, too, even an Appalachian Studies student. All of them are interested in historical architecture so, of course, they're thrilled to be working with you. They've all been shown examples of your work and what you do so they're coming into the class at least a little familiar with you and your work."

Thelma blushed at the end of her sentence, and Taryn understood. Undoubtedly, some of them would've signed up just to see what the big deal was with Taryn. Since the events at Griffith Tavern had unfolded, she'd been in several national newspapers and an entertainment show had even aired a piece about her—without her input or permission.

Taryn's official vocation was as a multi-media artist. Individuals and organizations called her in to reconstruct houses and other buildings in poor condition. Of course, she reconstructed them on canvas. In some cases the building was going to be demolished, and her clients simply wanted a beautiful reminder of it. In other situations, however, funds were procured for remodeling and restoring it, and Taryn's paintings were instrumental in helping the architects and contractors "see" what it would've looked like in its prime. This wasn't always as easy as it sounded since Taryn had worked with houses that were missing several key structures – everything from the front porch to an entire wing. A lot of her job consisted of research; she had to be well-versed not only in historical architecture but also in a variety of time periods so she could gain an understanding of paint colors, décors, and adornments. She spent nearly as much time in libraries and online as she did with her paintbrush in hand.

"I've seen your work and it's phenomenal," June divulged, a little of the ice thawing in her voice. "You reconstructed an entire Main Street from the early nineteenth century in that town in Mississippi and most of the buildings were wiped out from the tornado. How *ever* did you do it?"

"A lot of research," Taryn laughed. "Luckily, there were several people in town who had letters and other documents from ancestors from that time period. I used those to piece together some information I already had. And then, well, the rest was using samples of architecture from other surrounding towns that still maintained their downtown buildings. Of course, my imagination helped."

"So I imagine you'll be doing a lot of lecturing, as well as painting," June mused.

"That's what I was counting on," Taryn agreed.

Her classes started soon. After they left the classroom Taryn let June and Thelma show her around the liberal arts building and the "grill" where students ate. The campus was small, but the buildings were historical and Taryn loved the mountains surrounding them and valley they set in. The town itself only had ten thousand people.

"Apple Valley is basically a college town at this point," Thelma explained. "Of course, some people go on to Atlanta for college, but many of the young people stay here. They continue to live at home and attend school. With the price of higher education being so much these days..."

"Yeah, I understand. I'd probably live at home, too, if I were them."

"The largest portion of our students come from out of town, however, for our diverse programs and low-cost tuition. We're top rated in the south and have a terrific work-study program to help out with costs. We're a small town, but since we're right off the interstate we are starting to get built up a little more. There was a time, not too long ago, if you told me the name of a street I could tell you where it was. Now, though, we've grown so much and there are so many suburbs, it seems like they pop up overnight," Thelma said with a hint of sadness, a shadow passing over her face.

"What kind of jobs are here ?" Taryn asked. They were outside now and had stopped under an oak tree, its leaves blowing around them and then sailing off into the gray sky.

"Just the college and a few retail spots. Two factories. We're basically a bedroom town for some of the bigger places now. We used to have a thriving downtown area, a theater, and lots of farms, of course. Those are gone. One of the reasons my husband and I built the cabin out on our land was because we were trying to get away from all this 'progress,'" she laughed. "We'll eventually move out there full-time, but as long as I'm working here we need to be closer."

"What does your husband do?"

"He's an engineer. He commutes to Athens. He used to work at the Linklater factory here. Worked there twenty years until it closed a year ago."

It was a sight Taryn had seen over and over again, and one likely to get worse before it got better. Small towns were dying out and becoming bedroom communities of the larger cities. They were losing their businesses and character and, one day, there would be nothing left of them. Taryn's grandmother lived in Franklin, Tennessee and that's where she considered "home" to be, even though she technically grew up in a middle-class suburb of Nashville. Franklin was one of the few places that had retained its downtown area and local flavor. She hoped it held onto it.

"Do you need anything out at the cabin?" Thelma asked as she walked Taryn to the parking lot. Matt was already waiting for her, the car idling.

"No, we're fine. My, er, friend went grocery shopping while I was here and stocked up. He's anxious to sink his teeth into that fabulous kitchen."

Thelma laughed. "I do love a man who cooks."

"I wanted to ask you something, though," Taryn began timidly. This was only the second time she'd met Thelma and she felt awkward to bring up any of her other "talents," but she had to know...

"What is it?"

"I got a feeling last night. I can't describe it. I just... I don't know," she shook her head. "Maybe it's nothing."

She turned to get in the car but was stopped when Thelma placed her hand on Taryn's shoulder. Thelma's eyes had lost their luster and now she was looking at Taryn, almost pleadingly. Her dark hair whipped around her face and her bottom lip had the faintest of quivers. She looked forlorn, lost. "Did you *see*anything?" she almost whispered.

"No, nothing," Taryn answered, a question in her voice. "I just felt something. Did, did something happen there?"

Thelma dropped her hand and looked away. "I don't know," she replied, her voice trailing off. "I just don't know."

"**I**'m telling you, Matt, something's up," Taryn insisted as they carried the groceries into the house. He'd gone a little overboard, but at least they wouldn't starve. It was the first job she'd ever worked in which she'd have real food and not have to depend upon chains and processed stuff. Matt didn't even know what a Hot Pocket was.

"What do *you* think it is?" he asked, hands on his hips, surveying the cabinets. She wouldn't have to put anything anyway. The kitchen was his domain, and he had a system for where things went.

"I'm not sure," she mused. "Maybe just a local ghost story? An urban legend? I would've pressed harder but, to tell you the truth, she looked haunted herself. It didn't feel like the time."

"Do you feel scared?" His concern was palpable and it sent a twinge of guilt through her. Was she just being too dramatic? Too paranoid? She certainly didn't want him to think of her as a problem child – someone he'd always need to rescue from something.

"No, not scared. Unnerved. That's the word I keep coming back to. Have you felt anything?"

Matt didn't share her talent with the camera, but he wasn't completely shut off from the energies around him. He considered himself open to all possibilities, it's what made him more pagan than anything, and he believed in a greater energy – something bigger than himself.

"A twinge. Just a twinge, I suppose you'd call it. But, if you'd like, I could try harder," he grinned.

She threw a loaf of bread at him, and he caught it behind his back with one hand, with the deftness of a dancer. . "Oh, stop

20

it," she laughed. "You don't have to go down the crazy road with me."

"I'd go down any road with you," he winked. "Even if it involved a straight jacket."

With the last of the groceries in, he set about to putting things in order. Taryn went up to her bedroom and began unpacking her suitcases. She'd already taken most of her art supplies to the college, but she'd left her personal supplies there at the house. Since waking up she'd been overcome with the strongest urge to paint; it had been a long time since she'd painted for pleasure and not just for work.

With her satchel of brushes and paints under one arm and her canvas under another, she stepped outside the bedroom to the balcony overlooking the forest and lawn. It was a gray day, the fog from the morning gone but leaving behind a slate-gray sky without sun or clouds. The leaves were off the trees, leaving them stark and bare. Their pointed branches were brittle daggers against the sky. She could barely see the gravel drive from where she sat so it looked as though the house and bare lawn were an island, the surrounding trees a river of thorns.

It was peaceful. Even with the chill in the air, she felt an inner warmth, just knowing she had an interesting job to go to and that Matt was down in the kitchen, puttering around, doing his best to make the house as cozy and comforting as possible. She occasionally thought of Delphina and Permelia from her last job, but she tried not to dwell. Thinking of them made her sad. She wasn't thinking of Andrew as much these days and that had to be good for her. It was almost as if she'd left the biggest part of her

21

grief behind in Indiana. Maybe she was afraid thinking of him anymore might give the pain a road map back. She'd eventually have to focus on her Aunt Sarah's death and determine what was to be made of her house and property up in New Hampshire, but that could wait. She was also not ready to think about that yet. A little bit at a time...

With a portable CD player beside her, Taryn cranked up Jason Isbell and used the late afternoon to paint a landscape of the surrounding area. She loved the bleakness and solitude of their location and pored those into her brushes. Painting was therapeutic to her. If she was totally honest with herself, she preferred taking photographs, but she wasn't ready to pick Miss Dixie back up and try her out here. The camera picked up the truth, without judgment. Sometimes, to keep her mind still, she needed the canvas. She didn't want to see the truth as it was; she wanted to see the truth as she wanted it to be.

Taryn's mind often ran a mile a minute, as her grandmother used to say, and painting was the only thing that had ever really been able to steady and control it. As she painted she told herself stories and kept a running dialogue in her mind. It wasn't always an important or serious conversation; a few days ago she'd finished a painting by lamenting the state of modern horror and having a completely one-sided argument with the director of the latest slasher film.

It was beginning to grow dark now, though, and she knew she'd need to pack it in. As she gathered up her linseed oil, careful not to spill it, and wrapped her brushes up, her nose caught a whiff of something strong. It was the scent of a large fire, the flames powerful and rich. Someone was burning leaves, perhaps, or garbage. It wasn't an unpleasant smell, and it reminded her that it was late fall, when the warmth of a bonfire cut through the cold air. But when she straightened and looked around she couldn't see any black smoke drifting up through the trees.

Oh well, she shrugged. Someone was burning something somewhere. Maybe, along with her newer sixth sense, her other senses were becoming stronger as well.

Not giving it another thought she went back inside and closed the door behind her.

Chapter 3

$\mathcal{T}$he house was so quiet Taryn thought she could've heard a

mouse sigh. After spending a few weeks in Matt's condo with the close proximity of people around her and the heavy noise of traffic and the occasional airplane, it felt odd to be out in the country again, tucked away from everything.

He was so still beside her that she reached over and touched his back to make sure he was still breathing. The softness of his pajama top was light as a feather under her hand. She was sleeping in a nightgown and it had bunched up around her waist; now the fleece of his pants brushed against her naked leg. She could feel the heat of his skin through the bottoms, and it was somehow comforting.

He snuggled with her in his sleep without even realizing it. Whenever she needed to turn over or get up and go the bathroom in the middle of the night it always took a few seconds to unwind an arm or leg and slide out without waking him up. They'd made love (that's what he called it – she still didn't know what to call it) twice that night. She was exhausted. For some reason, being physical with him always left her feeling drained in ways she'd never experienced before. When she came out from under the haze and activity Taryn found herself feeling parched, dry, dehydrated. She needed to drink and to drink long. Sometimes, before even getting dressed, she found herself in the kitchen, downing an entire can of Coke or drinking juice right out of the bottle, her stomach turned into a bottomless pit.

The first time they'd been physical it had been awkward. She didn't know who started it, since they were more or less asleep at the time, but her money was on herself. In typical Matt fashion they'd actually talked about it first, several days ahead of time. He wanted to; she wasn't sure it was such a great idea. They were both already a little confused as to what they were doing with each other. Her very *presence* was confusing. But they were both lonely and underneath the weirdness of having sex with someone you remembered when they were a genderless child, it didn't sound like an ultimately terrible idea.

She'd told him she'd think about it.

Being a practical sort, he took thought as a step in the right direction and had gone out and stocked up on candles, massage oil, condoms, and lubricant—all of which he proudly brought back in a Walgreens bag and showed her over dinner. She'd tried not to laugh and failed.

Two nights later she'd woken up to find herself topless with her leg hooked around him and his face buried in the softness of her stomach. That time it was quick and to the point but early the next morning, as the sun was just starting to chase away the shadows of the night, they'd tried it again and this time taken their time. It was sweet, slow, and gentle. From then on, it wasn't always slow (or gentle), but it remained sweet. Taryn was afraid of hurting him, but she didn't think she could stop.

She was nervous about starting her new job but hoped once she got started she'd find her groove. And she was excited about being there. Matt was staying with her for two weeks and then returning home for a few days for a meeting he couldn't miss. He promised he'd be back, though, right after. They had no problem with him telecommuting for a while; it was the first time he'd taken an extended period off from work in seven years.

Although Taryn should have, by all accounts, felt content, the gnawing feeling continued. She still couldn't put her finger on it. The house was beautiful, the grounds picturesque, the college staff welcoming... she had Matt there with her. And yet...

Something was off.

She didn't want to over-analyze anything or travel down the road of paranoia, but there was a tinge of apprehension nipping around the late autumn air. She was uneasy, but about *what*, she wasn't certain.

"It will be okay," she whispered aloud. Matt shuddered beside her, and she patted him on the shoulder, comforting him in his sleep. Snuggling in closer, he cupped her face in his hand, and she rested her head against him.

It would be okay. It *had* to be.

*T*he surface beneath her was hard and broken; even just a tiny movement made it creak. A whiff of something unpleasant rose from the grimy floor. She was starting to get a little nauseous but continued to clutch the red plastic cup filled with the bitter whiskey; she wasn't drinking it any longer but having something to hold grounded her a little. She needed to leave soon, she kept repeating to herself, , but she hadn't yet been able to get up.

The flickering candlelight cast grotesque shadows upon the wall, their forms growing and then shrinking again as the flames shimmered.

Male laughter flowed around her; a dense, heavy sound that resonated through the sparsely furnished room and chilled her. She tried to smile along with them, but her face was numb and her lips wouldn't move into anything more than a thin grimace. In the darkness, the familiar faces took on carnival fun house shapes, their features distorted. She shook her head to clear *it as eyes bled into mouths and clown hands slapped legs and waved frantically about in the air.*

She wanted to get up, leave, do something but the voices, the shadows—even the flames—were closing in on her. When she opened her mouth to scream, only the faintest of whispers slid through her dry, cracked lips.

The dream left her cold and panicky. The feeling of almost immediate depression upon opening her eyes slapped her across the face; Taryn felt as though she were in the bottom of a well, seeing the world from far, far away. She didn't know whether she should left herself go back to sleep or jump up and run downstairs to find Matt—human companionship.

She opted to get up.

Her head was pounding, full of something left over from her sleep. Her hip hurt, something that had been occurring more and more often, and she felt rattled. The hardwood floors were cold under her feet, and the chilly air gave her goose flesh, but she didn't stop to throw on her robe or pull on her thick socks. Instead, she went straight for the stairs. Below, she could hear the sounds of Matt in the kitchen as he banged around pots and pans and turned the faucet off and on. The noises were reassuring, a sign there was life in the house.

"Hey you," he smiled as she stalked into the room. Now that she was down there and looking at him, she felt a little silly at her sudden burst of energy and panic.

"Hey," she sighed. It was chilly down there and she regretted not throwing something on.

"You okay?"

"Bad dream," she shrugged, trying not to let how upset she was show. "It's fading." It wasn't, but she didn't feel like discussing it at the moment.

"I'm making pancakes. I was going to wait and make them on your first day of school, but I was craving them this morning. Hope that's okay."

She sniffed the air. "You putting chocolate in them?"

"Of course."

"Sounds good to me!" Taryn wandered over to the refrigerator and took out a cold Coke. She opened it and downed half of it before she'd taken another step.

"I don't see how you can drink that so early," he admonished in obvious distaste.

"Not any different than people who drink coffee and put a lot of sugar in it. It's just cold. And I need the caffeine. Believe me, you don't want to be around me without it."

After they'd finished breakfast she gathered her painting supplies together and placed them on the dining room table. She was running low, but wasn't in the mood to go into town. She would try painting out on the front porch for a while, until it got too cold. Slipping her jacket on, she took what she needed and set her easel up on the wooden floors. It had been awhile since she'd painted trees, or a nature-based landscape of any kind, but she was looking forward to the challenge of finishing it. The sky was plain, devoid of color, and not a cloud broke up the monotony. But the dreariness gave the surrounding fauna an almost ethereal appearance – some branches and brown leaves still holding on, fading into the whiteness with the evergreens stark against the sky, reaching into the white like claws. There would be fog tonight, she could smell it, but for now it was clear. The air was as silent now as it had been the night before, but thick. Heavy. There was a dampness, too, and it closed in around her and settled on her hands and hair, dragging her down until she felt rooted to the porch beneath her feet.

She painted for nearly a half hour without any distractions, lost in the pale world she created on her canvas. Matt was inside doing something, but she didn't feel guilty leaving him alone. He liked his solitude as much as she liked hers, and he was never bored with his own company. He'd read, work, or play his guitar. He wouldn't watch television because that really wasn't his thing, but he'd find some way of entertaining himself. She'd talked to him earlier about her needing some time by herself, and he said he understood. With that being said, he'd left the curtains open so that he could look out at her.

The wind was picking up, causing the branches to sway with more potency. Fallen leaves swirled around on the ground, a multicolored dance moving across the dead grass in a frenzy. Taryn's hands were growing colder, her joints already stiffening and throbbing from the damp. She was just about to start packing it in when she was once again struck by the scent of smoke. It wasn't an unpleasant aroma as it wafted through the trees and curled around the porch, lapping at her. It smelled of fresh wood and something else—maybe aluminum or metal. She couldn't see any smoke but it was so powerful she coughed a little, sputtering into the wind.

"Matt!" she called in the direction of the window, hoping he would hear her. She was afraid to move, afraid the moment would be lost. "MATT! Come here for a second, please!"

She could hear his footsteps coming towards the door and saw the handle turn just as a wail, loud and female, pierced the air.

"I looked around," Matt shrugged. "There's nobody out there."

"You heard the scream," Taryn declared as she paced back and forth across the living room floor. "It was closer this time. And there was smoke."

"I agree about the scream," he drawled, a rare hint of accent creeping into his normally mild, controlled voice. He sat back on the small loveseat, his hands folded neatly in his lap. "It sounded like it wasn't far from the porch. But there wasn't anyone there. As for the smoke, I didn't get that I'm afraid."

"It was a girl, though, right? And not something silly like a coyote or bobcat or whatever could be out here in the woods?"

"I'm not up-to-date on my Georgia wildlife, but I'd venture to say it was a female," he agreed.

Taryn paused and gazed out the window. The fog was setting in now, like she knew it would. She could barely make out their car as the low clouds swooped in and covered everything in their path. "Do you think she sounded... scared?"

"I don't know," he replied, studying her. She could see his uneasiness. "Maybe. It could've been a cry for help. Or..."

"Or what?"

"It could've been something else. We don't *know*, Taryn."

"It's happening again, I know it," she muttered, mostly to herself. She felt keyed up, energized. There were sparks in the air now and they were coursing through her skin and veins. She felt like her entire body was on fire, pummeling her to something she was unsure of. "Miss Dixie..."

"Yeah?"

"I think if I took her out now, I'd catch something," she declared with authority. She was aware that she still wore her old boots and Carhartt jacket. She hadn't felt like taking them off, even though Matt had built a fire and they'd been inside for more than an hour.

"Do you want to?"

"Yes!" she shouted with enthusiasm. And then, a little more subdued, "No. I don't know."

"I'm here if you want to give it a shot. No pun intended."

Taking the stairs two at a time she raced up to their room and grabbed her beloved camera from the bureau. She was more than a little afraid of what she might capture, but she had to know if something was out there. If she took a shot and came back with a bloodied body on their porch or something then they were just going to have find other accommodations for the duration of their stay.

"Do you want me to come with you?" Matt called as she slid out the front door.

"No thanks," she hollered. "I'll be fine!"

The truth was, she wasn't sure if it would work – this capturing of the past – if someone else was with her. It had with Melissa back in Vidalia but that might have just been a fluke. She'd never tried it again with another person standing with her.

Taryn didn't go far as she steadily walked the cabin's grounds and took her pictures. The sound had been so close she was almost certain that if anything was there it would be captured within a few feet of the house. She slowly made a loop around the perimeter, taking shots every few seconds. She aimed the camera at the house, at the ground, and off in the distance, towards the tree line. The fog was even closer now and her flash was distracting as it ricocheted back at her. She turned it off for better results and kept moving, trying to take as many as she could before it got too dark and too foggy for anything to come out.

The scent of smoke was gone now; it had disappeared as soon as they'd heard the scream. Now, the only scent was that of the cold. Her grandmother had possessed a sense of snow and rain. She could smell it as far as two days in advance. "It's coming, a big one," she'd say as they walked out of the shopping mall, her eyes not even casting a glance at the sunny skies above them. "I can smell it."

Sure enough, two days later Taryn would wake up to several inches of snow, a freak storm by the weatherman's account.

Taryn's own sense of smell wasn't really developed. She'd always possessed terrible eyesight to boot. A little ironic considering what she was now picking up.

She was aware of being alone as she walked around, aware of being cut off from everyone despite the fact that Matt was inside, only a holler away. The remoteness of the cabin and property felt more pronounced and a big part of her was conscious of her vulnerability—a small figure walking through a desolate landscape miles from civilization. Shuddering, she turned Miss Dixie off and wandered back to the porch. Matt was waiting inside for her, a mug of cocoa in his hand. "Thought you could use this, adventurous one," he smiled sweetly.

They walked into the living room together, her hands warmed by the mug, the steam rising to her cheeks and prickling them.

He already had her laptop up and running and while she shrugged off her coat and boots Matt popped her memory card into the slot and waited. While the pictures uploaded, she sipped on the cocoa. "Thanks. It's good."

"No problem. Thought it might add to the festivities."

"You think this is fun," she accused, but a smile played at her own lips. It was a lot different with someone else there with her.

"A little," he admitted. "But it also freaked me out. I'd say I'm about half scared, half excited."

34

But the pictures revealed nothing. She hadn't captured a single abnormality in her shots of the cabin and property. Whatever had been out there earlier was gone.

Chapter 4

*C*aryn got to her classroom a little early, nervous about her

first day at school. She hadn't excelled at school when she *was* a
student, at least not until she got to college, so being back in a
classroom was a little intimidating. In true Matt fashion, he'd
packed her a lunch (in a vintage tin Scooby Doo lunchbox, as a
joke) and kissed her on the nose before he pulled away. On most
days she'd drive herself in, but he was in the mood to bake and
wanted to do some exploring. She felt like a little kid being
dropped off by her daddy, but it wasn't a bad feeling.

They hadn't spoken about the previous day's adventure, nor had they smelled or seen anything suspicious since. Indeed, had Matt not heard the sound himself she might have thought she was hearing things. She did have terrible headaches that concerned them both and despite her best intentions of going to a doctor and having them checked out, she hadn't yet. Maybe she was having some kind of petite seizures (she DID occasionally, use the Google) or a crazy parasite eating at her brain.

But then, Matt would have to suffer from the same thing and that wasn't likely.

While she waited for her students to arrive, she arranged the chairs and easels in a semi-circle, placing herself at the top. She wanted them to feel like she was a part of the group, and not necessarily an instructor. Taryn was a little confused as to why she'd been asked to do the job; she had zero teaching experience. She was no stranger to speaking in front of groups, though, so she hoped she could just fake her way through the actual teaching part.

While she set up the computer and ran through her PowerPoint presentation the first wave of students began trickling in. Most appeared to be in their late teens and early twenties, although at least two had gray hair and appeared decades older than their counterparts. They all wore comfortable looking, casual clothes: sweaters, jeans, tennis shoes, and hoodies. Some had wet hair while others wore dirty, faded baseball caps.

She felt overdressed in her red layered skirt, black sleeveless shirt, and white cardigan. She'd spent an extra half-hour trying to tame her hair and even applied makeup in an effort to make herself not only presentable but professional-looking. Taryn, used to working alone, had forgotten what it felt like to care about her appearance on the job. Matt had "oohed" and "aahed" over her and playfully tried to tug her back to bed with promises of delicious things he'd like to do, but she'd swatted him away, secretly pleased at the lavish compliments.

Feeling awkward and shy, she busied herself with the computer screen until the last student settled themselves into a desk and the clock showed her it was a minute past class time.

"Hi everyone," she looked up and smiled, raising her fingers in a small wave. "I'm Taryn Magill. Not 'Miss Magill' or 'Professor Magill' or anything like that. Just Taryn. Just so you guys know, I've never really done anything like this before. This, uh, is my first go at it. I'm very excited to be here, of course, and, uh, hope you enjoy the class..." She was rambling and knew it and could feel her face grow red and hot. The sea of college kids gazed back at her with polite interest. Some had notebook paper out and their pencils were raised. *Good Lord*, she thought. *I hope they don't expect me to say anything interesting...*

"So, um, today I thought we'd just go over what I do a little bit. I'm going to show you some pictures I've taken, along with some paintings I've done of those places. Of course, yours don't have to look like mine or anything. Yours will probably be better!" Her joke fell flat, though, as only a few people cracked good-mannered smiles. "Um, anyway... Let's get started!"

The first few images she showed them were of older houses she'd taken pictures of early on in her career. She was careful to avoid using any examples of places she'd worked on with Andrew.

38

Although she felt like she'd come to a better place in regards to her grief, she still felt fragile enough that she didn't want to rock the boat. Besides, there were enough images that she didn't have to rely on those.

It was easy talking about the buildings, why she'd taken on the jobs she had, and what creativity she'd needed to use to "reconstruct" them. She was in her element.

"See this house?" she asked, pointing to an American Foursquare in Nashville. "Nothing structurally wrong with it. As you can see, everything is still intact. Well, the inside was a little rough, but that's another story," she smiled. The students laughed.

"I was hired by a couple, newlyweds with money, to do this rendering." She flipped to the next image, which showed her painting. "They wanted to restore the house, which was looking tired and worn, to its original splendor. And they wanted to be as historically accurate as possible. So, as you can see, in my painting I added the shutters, mended the porch and columns, patched up the roof, and repainted it. They knew the original color was this dark green and my painting helped them see what the final result would be."

A young man directly to her left raised his hand. "So after you did this, did an architect or contractor come in and make the changes based on your painting?"

"That's normally what happens," she replied. "But in this case the couple was a DIY pair who loved HGTV and they did most of the work themselves. I should add, too, that this was a very quick job for me. They only wanted the front of the house done. It took me about two weeks and since I live in Nashville I didn't have to leave town. Not only did they want to see what the finish product would look like, they wanted something nice to hang in the foyer, too."

"So you're kind of like a plastic surgeon," a girl with honey-colored hair said. ."Except instead of showing 'after' images, you show 'before' ones."

The other students laughed, Taryn along with them. "You can look at it like that, yes."

The young man who'd spoken earlier gazed at her thoughtfully, his chin resting on his hand. "I imagine you have to have quite a bit of historical architectural knowledge to be able to do this job, right? And know about a LOT of different time periods and house styles."

"Yes," she nodded. "I'm constantly researching and learning something new. I've worked in Arizona, New Mexico, San Francisco–places where the architecture can be vastly different than what I grew up with in Nashville. After all, I grew up in a subdivision where all the houses looked the same. So yeah, there's a lot of research involved. I'm not just an artist; I'm also a historian to an extent."

"And an urban explorer." The statement came from a petite redhead with a long, peasant skirt and a leather jacket. She smiled shyly at Taryn when she looked at her. "I'm sorry. I Googled you."

"I'm not as much of an urbex as I used to be," Taryn admitted. "The cost of gas and too many spiders put a stop to that. But I do love exploring old buildings and taking pictures. I like to imagine what a place used to look like, before it became neglected. That's why I went into this job."

The redhead smiled in agreement. "Me too. That's why I signed up for your class. I love your photography, especially the pictures of the old mental institution up in Danvers."

Taryn noticed other students making notes now. *Great,* she thought wryly. *Now they're all going to go home and Google me for sure.*

The hour and a half passed by faster than she'd expected. Most of the students came up to her afterwards and welcomed her to the college. The redhead was the last to leave and held back a little, waiting for everyone else to leave the room.

"Hi," she offered hesitantly as she made her way up to Taryn. "I'm Emma. I'm an Appalachian Studies major here. I just wanted to introduce myself and say how much I'm looking forward to this."

"It's nice to meet you, Emma," Taryn replied, a little thrilled someone was excited about actually coming to hear her talk. "Do you enjoy painting?"

"I dabble in it a little. I'm not that good," Emma laughed, "but it's therapeutic. To be honest, I'm here because of your..." Emma let her sentence drop as her face flushed red and she looked down at her scuffed boots.

"My what?"

Emma shrugged, her thin shoulders small in the heavy jacket. "Because of what happened to you in Indiana. I saw it in a chat room. I'm sorry, I know you probably don't want to talk about it, but I think it's amazing."

"Oh." Feeling awkward now, Taryn perched on the edge of her desk. "Well, I don't know what to say. I mean, I don't know if I did that much. I was just kind of there, you know?"

"With your camera," Emma nodded. "It must be wonderful to see the past through it like that."

"Sometimes," Taryn admitted sardonically. "But I don't seem to have much control over it." She thought about the night before—the smoke, the scream.

"It's not just because of the ghost stuff," Emma continued in a hurry. "I also love old houses, exploring, and what you do is amazing. I mean, your actual work is amazing. So I couldn't pass up this opportunity."

"Well, I'm glad to have you, whatever brought you here," Taryn resounded warmly. She *felt* awkward, but Emma looked it, and she didn't want her to be uncomfortable. "Can we kind of keep what happened between the two of us, though? For now?"

"Yeah, yeah, no problem. I understand. See you Thursday!"

Taryn was left alone in the quiet classroom, the circle of desks staring at her.

Matt prepared a "first day of school" feast for her back at the cabin. It consisted of her favorite foods: mashed potatoes, macaroni and tomato juice, salmon patties, and peanut butter pie.

She was going to gain forty pounds if she continued to eat like that, though. She'd have to cut him off at some point.

Sitting around the fireplace afterwards, her feet in his lap as he thoroughly rubbed every inch of them, they talked about their days. Or rather he talked and she tried to respond, as waves of relaxation coursed through her feet and legs pulling the thoughts right out of her brain. "It's a nice town," he concluded. "Small, not a lot there other than the college and a few stores, but you can tell it used to be really something. I saw a couple of old homes you're going to want to go back to and take pictures of. I made notes."

"I hope," she gasped out the words as he ran his thumb down the middle of her sole, "you're not going to be," she reached again as he massaged the center carefully, "too bored hanging around here while I work," she finally finished somewhat discomfited at his effect on her ability to talk coherently.

"I'll be fine," he declared with a wave of his hand. "I do have to go back next week for two nights and when I do I'll pick up some more books for myself. Get my marble slab."

"What's ... that... for? You planning... on whacking somebody... in the head?"

He looked as her like she'd grown two heads. "To make candy," he sputtered.

"Oh, uh, yeah..."

Later, they sat for nearly an hour without talking, the radio set to an oldies channel, both reading their own books (his: *The Forever War*, hers: *Flowers in the Attic*) and enjoying the warmth from the fire. It was cozy and intimate, and Taryn's belly was still

43

full from supper. She had no reason to feel insecure or unsettled. Yet, she did.

"Something's wrong," she declared after a while, looking up from her book. It was the same statement she'd made on their first night but it hadn't gone away. She'd read the same paragraph half a dozen times, not a big deal since she practically had the book memorized, before she'd given up on it.

"What do you mean?" Matt asked absently, focused on the words in front of him yet still managing to rub her foot at the same time.

"I *feel* like something's wrong," she insisted. "I still can't explain it."

He patiently bookmarked his book with a receipt and placed it on the end table next to him. Turning his dark brown eyes to her, he studied Taryn intently. "You want to try?"

"I feel... disconcerted," she finished lamely. "I don't know. Maybe I'm just restless or something."

"You want to go back out and try to take some more pictures?"

"No," she shook her head. "I don't think it will help anything."

"I wasn't going to say anything earlier because it wasn't a big deal, but I felt something myself this morning. While I was fixing breakfast," Matt explained.

"What?' Taryn asked, fascinated. Matt's beliefs in the paranormal were uncertain. He believed in her, for sure, and had an extremely open mind but so far hadn't really experienced anything himself that he couldn't explain. He claimed that when he showed up at Griffith Tavern, and was trying to get in to her on that last night, he'd seen the faintest flicker of a shadow cross over his line of vision, but it hadn't been anything substantial. And, of course, the door had given him some trouble. But his rational mind had chalked it up to age and nerves.

"I was here in the kitchen and felt like someone was watching me. Not in a threatening kind of way. Just like, I don't know, like maybe they were curious about me. Just wanted to see what I was up to. And then I felt sad. It hit me all at once, like a ton of bricks. The feeling didn't last long, just a few seconds, but it was there and it unnerved me."

Taryn felt the blood pushing at her temples, the beginning of a headache. "You think there's something here, then?"

Matt's eyes clouded over and he caught his breath, as though hesitating. "Maybe..." he admitted, slowly. "But it might not be anything, you know. It might just be a... presence," he finished lamely.

"I don't normally feel or sense something unless it wants something," Taryn pointed out. She stood up in front of him, gazing down. Every so often she was struck at just how beautiful he truly was. Matt, with his dark eyes, thick hair, smooth skin...

45

She'd known him since they were children and occasionally she found herself forgetting he was a man; she still saw him the same way she had when he was ten. It was different in bed. With the lights out and the silky thick curls of his legs on her bare skin he was all man. But in the daylight, here he was: Matt, young at heart and as safe as a childhood blanket.

"It doesn't have to be scary, though," he lectured softly. He reached up and took hold of her hand, his palm sliding over her wrist and down to her fingers. It was a soothing gesture, one he'd been doing for a long time. The familiarity of him and his touch was enough to have the oncoming pain in her head subside.

"At any rate, I think my class will be okay. Nobody fell asleep or threw tomatoes at me. No anarchy."

"Well, there's still time," he teased.

Laughing, she plopped down and pulled him along with her, resting her head on his shoulder.

Chapter 5

$\mathcal{OS}$ince her class didn't meet every day, she had the next day

off. "I've got to get myself on some sort of schedule," she mumbled
sleepily as she gazed at the digital clock next to the bed. It was
almost 2:30 pm. She'd been up half the night watching the
Hallmark Channel. It wasn't even Halloween yet, but they'd
already started showing their holiday movies and she was a sucker
for those, the more saccharine the better. It was an illness, she was
sure.

Matt was gone but had left her a note; he'd be back in a few hours. All alone in the house, she decided to get dressed and take herself for a walk. The air was chilly and on its way to being downright cold, so she made sure to bundle up. After slinging Miss Dixie around her neck, just in case, she stepped out into the bitter wind and began making her way around the property.

There wasn't much to see within close proximity to the house. She'd seen most of the yard already. The trees that formed the barricade against the rest of the world were leaning gently away from the wind, except for the evergreens standing proudly, boasting their greenness and showing off to the others. The gravel road was starkly white against the brittle, dry ground and looked freshly laid. The owners did a good job of keeping the place up, especially since they claimed not to use it often.

After walking the perimeter and taking a few casual shots of the house, grounds, and sky she ducked into the thicket of trees. There were several paths in the woods, made by four-wheelers if she were to guess, since the deep ruts were parallel to one another.

Inside the trees the air was still and not as cold, since the wind had trouble penetrating the thickness. Still, she huddled deeper inside her jacket. Taryn didn't mind being by herself on a walk; indeed, she enjoyed it. There were few things she liked better than being alone with her thoughts, taking walks, and capturing pictures. With her ongoing dialogue with herself, sometimes aloud, she often worked out her problems.

Not that she really felt like she had any problems at the moment. Her bills were all paid, for once, and she even had a little extra spending money.

But, like most women, Taryn was a brooder and a thinker and it was hard for her to be content; she was always worrying about something. Had she remembered to turn the stove off when she left? What would she do for money once THIS job ended? Where was her relationship with Matt going? She needed to get up to her Aunt Sarah's house and see what needed to be done about the estate and that was weighing on her mind. Why did she continue getting these awful headaches and were her joints really hurting more than usual? Was her favorite character on her favorite television show really going to get killed off? Who all did she need to send Christmas cards to this year?

She was so lost in her thoughts she didn't realize how far she'd gone or how long she'd been out, until she stopped and looked behind her. And couldn't see the entrance where she'd come in. The sky was growing gloomier overhead, it was getting darker faster these days, and her toes and fingers were growing numb. A glance at her watch showed her she'd been out for more than an hour. Matt might be back by now, or at least on his way home, and she was hungry.

Taryn was just about ready to turn around and start back, when something up ahead caught her eye. The light was a little brighter there and the trees thinner, suggesting an opening. Thelma had told her there wasn't another house or business for miles and she knew she hadn't walked that far – maybe half a mile at most. Curious, she quickened her pace and continued on. Although she assumed it was probably just a field, Taryn was feeling a little adventurous When Matt got home she wanted to be able to say she'd done something with her time while he was gone.

49

Only it wasn't *just* a field. When she reached the clearing, the land opened out in front of her and revealed a farmhouse.

It wasn't architecturally interesting by any means, and certainly hadn't been lived in for many years, but Taryn was instantly drawn to it. An old, abandoned farmhouse? That was just her thing.

Taryn walked closer, snapping pictures as she neared the structure. It was in remarkably good shape from the outside, despite the fact that the once white facade was now a dingy gray and the windows had almost all been broken out, leaving shards of glass on the ground that she had to tiptoe around.

The roof was missing some pieces and there was a gaping hole over the back, but the porch was sturdy and when she stepped on it, none of the boards buckled under her weight. The front door was missing, letting her peek inside. It was definitely empty, but she didn't feel like exploring any farther at the moment. She'd save that for another day, a day when she was trying to find something to do with herself. She might want to take pictures, after all, and the current lighting situation was not ideal.

About one hundred feet away to the left of the house she caught the remnants of a bonfire pit, complete with blackened beer cans and food wrappers. Logs were positioned around it in a circle. Multiple tracks in the grass suggested a variety of vehicles coming and going to this spot. In front of the porch was a very large stack of wood, suggesting more activity to come. A popular party site, then, although it didn't appear to have been used for a while. The house didn't look to be damaged by anyone; the windows could have come out for a variety of reasons. There were no signs of vandalism.

Hands on her hips, Taryn surveyed her surroundings with an eye for detail. It was a beautiful spot, isolated enough from the main road to offer quite a bit of privacy and flanked by the woods and fields. The remains of a barn could be seen in the distance, and Taryn could imagine a time when this had been a working farm with a rich vegetable garden, grazing cattle, and maybe even horses running through the tall grass. If she closed her eyes she could catch the smell of bacon wafting out of the house on Sunday morning, see a lazy hound dog sunning himself on the porch, hear the flapping of towels and sheets as they dried on the line. This had once been a home and a family had lived here, laughed here, and worked here. Now it was empty, nothing more than a vacant shell. It made her sad in the pit of her stomach.

Before it got too dark Taryn walked around a little more and took pictures of the towering chimneys, littered fire pit, and deep tracks in the grass. Then, realizing she'd spent far more time than she'd planned, she turned and headed back for the woods. It had been quiet she had walked around the remains of the farm, almost eerily so, but the moment she stepped inside the trees the silence was cut by a wail so deep and loud it penetrated her down to the bones and made her jump nearly out of her skin. In shock, she turned around, fully expecting to see a woman standing just feet from her, clearly in agony. But there wasn't another soul for as far as she could see. The farmhouse, dark and dreary against the pale sky, was the only thing watching her. And if it had secrets, it wasn't talking.

Without another thought, Taryn turned back to the woods and began moving her feet as quickly as she could.

Matt was waiting for her inside when she got back to the cabin. "It's not our imaginations," she proclaimed as she burst through the front door, her cheeks flushed and cold.

He'd been sitting in one of the overstuffed recliners but stood up as she drew closer to him. She thought she could see a trace of worry of his face and silently cursed herself for not leaving him a note. She wasn't used to living with another person who might care where she took off to.

"What do you mean?"

Taryn gently unwound Miss Dixie from around her neck and placed her on the coffee table. She let Matt help her with her jacket and boots while she talked.

"The sounds and stuff we heard? It's not just our imaginations and it isn't nature getting the best of us. I heard something today, real close. Oh! And I found a house," she added. Stopping for a moment, she turned and faced the kitchen and sniffed pointedly. "Food. I smell food."

"Chinese take-out," he waved in the general direction of the kitchen. "What did you hear? And what house? How far did you go?"

Trailing behind her, he followed her into the kitchen and watched while she helped herself to the cartons he'd lined out on the counter. "About half a mile maybe? Not as far as I thought I'd gone at first. And the house is an old farmhouse, empty. Looks like it's been that way for a long time. The noise was definitely a scream. Or a shout. But something of that nature."

She waited while he fixed himself a plate and then they traipsed into the dining room. He'd already poured glasses of wine and they were waiting on the table. "Oh, man," she apologized, realizing the trouble he'd gone to. "Sorry about making you wait. I actually thought I'd beat you back here."

"Don't worry about it. So the scream or shout... male? Female? Age?"

She hadn't realized how famished she was until she took the first bite and then she didn't want to stop. "Don't know," she shrugged, trying not to talk with her mouth full but unwilling to slow down. "A woman if I had to bet money."

"Scared?"

"Maybe. Same as before."

Matt gazed down at his spring rolls and noodles and contemplated. "If the house is old then there's the chance something could've happened there. That might explain what we've been hearing here."

She nodded, took a sip of wine. "Yeah, I thought about that. I wonder what it means, though."

"Maybe it doesn't mean anything."

Taryn sighed and downed the rest of her wine. "You mean you think maybe ..."

"That maybe you're just going to have to accept the fact you're tuned in to these things now, and they're going to be on your radar. Or you're going to be on theirs, depending on how you look at it. Not everything is going to mean you have to do something about it."

"Yeah, I get what you're throwing down," Taryn smiled.

"Are we gangster now?" Matt laughed, his eyes bright and warm.

"Just making sure you're still paying attention."

"The man on the beach last month..." He let his voice trail off, and Taryn lost herself in the memory. It was sunset and they'd been on Ormond Beach, taking a walk. She preferred that stretch of sand because it was rarely crowded, almost dead in the late fall, and it was a place where she could stroll and get her feet in the sand without stepping on anyone, or any*thing* --like a beer bottle.

Matt had walked beside her, the wind whipping his hair and throwing it in his eyes. He'd been humming that Kenny Chesney song about the summer romance, the line about Mary liking to carry her shoes in her hand to feel the sand beneath her feet. Between the pleasant sound of his singing and the gentle lapping of the water against the shore, she'd felt peaceful, despite the chill.

It had been a good moment, all in all. Then there'd been a man up ahead of them. His back was to them and he was staring at the water. Nothing unusual about him. Taryn had instantly felt for him though, the way his shoulders slumped and the distant look on his face as he watched the waves. Matt didn't seem to notice him. They were within fifty feet of the stranger when she'd looked over at Matt to say something, make some joke. Then, when she looked back, the man was gone. She hadn't seen him disappear; one minute he'd been there and the next minute he hadn't.

"That time it didn't mean anything, probably," she agreed. "I never saw him again, he didn't say anything to me. It was just a moment."

"And you will probably have more of them," he concluded.

Taryn thought about his, mulled it around her head. "Yeah, but you didn't see the guy. And you heard or felt something here. That *might* mean something," she pointed out at last.

"It might," Matt agreed. "But until it does, let's try not to make a big deal out of it. Let's just enjoy ourselves."

Taryn intended on enjoying herself. She enjoyed her dinner, her extra glass of wine, the nice long bubble bath she took while Matt cleaned up (hey, he insisted and she wasn't going to argue), and even enjoyed putting her notes together for her next class. While she went over them and perfected her Power Point presentation, she let her pictures from that afternoon upload. It wasn't late yet and she had plenty of time to play around with some of them, if any happened to be any good.

Closing down her presentation and exiting out of the web browser she was using for research, Taryn popped her knuckles and stretched her arms over her head. The pictures were finished uploading and she could take a look at them.

It only took two of them to pop up on her screen before she jumped up off the bed and let her feet hit the floor with a thud. "Matt!" she called down the stairs, letting her voice rise over the sounds of Shakira. Matt liked to dance while he cleaned, something she found endlessly entertaining. "Matt!"

"Yeah?" he hollered back, gliding out into the living room in his socks. "What's up?"

"Come on up here. I think we can start making a big deal out of it now."

Chapter 6

On the past, Taryn had always emailed her pictures to Matt so that he could take a look at them and help her try to figure out what was going on. This was the first time he'd ever been there in person, a front seat ticket to all the action. If he was shocked he wasn't showing it, although he did crawl onto the bed and sit as close to the computer screen as possible, his brows furrowing and his fingers tapping repeatedly in a frenzied pattern on his knee.

"Well," he nodded at last. It was a statement.

Taryn, looking at his face to get his reaction rather than the computer screen, let out a big sigh. "So what do you think?"

"It's hard to say," he muttered. "I mean..."

Taryn let out a grim laugh. "I know what you mean."

Her pictures of the house showed nothing but the way it looked now. Her pictures of the bonfire debris, however, were another story. Standing on the edge of the charred sticks and logs, the faded beer cans, and cigarette stubs was the image of a young woman, maybe even a teenager. Her long black hair was tied up at the nape of her neck in a ponytail. Her legs extended from a pair of shorts and ended in cowboy boots. A jacket was tied around her waist. By the way she was staring at the fire (which, in the picture, was roaring and shooting its flames up into the sky) she looked pensive, possibly even worried.

The image was much clearer than other shots Taryn had taken in the past. Even the details of her jacket and shirt were plain. Except for the fact that in a few places you could see through her to the trees and barn on the other side of the fire, at first glance she might've looked like a real, living person.

The mystery girl was in one more shot. In this one, she sat crossed-legged in the grass, her hair down and spilling around her shoulders, almost touching the ground. Her face could be seen in full detail in this one and while it was an exceedingly pretty face, she appeared tired with just a touch of sadness. She leaned forward, her head resting on her hands, her elbows on her knees. Her jacket was on in this one, her hair loose around her shoulders.

There wasn't anyone else in any of the other pictures.

"She looks young," Taryn offered. "I'd say a teenager maybe. Very pretty."

"Do you think she's..." Matt couldn't even finish the sentence.

"Dead?" Taryn supplied for him. "Maybe. My first thought would be something someone who used to go there a lot, has a special tie to the place."

"What about the bonfire?" Matt mused.

"That's creepy as hell," Taryn muttered. The thought of the pretty young girl losing her balance and falling into the flames (or worse, pushed) was terrifying.

Taryn herself was nervous around fires. She liked to watch pretty ones in a nice, contained fireplace with a smoke alarm and fire extinguisher handy nearby but she didn't really get into the whole bonfire thing. The way it could grow taller and taller, reaching for the sky, with little to contain it was something Taryn couldn't get on board with. Not to mention the heat. Despite the fact she couldn't swim, she preferred the water, although that opened up a whole other can of fears for her.

Matt busied himself by flipping through the pictures one by one, just in case Taryn had missed something. He couldn't find anything.

Unable to reach any kind of conclusion, Taryn sighed. "I think I'm going to go watch TV for a while." She bounced off the bed and threw on her robe and house slippers. They had cat heads at the end and were hard to walk in, but they kept her normally frigid feet toasty warm. Matt actually wore matching pajamas and a complimentary robe. Together, with Taryn in her flannel nightgown, they figured they looked pretty much the way they would when they were elderly. She knew she should probably invest in sexy lingerie, but she loved flannel and nightgowns that dragged the floor; they made her feel like she was stepping back in time.

She left Matt on the bed, still mesmerized with the shots. Knowing him, he'd spend at least an hour scrutinizing them and making notes before he wandered back out of the room, full of theories.

Back in the living room, Taryn plopped down in front of the television and flipped through the limited number of channels. She managed to find an old black and white movie called "The Uninvited" and although it was a ghost story, and probably not something she should've been watching considering the circumstances, she loved it.

If only *real* ghost stories could be as neatly wrapped up as the ones on TV, she thought. And if only cheap seaside mansions like the one in the movie truly existed. She wouldn't mind chasing after ghosts if it meant she got to live in a mansion by the water and have tea time on the terrace every day.

Wearily, Taryn rubbed at her throbbing temples and thought about the teenager her camera had captured. Who was she? What happened to her? Did she want something from Taryn?

The last question was a no-brainer. Of course she wanted something. They always did.

Taryn's students were waiting for her when she entered her classroom two minutes late. They already had their notebooks out, polite expressions on their faces.

"Sorry I'm late," she apologized as she set up the computer. "We got behind a tractor coming in."

Everyone nodded their heads in understanding. Slow tractors and school buses were a given when one was running late in a small, rural town.

"I had to take a piss once," a guy in overalls called out. "Got behind a tractor with about two dozen bales of hay on it. Didn't think I'd make it. Finally, after about ten minutes of driving 5 mph, I emptied out a Coke bottle and used it behind the wheel."

"Good thing your aim was good," a girl with long black hair braided on both sides snickered. The rest of the class laughed, including Taryn.

"Nothing worse than having to use the bathroom when you're out in the middle of nowhere or behind slow-moving traffic," she agreed.

Today, she planned on showing the students some of the paintings she'd done of houses that were almost completely destroyed and missing key architectural structures. Then she had a little assignment for them.

"First I'm going to pass out some of these magazine pictures," she lectured. "Pick one out you like then pass them on to the next person. I'll talk while you're doing that."

It only took ten minutes for her to go through her lecture. She showed them five images, each one including a house or building with severe damage. First, she showed them the photograph then she showed them her painting. They all appeared to be duly impressed.

"Okay, now we're going to do a little art project. You just need a pencil for this one," she advised. "First, I want you to look down at your image. As you can see, it's a woman's face cut in half. Some of you all have pictures cut vertically so that you can only see one eye, half the nose, and half the mouth and chin. The rest have pictures where the image is cut horizontally so you get half the nose and both eyes. What I want you to do on your paper is place your image in the middle and draw the missing half. When you're finished, you should have one complete image of a woman."

Smiles flashed on most of the students' faces as they dug out their pencils. "I'm not good with faces," one guy professed as he studied the picture of Christie Brinkley he'd chosen. "It won't be good."

"It doesn't have to be good," Taryn promised. "I'm just trying to get you all in the mindset of figuring out what the other half looks like just by looking at the limited amount of information you possess."

She gave them twenty minutes for their assignment. While they drew, she hunted through her computer image files and studied them. For her next assignment, she was going to post five images of five different architectural styles and have them draw the houses as quickly as possible. This would help them learn the various time periods and what was popular during those times of construction.

The only sounds she could hear were the chattering of students from down the hall as another class was released and the faint scratching noise of pencils hitting the paper. "Mind if I turn on some music?" she asked. "I can't go long without it."

The students nodded their heads and kept working.

Taryn chose her Jason Isbell CD and turned the volume down low so that it wasn't overbearing. She didn't know how she'd gone so long without discovering him but at the moment she was hooked on his voice.

By the time class let out she had a good handle on what her students were capable of. Most of them were quite good and the others made up in heart and enthusiasm, what they lacked in skill.

When they began packing up their stuff to leave, Taryn called Emma to the front of the classroom. The redhead was wearing a pair of beige capris, penny loafers, and a Nitty Gritty Dirt Band T-shirt with the words "Fishin' in the Dark" on it. She looked surprised that Taryn wanted to talk to her, but she waited until everyone was gone before she approached her.

"I loved the class today," she confessed shyly. "I'm sorry my picture isn't very good. I guess I'm not much of an artist."

Actually, Taryn thought it was very good and told her so "But don't worry," she added with a laugh. "I'm not going to hang them outside in the hall."

Emma relaxed then and perched her slender body on the edge of a desk. "Did you need to see me for something?"

"Yeah, you got a minute?"

Emma nodded. "I don't have to be anywhere for at least an hour."

Anxiously twirling a strand of curly hair around her forefinger, Taryn hesitated. She didn't want to put the girl on the spot but she wanted to talk to someone. "Okay," she began at last. "I have a question and was hoping you might be able to answer it."

"Shoot!"

"So the woman whose cabin we're living in. Do you know where it's at?"

"Sure," Emma replied. "I grew up around here. Everyone knows that area."

"Not far from the cabin, through the woods, there's an old farmhouse. Do you know it, too?"

A shadow passed across Emma's face, but she smiled. "We call it flat rock. Because out back behind the barn there's a pond with, you know, a big flat rock." Both women laughed. "Seriously, though, that was always the party place. Kids from school here, and even from other counties, would go out there and party. Innocent stuff, you know. Just drinking, dancing, making out."

"I know about those places. I was young once, too," Taryn grinned. "Although I was never popular enough to get invited."

"Yeah, neither was I," Emma admitted. "But I went anyway. Some friends of mine thought it might be fun to crash it. Once we got there we figured out nobody cared who you were as long as you brought booze."

"Well, so here's my question..." Taryn bit her lip in nervousness. "Did anything bad ever happen out there? Like an accident?"

64

"Are you talking about Cheyenne Willoughby?" Emma asked her in uneasiness.

"I don't know. Am I?"

Emma nodded her shiny hair bouncing on her shoulders. "Probably. She died last year. Well, a little over a year ago to be exact."

Taryn shuddered but felt vindicated. "What happened? And what does the farm have to do with it?"

Pursing her lips, Emma looked down and studied her shoes. *Great*, Taryn thought. *I've made her completely uncomfortable and put her on the spot. Terrific teacher I am.*

"Well, the thing is, nobody knows. I guess to say she died is a little premature. To be honest, her body was never found. Everyone just assumes she's dead," Emma finally said.

"Disappeared?"

"Yeah, more or less. She was there for a party not long after graduation. She didn't come home that night or the next day. Nobody's heard from her since," Emma explained. "Because of what happened that night, we mostly just assume she's dead."

"What happened?"

"She was at the farm and then left with another guy. He claims she never went home with him, that he left by himself. Nobody believes him," Emma whispered confidentially.

"And everything was searched? The farm, the pond, the house?"

"Well, the pond was dredged and the woods were searched more than once. The house was searched from top to bottom but there weren't any signs of her. It's like she vanished right out of thin air."

This being a small town, Taryn was sure everyone had their own theory as to what might have happened. She didn't say it out loud, of course, and instead thanked Emma for her time.

"No problem," Emma shrugged as she slipped on her backpack and started out the door. She was almost all the way out when she stopped and turned around and glanced back at Taryn. "I'm kind of surprised you didn't know the story, though. I mean, with Thelma being Cheyenne's mother and that farm belonging to Thelma's brother, it seems it would've been mentioned at some point."

With that, she sauntered off down the hallway, leaving Taryn alone and stunned.

Chapter 7

"can understand why she wouldn't mention it," Matt confessed as they drove back to the cabin. "It's not usually something that would come up in conversation: 'Here's your keys, thanks for coming, and by the way – my daughter disappeared right here on this farm about a year ago. Enjoy your stay!'"

Taryn laughed in spite of herself. "True. And I haven't seen her since we had lunch and she showed me the college, so it's not like we've had a lot of heart-to-hearts and been given an opportunity where it *could* be mentioned."

Matt grew silent as the melodious harmonies of The Secret Sisters and their song "Tennesseeme" filled the car. Taryn laid her head up against the window and had a sudden pang for her small apartment back in Nashville. It wasn't a fabulous place – before she'd left this time around she'd noticed the linoleum in the kitchen was starting to peel around the refrigerator – but it was hers. She loved staying with Matt in Florida and having this time in Georgia for a little while, but she was beginning to wish she could be by herself again sometimes. She missed being able to walk around naked if she pleased (although Matt certainly wouldn't argue with her or complain if she did it now), not having to say "excuse me" every time she burped, and having suppers that consisted of slices of cheese and chocolate chip cookies when she was caught up in work.

"I think she's dead," Taryn whispered when the song ended. "Cheyenne, that is. As far as I know The Secret Sisters are still alive."

"Because you saw her in the picture?" Matt asked turning onto the long gravel drive. "And because that girl in your class said so?"

"Yeah. I've never seen a live person in one of my shots. Well, not unless they were actually there, standing in front of me. You know what I mean."

"What do you think happened?" he asked, keeping his eyes glued to the road in case a deer or other wild animal decided to try to play suicide games and jump out in front of the car.

"I don't know," she mumbled, staring off into the deep thicket of trees that surrounded the small road. "But I guess that's what I am going to have to find out."

A letter from her Aunt Sarah's attorney was waiting for her at the cabin. Everything was out of probate now, and she could take control of the house if she so desired. He'd sent the keys. They were surprisingly light in her hand, considering the weight of her aunt's personality.

Taryn wasn't sure when she'd be able to get up there, or *if* she even wanted to go. Losing her aunt had been a huge blow, and had come at a terrible time when Andrew was always on her mind. The amount of guilt she felt over not spending more time with Sarah, or at least keeping in touch more regularly, couldn't be measured.

Still, she couldn't just ignore the house. She'd have to do something about the rambling structure, tucked away in the New Hampshire mountains. She hated the idea of selling it, but was certain the amount of renovations it would need (Sarah had never been good about keeping stuff like that up) was more than Taryn was capable of doing, or affording. Of course, Matt had offered on more than one occasion to go with her and help her out, but this was really something she felt like she needed to do alone. She already let him do too much for her, from cooking dinner to taking time off work to stay with her in Georgia. She couldn't expect more out of him, especially since they hadn't defined their relationship yet.

She wasn't real sure where she was supposed to start now. Should she talk to Thelma about her daughter? Nah, that would be crossing a line. She couldn't just call her up and say, "Hey, so I heard your daughter disappeared on the property next to me. Want to fill me in?"

She didn't want to bring it up in her class and have word get back to Thelma or other college administrators. That would come across as unprofessional and gossipy.

So what then?

Taryn sat bolt right up in her recliner and slapped herself on the forehead. Well, duh! Ye Olde Google was what she usually turned to first.

Turning the television off she sprinted back up the stairs and into the bedroom where Matt was going back over her pictures on her laptop. "Hey, you're gonna get stiff sitting like that for too long," she admonished.

"Well that sounds like fun," he teased her but he did hold his arms up over his head and stretched. His neck cracked a couple of times from the effort. "I am in a little bit of pain, though. I should stop while I'm ahead."

"Did you see anything we missed?"

"I don't think so. I zoomed in on the house, thinking I might catch something, but I didn't. Nothing in the woods, either. Just the girl."

"Cheyenne," Taryn supplied because, after all, the victim had a name.

"Right, Cheyenne. So did you need anything?"

70

"The computer, actually," she answered. "I want to do some searching on the case. See what I can find out."

"Good idea," Matt agreed. "I'm going to go down and fix myself some cocoa. You want any?"

"Yes, please, and doctor mine with a little bit of Baileys if you could," she smiled sweetly.

"One semi hot toddy coming up," Matt sang as he sailed out of the room, leaving Taryn to the bed and computer.

It didn't take her long to find answers. Simply typing in her name brought up at least a dozen news articles. Leaning back into the throw pillows and propping the laptop on her lap she began reading. The first article was written two days after she disappeared.

Local Girl's Whereabouts Unknown

Cheyenne Willoughby, 18, is missing. Upon attending a summer party at the farm of Chris Hinkle on Dark Hollow Road, Willoughby was expected to return home the next morning. When she didn't arrive by noon, her worried parents began calling her friends, assuming she'd gone home with one of them. Although many of the other party-goers, mostly local high school kids, remember seeing Willoughby at the party none of her friends reported anything suspicious.

The pretty, active brunette was on the honor roll all four years in high school. Her parents, Jeff and Thelma Willoughby of Telford Avenue are asking anyone with any information to please come forward and alert them or the police. Willoughby is 5'1", weighs approximately 100 lbs. and was last seen wearing a red jacket, red cowboy boots, and a white sleeveless top. Locating her is of the utmost importance considering the fact that Willoughby has severe asthma and has suffered complications in the past.

The next article contained more information the police had uncovered.

Willoughby Last Seen with Male Friend

Cheyenne Willoughby, the missing 18-year-old high school graduate from Apple Valley, Georgia, was last seen with a male friend, witnesses say. Willoughby, who had attended a party on Dark Hollow Road on May 31, has been missing for one week.

After a series of interviews it was determined Willoughby was last seen with 23-year-old Travis Marcum. Party goers reportedly saw Willoughby climb into Marcum's truck at approximately 3 am. Marcum submitted to interviews with detectives and denies having taken Willoughby with him. He has told reporters that he was "not friends with Willoughby but knows her as an acquaintance" and that the last time he saw her was before he left, on his own.

More searches throughout the community are expected to take place within the next few days. If you have any information regarding the disappearance of Cheyenne Willoughby, please contact the Evarts County sheriff's department.

Taryn had all kinds of questions about that article, but figured she'd wait until she read the others before jumping to any conclusions.

Case of Missing Girl Could Be Runaway

The search continues for 18-year-old Cheyenne Willoughby of Apple Valley. Willoughby went missing two months ago, but so far has turned up no leads. There has been some speculation that Willoughby could have left on her own accord. "We've interviewed dozens and dozens of people who saw her that night, including the two fellows who were the last to see her," Detective Anderson said. "But we don't have any solid leads yet. We can't rule this out as a runaway case just yet, but we are exploring every angle."

The lines on Taryn's forehead grew deeper as she read Detective Anderson's statement. Of course, running away would make sense. But then again, she was eighteen years old. Why would she have had to run away when she could've just gone ahead and moved somewhere else?

Willoughby Family Holds Massive Search

The parents of the missing Cheyenne Willoughby gathered more than five hundred volunteers last Saturday morning to search several different parts of the county, including the forest around

Dark Hollow Road and the rock quarry on HWY 67. Searchers walked a grid and looked for clothing, accessories, and other belongings Willoughby might have had with her, including her purse and cell phone. Dogs, including cadaver dogs, were used in the search, which did not yield any results.

"We don't understand what happened to her," Thelma Willoughby told our reporter. "Cheyenne was a happy, friendly girl. She never hurt a soul. She was excited about the party and said she'd be home in the morning. We talked to her twice that evening, and she sounded fine."

Investigators have recovered Willoughby's cell phone records but have not yet released a statement concerning Willoughby's last calls.

Willoughby Family Holds Fundraisers

The family of missing teen, Cheyenne Willoughby, is holding a fundraiser on Friday, September 15, at the Evarts County Fairgrounds. The fundraiser, which features music by country music band Freedom Express and includes vendors, crafts demonstrations, and bounce houses for children will run from 6-10 pm. The cost is $5 per person and all proceeds go to the Bring Cheyenne Home fund. Monies are expected to be spent on a billboard to be placed along I-75 and further searches in an expanded area.

Willoughby, who has been missing since early last summer, soon after graduating from high school, is 18 years old. Although several area searches have taken place and countless witnesses interviewed since her disappearance, investigators are at a standstill.

Phone records reveal that her last text message was sent at 11:30 pm. The text, to her mother, stated that she had a ride home and would return early. However, Thelma Willoughby was in bed at the time and didn't get the message until that afternoon. "I heard the phone go off, but it was so late I figured I'd check it later," Ms. Willoughby has been quoted as saying. "Of course, in hindsight, I wish I'd looked at it. It was the last time anyone heard from her, and I would've known something was wrong sooner."

The phone continued to receive calls and voicemails from Willoughby's concerned parents throughout the morning and afternoon. Her last known whereabouts were at a friend's house in the Dupont Subdivision. However, the phone has not yet been recovered.

Investigators Believe Fire Not Linked to Missing Teen

Investigators have ruled that the fire in the one story house on Poplar Road, the same night as Cheyenne Willoughby's disappearance, is "most likely" not linked in the case. Instead, they believe it was a coincidental act of arson that unfortunately just happened to occur on the same night.

The house, which had been recently unoccupied, did not have electricity. Arson investigators claim it's unusual for house fires to start where electricity isn't present. An unnamed accelerant was found, however, and it's been concluded that the fire was intentionally set "for reasons not yet known," according to Police Chief Randy Mason.

There is not yet a suspect or person of interest at this time. At the time of the fire Willoughby was allegedly at a friend's house twelve miles away.

Willoughby's whereabouts are still unknown. Although she had a purse with personal belongings with her, according to witnesses, these have not been recovered.

Mason says he hopes she left on her own freewill and "wants to be missing" rather than "the alternative." "I know it's hard on the parents," he told WTVX, "but I hope she left because she wanted to because that at least means she's out there safe somewhere. That's the best case scenario at the moment."

Cheyenne Willoughby, 18, Still Missing

It's been one year since 18-year-old Cheyenne Willoughby went missing. On her nineteenth birthday, her parents are sending out another plea for anyone who might have information to contact authorities. "You can be anonymous," her mother, Thelma

Willoughby says. "We just want information and to know she's okay."

Despite the efforts of local law enforcement and concerned citizens, there is still no sign of Willoughby or clues as to what may have happened to her.

"When your daughter is gone and you don't even know where to start looking, it's heartbreaking," her step-father, Jeff Willoughby said. "It feels like if someone would come forward and say something so we could at least look in the right direction. But nobody's talking."

Although it has been a year of sadness and frustrations for the family, they remain hopeful that Cheyenne will be found and brought home safe. There is currently a $15,000 reward for anyone offering information leading to Cheyenne's whereabouts.

Chapter 8

By the time she'd read through all the articles and even

checked out Cheyenne's Facebook and Instagram sites, Taryn felt
drained. She'd started making a list of questions as she went along,
and now her notes were two pages long. There were more than
twenty articles she'd recovered in all, although most of them just
repeated the same information. It all came down to this: Cheyenne
had attended a party, left with a male friend, and then
disappeared. Nobody had seen or heard from her since she left the
party. And the fire at the other location apparently wasn't
connected to her disappearance. Supposedly.

"Hey," Matt stood in the bedroom door, a glass of Coke in his hand. "How's it going?"

Setting her laptop on the bed, Taryn stretched her legs out and reached for the drink. "It's going. I found a bunch of articles and stuff about the missing girl."

"Yeah? What'd you find?"

Matt perched at the foot of the bed and began stroking Taryn's foot, something that made her purr like a kitten. She was a sucker for getting her feet rubbed.

"A lot of things. But basically she was at this party, left with a dude, and then disappeared."

Matt cocked his head to one side and studied Taryn. "So what's the mystery? Sounds like the guy Travis did something to her."

"Yeah, you'd think," Taryn agreed. "Only the police don't seem to think he's a suspect. He claims she never left with him at all, that he barely knew her and left before she did."

"That should be easy enough to prove, shouldn't it?"

"You'd think so."

"Still, to me, it sounds like the guy did something," Matt pointed out. "I mean, if witnesses saw him..."

"Oh, and another thing. There was a house that burned down. Same night, and arson at that. But the police don't think it's connected."

Matt laughed, his face lighting up in delight. "Are you kidding me? Well that's a big coincidence then."

"Maybe," Taryn answered. "It's all so confusing really. Too easy to think of this guy as the one who did it."

"So give me a rundown on the list of our suspects," Matt prodded. "I know you; you have some ideas."

"Okay," Taryn agreed, rubbing her hands together. She tried not to think about the fact that this was a real person they were talking about, a real missing girl. She would think about that later, and it would sadden and depress her, but for the moment she needed to be analytical about it. "First we have the guy she went home with."

"Alright, we have a guy. The last one to supposedly see her. Assuming he was the mystery ride."

"Right!" Taryn exclaimed. "She texted her parents and said she had a ride home and would be home early. We are assuming it's the guy witnesses claim to have seen her leave with."

"Okay, what about a random stranger?"

"I thought about that, too," Taryn confessed. "Maybe she did get a ride from the other guy, he made a move on her and she didn't like it so she asked to be let out of the car. She gets picked up, gets killed, and now he's denying taking her home because he feels responsible for her death."

"Anyone else?"

"The parents. I hate to say it, but people area freaks and you just never know. Although I've met Thelma and she seems okay."

Matt leaned back against the bedpost and closed his eyes. "And that's not even counting all the people we don't know about. For instance, what if the guy was lying and there were more people at his house. Did he live alone?"

"No, with his parents."

"Can't rule them out either. Brother? Sister?"

Taryn sighed, rubbing at her temples. "And then the people at the party. What if she made someone mad and they came out and found her? They may *never* find this poor girl."

"So are you discounting her being runaway?" Matt asked.

"Yes," Taryn answered quickly.

"That was fast. What makes you think she didn't just up and leave? Get mad and go off to blow some steam?"

"Because I wouldn't be seeing her if she wasn't dead."

Taryn's sleep was restless. Although she'd never been a great sleeper, she'd been doing a lot better with Matt around. It was soothing to reach her foot or hand out in the middle of the night and touch his toe, his thigh, his stomach... Not only did Taryn have trouble falling asleep and staying there, terrible nightmares had plagued her since she was a child. Her parents had sought medication for her before she moved in with her grandmother full time (she'd promptly had Taryn stop everything, thinking it was probably making things worse rather than better and she was right) She had even seen a therapist. Nothing but having an actual physical body there with her helped.

Sometimes the nightmares were so bad she wondered if she maybe she wasn't reliving some former past lives and horrors that befell her back then. The recurring dream of burning in a fire, feeling her flesh smoldering and then peeling was much too vivid to come out of her random imagination.

Tonight, the dream started out innocuous enough.

The grass beneath her feet was brittle from the lack of rain, but the air was damp, foggy. It was sweet-smelling from the fire and the mixture of dampness and smoke clung to her hair, to her skin, to her clothing. She breathed in deeply, taking in the scent, and then let it roll off around her, engulfing her in its saccharinity. There was a chill in the air, a small but biting one, and she found herself pulling her jacket closer around her, discovering warmth and protection in its thick, lined fabric.

The sound of laughter was all around her, although she couldn't see where it was coming from, and the noise was a comforting one. The sense of being surrounded by people, being a part of something, was tantalizing. The wine cooler she'd downed earlier set solidly on top of her stomach, a nuisance but not an unpleasant feeling. She felt loose, carefree, relaxed.

Then, the air changed. It wasn't a subtle change, but abrupt. Suddenly, she was conscious of the fact that she was alone. As the fog grew denser around her and the cacophony of voices dissolved a panicky fear she'd not known since she was a child, clawed at her chest and stomach. In frantic circles she turned around and around, trying to peer through the thickness of the night. The fire was gone, replaced by a coldness that sank into her skin and bubbled there, mixing with the fear until a putrid stench erupted from her in tiny clouds; she could smell her own terror.

The grass under her feet was slick as she tried to run. Her cowboy boots slid on it, torturously making her feel as though she

82

were running in slow motion. When she fell to her knees, there was laughter from above her but it wasn't friendly; it mocked her and chided her. "Mommy," she cried piteously, calling for someone she hadn't yearned for in years. "Mommy!"

Then, the darkness settled over her and dragged her down, down, down until she was unable to breathe and simply clutched at her throat for air.

She *knew* this was a dream. She wasn't caught up in it like she often was in her nightmares, but it didn't make it any less terrifying. With Matt still sleeping on the other side, Taryn sat up in bed and let her feet rest on the cold hardwood floors. It was only 6:17 am and she didn't technically need to be up for hours yet, but she doubted she could get back to sleep.

A can of Coke and a shower later and she was starting to feel a little normal. The sadness clung to her like a heavy dress as she moved through the downstairs rooms. A young girl was undoubtedly dead, parents grieving, and a town confused. What had happened to Cheyenne? Was there any way she could help? If she went back to the farmhouse and walked around, would her camera pick anything up?

Matt wanted to work in the house that afternoon, so she drove into town by herself. Now, driving down Main Street of the sleepy little college town, she looked at it with different eyes.

Although it boasted the small liberal arts college, the town itself was barely on the map. There were only two main streets (Main and Broadway) and one school (elementary, middle, and high) for each of the corresponding grades. The high school and middle school were located next to each other in a large, modern, soulless concrete complex about a mile from the college campus. The elementary school was a throwback to the 1960s and had only one story and a large playground that still boasted a steep metal slide and a real jungle gym.

Taryn figured that most of the kids in town would've grown up together, attended school with one another all through the years and, unless they scattered after graduation, now probably lived within a few miles of one another, raising kids who would also continue the cycle.

Unlike many of the smaller rural communities, the downtown area had a few shops, thanks to some antique places and crafts vendors.

The nearest Wal-Mart was in the next county over and there was only one grocery store—a discount one. Lots of second-hand shops. Chain restaurants consisted of a McDonald's, Pizza Hut, Wendy's, and Hardee's. Several mom and pop type places, her kinds of places, dotted the side of the road. A large grassy area in the middle of town proclaimed itself to be a "War Memorial

Park" and at 2 pm there was a handful of toddlers playing on the swings while bored-looking mothers pushed them back and forth, either chatting with one another or gazing at their smart phones while they idly kept the rhythm with one hand.

The county was dry, so there weren't any beer or alcohol sales.

Cheyenne would've grown up in this, Taryn thought idly as she pulled into her parking space at the college. She undoubtedly knew everyone at the party because she'd grown up with them. She'd probably played on the swing set in the park, shared a plate of bread sticks and tossed coins into the Pizza Hut jukebox, laughed in the hallways of the middle school as an eighth grader (feeling smug and worldly) and then entered the high school on the first day feeling timid and unsure of herself.

There was probably no reason for Cheyenne to feel afraid that night of the party at the farm; she may have been there dozens of times in the past. After all, it was her uncle's farm. Taryn tried to put herself in Cheyenne's shoes, a young girl getting ready for a long night of fun and mischief, not knowing it would be her last. Who had killed her? And why? And was she even dead? Yes, she was dead. Taryn was sure of that.

It wasn't just the terror Taryn had felt from Cheyenne (and she was sure it was her) in the dream that bothered her, it was the helplessness. And even the guilt. For a brief moment Cheyenne hadn't just been afraid, she'd felt dejected. She knew she'd done something she shouldn't have (but what?) and just wanted it to all go away so that she could be home, back in her bed.

Oh, how many times had Taryn felt that same way.

She remembered being a high school freshman and not having any friends other than Matt. She thought she'd start the new school and the new year fresh, a brand new beginning. She'd really put herself out there, tried to talk to people and be sociable. But by the second month she still hadn't bonded with anyone. All the other girls were pairing off with guys or forming new thicker-than-thieves friendships. But not Taryn. Oh, people were friendly enough, but she didn't get invited anywhere. Nobody went out of their way for her.

Then, one day after school, two girls in her chorus class had approached her and asked her if she wanted to hang out. Their names were Lisa and Etta May and they'd eaten lunch together on occasion. Taryn liked them well enough but was thrilled to be included in something. Etta May had just gotten her license and offered to drive Taryn home, saying they could stop along the way and grab a bite to eat.

She'd regretted getting in the car the minute they took off. Instead of heading to her house, or even a restaurant, Etta May went for the interstate. There were three other people in the car and they whooped and hollered as she laid on the gas and hit the crowded freeway with gusto. Taryn, riding in the front seat, watched in horror as the speedometer climbed from 65 mph to 75 and then on up to 90. Closing her eyes, she grabbed the armrest and felt beads of sweat sliding down her face and pooling under her blouse.

Thankfully, after a few minutes, Etta exited off. They stopped at a truck stop and all the other teenagers clamored out of the car like a pile of puppies, laughing and screaming. Rather than going inside, however, when they spotted a semi with its back open they darted to it. "Let's look inside!" Lisa cried and everyone laughed. Everyone, that was, except for Taryn. She poked behind them, feeling guilty and awful. She just wanted to go home, climb into her bed, and pull the covers up over her head. Taryn never broke any rules (unless you counted climbing into abandoned houses to take pictures breaking a rule) and was desperate to stay out of trouble. She watched as the others actually got into the back of the semi and danced around.

When the owner of the truck, a large man with a gut that hung over his jeans and a messy looking sandwich in his hand, came out of the restaurant he screamed at the top of his lungs and waved his fist at the kids. Squealing with laughter, they took off at top speed, passing Taryn, and going for Etta May's car. This time she ran as well, happy to be leaving.

Again, she offered a silent prayer as they navigated the interstate, passing cars at breakneck speeds and exiting off so quickly the tires squealed.

Back at her house, she'd not only felt safe (land, land!) but when the dust had settled she'd felt angry with herself. She tried to remind herself that it wasn't her fault, that she couldn't possibly have known what the afternoon would entail, but she still felt somehow responsible. From that day on, she swore she'd be a better judge of character.

Now she wondered if perhaps Cheyenne had experienced something similar. Was she going along with something for fun, afraid to say no, when it had taken a turn for the worst? Or had she simply been in the wrong place at the wrong time?

With one foot already halfway out the door, Taryn drifted through her lesson in a daze. Her mind was running a million miles a minute and even though she knew it was wrong to only give her students a small percentage of her, she had things she wanted to be doing instead. Still, once she got them all started on their assignment, completing the other side of a building that had been torn down or burned to the ground, she was able to relax. To their credit, her students were much more enthusiastic about the work than she'd thought they'd be and most even looked like they were enjoying themselves.

While they sketched, their chosen images propped up in front of them, she made a list of her next steps. Although her careless treatment of clothing (always on the floor, never on hangers) and shoes (always in a haphazard heap, despite the attempt Matt made to corral them in to a crate or on a shelf) she was actually a very organized soul.

On one side of her paper she made a list of the key players involved in the case; on the other she began listing possible scenarios. The scenarios were a short list. There were only so many things that could've happened to Cheyenne and none of them were good.

She was lost in deep thought when a shadow crossed over her paper and made her look up. A tall, thin boy of about eighteen

88

years old stood before her. His face was an eruption of pimples and one large nasty-looking cyst but his hair was beautifully thick with blond streaks running through it. He was dressed in a pair of khaki slacks, leather loafers, and a pullover sweater that looked cashmere. His appearance spoke of quiet money, the kind that meant one or both of his parents probably had administrative jobs outside of the county.

"I had a question about this side," he apologized, holding out his sketch. "Just how parallel would the sides have been? I mean, would it have been a perfect reflection?"

Taryn set her pencil down and studied his drawing. It was quite good and he'd spent an awful lot of time on the shadowing, making the old house nearly jump right off the page. "That's a very good question," she answered truthfully. "The fact is, with these Gothic style houses, you typically wouldn't see the same design repeated on the opposite side. Even the most ornate tended to focus on one side or the other. You've got this turret here," she pointed to the one in the photograph, "so chances are the other side wouldn't have had one." Quickly flipping through the images on her Power Point presentation she showed him an example that was similar to the house he was attempting to recreate.

"Ah!" he cried, taking his sketch back under his arm. "I thought so. Well, that saves me some time anyway."

Before he turned to go back to his desk, however, he hesitated. "Hey, I don't mean to pry, but what are those names you have written on your pad there?"

"Yeah?" Taryn asked, resisting the urge to cover them with her hand. She felt like a student caught cheating.

"I know those people," he shrugged. "You're probably thinking about Cheyenne Willoughby and what happened to her."

A few students closest to her laid down their pencils and studied Taryn inquisitively. She felt her cheeks blushing under their gazes. "Well, yeah, I was. I just learned about the disappearance a couple of days ago, and it's been on my mind."

"You know, I was there that night. That night at the party," he explained. "My name's Johnny, and I'm from here. I'm a freshman."

Taryn's embarrassment turned to interest as she now studied him. "Were you friends with Cheyenne, if I may ask?"

He laughed, a thin sound that border-lined on giggling. "No, I was younger than her. She knew who I was, but we didn't hang out or anything. She was out of my league, if you know what I mean. A cheerleader captain."

Taryn understood what he meant. She would've been out of Cheyenne's league, too.

"I was just there with my brother that night, kind of tagging along. His name is David. They hung out some but weren't really friends either. His girlfriend has him on kind of a tight rein, if you know what I mean."

"To be honest, I'm surprised no new news has cropped up in the past year about her," Taryn dared. Some of the students exchanged looks that Taryn couldn't decipher. Knowing she might be stepping on some toes and going into territory that could only be described as "inappropriate," she plunged on anyway. "Do you guys have any ideas?"

"Well, common theory is that the police know who done it but won't do anything about it because they're afraid they don't have enough evidence," a young woman close to Taryn spoke. She frowned down at her sketch and pushed a long jet-black lock of hair behind her ear. "You know, like that case of that woman down in Florida with the little girl who died? Everyone knows she did it, but the prosecution thought they had such a slam dunk that they didn't even try at the trial. It was all circumstantial, and the jury didn't buy it. Maybe if they'd spent more time gathering more evidence and stuff..."

Everyone was looking at the speaker now, some of them with looks of admiration on their faces. "Hey, I'm an art major but I watch a lot of television," she shrugged with a smile. "I'm kind of into that true crime stuff."

"Nobody thinks she's still around, if you're wondering that," Johnny croaked with authority. "Even her parents know she's gone. But they won't admit it."

"There's so many places around here where a body could be taken," a heavyset brunette with a thirty-two ounce Coke declared. "Caves, wells, ponds, whatever. She'll never be found."

"Just out of curiosity, how many of you are actually from here?" Taryn asked, gazing around the room. More than half of the students raised their hands. "And how many people knew Cheyenne?" All but three of those whose hands had been raised kept them up.

Interesting indeed, Taryn thought as she changed the subject and encouraged them to all get back to work. She didn't know what she'd do with that information yet, but she'd definitely file it away for future reference.

Chapter 9

On the clear light of day, without the fog and gloom, the

farmhouse and fields around it were harmless. Matt stood next to Taryn, his hands stuffed in the pockets of his black pea coat, and studied their surroundings. "Pretty place," he remarked offhandedly. "Kind of secluded back here, huh?"

Taryn nodded absently, running her fingers through her thick hair. It had been in a ponytail, but the wind caught it and now it was blowing about her face, catching between her lips. The sun was out but the wind was making it cold. She never wore gloves when she planned on taking pictures because they made her hands too clumsy. Now, though, her fingers were chapped and red and she couldn't wait to get back inside of their own cabin where Matt could build a fire and have it toasty in no time.

"It doesn't feel like anything bad happened here," Taryn remarked at last, trying to vocalize what was running through her mind. And the place didn't have any kind of unsettling feeling to it. It was quiet, still, and isolated. The surrounding woods shielded it from the outside world, the same way they separated their cabin from it. The hills rose up in the distance like foot soldiers closing in on their target and this time of year they were bare and stark against the late autumn sky. But they weren't foreboding. The lowlands were flat in some places, slightly rolling in others, and the remains of an old wooden slat fence could be seen here and there. A smokehouse still stood behind the house, a primitive (almost charming) structure that spoke of days gone by. The litter from the bonfire site was the only sore spot in the picture. Nothing screamed "young girl brutally murdered or abducted" here.

"I feel something, but I can't put my finger on what, exactly," Matt murmured. He'd reached out and taken her hand and now gave it a light squeeze. She wasn't even sure he'd realized he'd taken it in the first place.

"I'm going to walk around and try to take some shots, okay?" Matt nodded and Taryn gently pried her fingers from his and started making her way through the damp grass.

Armed with more information than she'd had on her previous visit, she tried to be more focused on the pictures she took and the locations in which she took them. She started with the burn pile and aimed her camera directly into where the fire would've raged and then, turning her back to it, made a slow circle around the pit, taking pictures every few feet. If Cheyenne had been close to the fire at some point and something had happened there, she would catch it. Hopefully.

With her fingers growing colder by the minute, Taryn walked back over to the farmhouse. Today, she would focus on the outside. Training her camera to the left and working slowly to the right she took pictures of every inch. When she was finished, she walked to the back of the house and did the same, trying not to miss anything.

Considering it more or less bad luck to check her LCD screen while she was still in the field she resisted the urge to look through her pictures and examine them. They'd been out there for some time now anyway, and she could tell that Matt was getting cold. His cheeks were rosy, and he kept dabbing at his nose with a handkerchief – something she found old-fashionably charming. He was too polite to tell her he was ready to go so she made the executive decision herself.

"Come on, love," she called across the yard. He looked up from where he was examining the remains of an old stone well and lifted his hand in a wave. "It's freezing out here. Let's head back!"

Nodding in agreement, Matt jogged over to Taryn and slipped his arm comfortable around her shoulder. "What do you say we drive into town tonight for supper? My treat."

"I say if you're buying then it sounds great!" Taryn chuckled and put her own arm around his waist. Together, they entered the patch of woods and headed back towards the cabin.

The farmhouse stood stoic and proud in the middle of the field. There was nothing spooky or alarming about the image on her computer screen in any way; no ghosts were popping out of the windows, no bloody hand prints on the walls, and no signs of a grisly accident or murder. The disturbing thing was the young, laughing girl perched on the front porch.

"Huh," Matt pondered as he leaned over Taryn's shoulder and gazed at the images. "You know, except for the fact that it's scary as hell, you could look at this on the bright side and think about how much easier this is going to make your job in the future."

Unable to supress a laugh, Taryn made a grunting sound and pretended to glare at him. "At least the house is pretty."

And it was, really. There was no real architectural style when it came to farmhouses; they got their names due to their locations and not because of any particular traits or characteristics. This house looked to Taryn like a "Sears" house – one that was brought in by train or boat and assembled on site. With its side-gabled roof, she thought it might have been a model called The Concord which was popular around the early twenties century. The frame would've cost less than two thousand dollars and boasted eight or nine rooms and a large front porch. Many had excavated basements, although the house in question also had a root cellar, as Matt had discovered.

From the broken windows, sagging porch, and roof that was obviously in need of repair, it was clear to Taryn that the picture was depicting a fairly recent time period, if not the present. It had the look of an abandoned, neglected house although it was, of course, in far better condition than it was today. Weeds grew in clumps around the foundation and a rash of poison ivy wounded its way up from the ground all the way to a second-floor window. "Leaves of three, leave them be," Taryn chanted silently in her head.

The sadness that often accompanied her view into the past settled over her like a damp fog. At one time someone had ordered the house, probably in excitement at the thought of building their own home. They'd watched it roll in and be unloaded and then watched as it was put together, piece by piece. Some woman, most likely, had visited furniture stores and outfitted the rooms to her liking and maybe even fawned over fabric samples as she dreamed of curtains and bedspreads. Taryn knew nothing about the former occupants, or original owners, but she had a fairly good grasp on people in general; the house had once been loved. Now it was forgotten, simply an addendum to the open field where mischievous teenagers liked to party.

The pictures Taryn took around the fire pit were unremarkable. She zoomed in on a few, thinking she saw something small, but nevertheless revealing, but nothing stood out. Only the farmhouse, with Cheyenne happy as a lark on the porch, was troubling.

"It takes your breath away a little, doesn't it?" Matt mused. "To see her there, alive, when there was nothing present when you took the photo."

"I thought I'd get used to it eventually, seeing things like this," Taryn said. "But I haven't. . I keep expecting that it will stop, that I'll wake up one morning and be unable to do this. And yet... here's another one."

"I think we can agree that the house had something to do with Cheyenne's disappearance," Matt concluded. "Or at least the farm."

"So what do you think I should do now?" Taryn asked, feeling helpless.

"It might be time to talk to her parents. You're going to have to do it anyway, and it's better that you go to them rather than them hearing about asking questions."

"You're right," Taryn sighed. "But that's one visit I'm not particularly looking forward to."

The house, a small brick ranch, was located in an older subdivision where sheer age had allowed the trees to grow again after being cleared out for the construction. Houses were positioned fairly far apart, with each lot having what looked to be an acre or more. Cheyenne's house had a black Ford Explorer, an older model, and Kia Rio in the cracked driveway. A metal patio table, with a ripped stripped umbrella, perched at the edge of the yard; the umbrella beating back and forth in the wind. An attempt had been made to put in a flower garden along the front of the house, but the beds were overgrown and weeds were shooting up through the hard-packed soil, obscuring the myriad of gnomes, toads, and ceramic chipmunks. It was obvious the shutters and front door had been painted recently, but it also appeared that the old paint hadn't been scraped off first as it appeared thick and bubbly.

When Taryn knocked on the door Thelma opened it almost immediately, leaving Taryn to wonder if she sat by her front picture window, watching the road for signs of visitors, or signs of Cheyenne.

The warm interior was a stark contrast to the biting cold of outside. Indeed, it was almost stuffy, and Taryn found herself wishing she hadn't worn so many layers. The house opened up into a living room jam-packed full of furniture, decorations, and books. The blueberry-colored walls were alive with Home Interior, every few feet a different collection of prints and the matching accessories. Taryn was seated in a fluffy recliner under a print of a seascape. Beneath the print was a small shelf containing a matching seashell, ceramic lighthouse, and candle. Across from her, above Thelma's head, was a farm print. Surrounding it were wall hangings of miniature cows and horses. For some reason Taryn couldn't help herself and found she was adding up the cost of the collections; she figured there was at least three-thousand dollars' worth of Home Interior on the wall. That stuff didn't come cheap.

The shabby furniture was happily alive with "primitive" figurines and "artwork." Everything from plaques proclaiming "Everything simple" on reclaimed barn wood to imitation farm implements littered the room. Thelma obviously took great pride in her decorating and her "things." The couch was sagging, the fabric on the matching recliners torn in several places, and the wood furniture all pressed and factory made (cheaply) but there wasn't a spot of dust or stain to be seen.

"I'm sorry it's such a mess," Thelma apologized, gesturing about the room. "I just didn't have time to really clean."

It was a southern thing, Taryn knew, to apologize for the house's cleanliness. She had no doubt that Thelma, like most southern women she'd known (her grandmother and mother included), had probably spent half the morning polishing, dusting, vacuuming, and shoving things in forgotten rooms and corners. She'd even taken the time to light candles and set out incense; the air was filled with a combination of vanilla, strawberry, and lavender aromas.

"It's a beautiful home," Taryn asserted, "and there's no mess at all. You should see MY place." That was also the polite southern thing to do: assure your hostess their house is perfect and you're the unkempt one.

"You're too sweet. Would you like something to drink, dear?" Thelma asked. "I've got sweet tea, Coke, Diet Coke, and hot chocolate."

"I'd like a Coke, please, if it's not too much trouble," Taryn replied, thinking a boost of caffeine couldn't hurt.

Thelma excused herself to the kitchen and was back a moment later, the Coke poured into a tall glass with imprints of roses on it. Ice cubes bobbed at the top, their clinking noise cheerful in the otherwise quiet room.

Now that visitor protocol had been reached and carried forth, it was time to get down to business.

"First, I wanted to say how much I am enjoying teaching the class," Taryn began sincerely. And she truly was enjoying herself. "I don't know how good of a teacher I am, but I'm having fun and nobody's dropped out."

"Oh, lots of little birdies have told me you're a wonderful teacher," Thelma assured her, her eyes dancing. "Some are even asking if you'll come back a second term."

Taryn felt her back stiffen in pride. Perhaps she didn't stink as badly as she thought she did.

"There is something else, though, and I don't quite know how to say it..." Now that she was there, in Thelma's living room, she felt awkward. How did one go about bringing up the other person's private life in such a direct way?

"Well, I imagine the best way to say it is the most honest. What's on your mind?"

"I know about your daughter, about Cheyenne," Taryn disclosed softly, looking down at her feet. Her boots were heavy and dark against the light beige carpet and now she belatedly wondered if she shouldn't have taken them off at the door. Some people were funny about their carpets and shoes.

"Oh," Thelma sighed.

Taryn could feel a shift in the room, a heaviness. The sweet aroma of the lavender candle next to her was starting to make her a little sick to her stomach and the Coke was thick on her throat. Perhaps it hadn't been such a good idea to pay Thelma the visit. "You see, I... well, I felt something on one of my first nights. And then someone told me about her disappearance. I did some research of my own," she finished lamely.

Thelma's ears had perked up now, and she was studying Taryn intently, gazing at her with rapture. 'What did you feel?"

"I can't really describe it, I'm afraid. But I heard what I thought was a cry. And then I had a bad dream. Well, when you look at everything individually it's not much but when you put it all together, it usually means something. I think Cheyenne might be trying to communicate with me." Taryn held her breath, cringing at her choice of words. The fact was, there was no way to talk about this without letting Thelma know she thought Cheyenne must be dead.

But Thelma only nodded. "In the beginning I felt things as well. I'd hear a voice, a singing even. The air currents around me would shift. Sometimes, I'd catch things out of the corner of my eye, but I could never get a full picture. I talked to my preacher about it. He said it might be part of my grief, my depression." Thelma's eyes filled with water and she hastily dabbed at them with the edge of her sweater sleeve. "I know she's dead. I know it. A mother would know these things, right?"

"Maybe she's not," Taryn proclaimed, but to her own ears it didn't sound particularly convincing.

102

"We know she's dead," Thelma stated again, this time with more firmness. The glass in her hand shook a little, sending drops of cola over the side, but she steadied and forced herself to be steady. "Cheyenne was a difficult child, the kind of teenager you wanted to pull your hair out over, but she was thoughtful. She would never do this to me."

Taryn made a mental note that she hadn't mentioned Cheyenne's father, but decided to let it pass for now.

"You would know your daughter best of all," Taryn reassured her with care, trying to choose the right words. "My parents and I had a difficult relationship when I was growing up. I actually ended up going to live with my grandmother when I was still young, and it was an arrangement that suited everyone well. But, like Cheyenne, I wouldn't have put my parents through this kind of grief. Not for this long anyway."

"Exactly," Thelma quavered, sounding relieved Taryn understood her. "I know the police still consider this a possible runaway but I know she's not. Jeff, that's her stepfather, he still holds out the belief she'll turn up one day with her tail between her legs, seeking forgiveness. I give that sliver of hope to him. He holds so much guilt otherwise."

"Why?" Taryn asked, unable to stop herself.

Thelma sighed and seemed to age ten years in a matter of seconds, her face darkening and the lines drawing deeper on her forehead. "Jeff and I married when Cheyenne's father died. She was twelve when he officially adopted her. He did his best by her, Jeff's a good man you see, but he's not always an easy man. Sometimes he may have expected too much out of such a young girl. Jeff's former Navy, retired now, and likes everything in order. Cheyenne was just the opposite. She didn't understand his rules, his rigidity, was to keep us safe and his way of showing love. They butted heads a lot. But he would've walked through hell and high water for her." She snapped this last part with vehemence.

"It's not his fault what happened," Taryn tried to soothe her. "He couldn't have known."

"Well, in a way he could have. You see, Cheyenne called him earlier that evening to come and get her. I guess her and her friends got in a tiff. That's what one said. That's why she was leaving with somebody else. She sent us that text, the one saying she was coming home early. But we didn't get it. We were asleep at the time. If we'd gotten it, we'd have been expecting her. We would've known when she was meant to be here. We would've asked who was driving her. We both feel guilty about that." Thelma set her Coke down on the end table next to her, a coaster under it, and shook her head with sadness.

"I understand about the guilt. I lost my husband years ago and am only just now getting around to letting go of some of the blame I put on myself," Taryn admitted, feeling helpless. She wished she could offer this woman more comfort, but felt helpless.

"I am glad you're here, no matter what anyone says," Thelma asserted suddenly, her eyes blazing.

"What do you mean?" Taryn asked, taken aback. Hadn't they wanted her to come and teach at the college?

"I know it was wrong of me to bring you in on false pretenses, but the students really are enjoying you and–"

"Thelma, what are you saying?"

"Oh, honey," Thelma exhaled loudly. "Can't you see? You're not seeing and hearing my daughter on accident. I brought you here because I know who you are. I put you in our cabin to be close to where Cheyenne was. You're here to find my daughter."

Chapter 10

Although her stomach grumbled and she was dying for
something carbonated and caffeinated (everything was a "Coke" to
her unless it was clear) she drove straight to the cabin without
stopping. For the first time since Andrew died, Taryn found herself
wanting, *needing* really, to be engulfed by the presence of a man.
Or, more concretely, a man who loved her. And despite the fact
she couldn't really explain her current situation with Matt, one
thing was for certain – he was the only person left in the world
who truly *did* love her.

When she walked through the door she found him sitting
cross-legged on the couch, his skinny pale legs poking out from his
pajama bottoms. She still liked that he always wore matching
pajamas. A bathrobe was tied loosely around his waist, and papers
were scattered on the floor and around him.

"Hey," he smiled as she began the process of disrobing of her outer layers. She let her scarf, jacket, and gloves land on her jacket in the floor while she studied him. Most women probably wouldn't find him classically attractive. He was too thin, too angular. His longish black hair fell in a curtain around his bright green eyes, hiding them for the most part. A pity, too, since she found his eyes to be his best feature. Despite having both Italian and Native American in his lineage he was pale, even in the summertime. His jaw was angular but his mouth was full. At six-foot-two he towered over her, but had a tendency to hunch his shoulders when he walked, making him appear much smaller. He was a terrible dresser, wearing things that went out of style years ago or were much too young for him (a favorite outfit of his was black jeans with a T-shirt boasting a bunch of dancing frogs).

Still, there were times when she looked at him and thought he might be the most beautiful person she'd ever seen. Like now.

"How'd the visit go?" Taryn knew he hated being interrupted when he was working on something. His OCD mind liked to finish one thing before starting another, but he always made the effort to squeeze Taryn's needs in.

She wasn't ready to talk about the day, though. Instead, she walked over to Matt without a word, cleared the papers from his lap, and sat down on it. Like a little child she curled herself into his chest and wrapped her arms around his waist. He bent forward so his head rested on hers, that silky hair now falling down into her face and covering her own eyes. And, for the longest time, they didn't move.

The sound was far away, off in the distance, and might have been part of her dream. Taryn was aware she was asleep only because her body felt incredibly relaxed and lucid – a feeling foreign to her when she was awake. She thought she was too young for arthritis but for the past few years she'd experienced such periods of stiffness and pain it felt as though her bones were breaking.

But the noise... it was nothing more than a "ping" really – a small, tinny sound that barely registered on her mental plane. Lovely images of a dark, starry sky floated behind her eyes like scenes from a vintage movie and made her smile in her sleep but the sound was out-of-place, a disruption that disturbed her.

She stretched her leg out and in her sleep was aware of the rough fabric of the couch beneath her. While she didn't awaken, her heart rate quickened, and her breathing became more jagged, frenzied. Something wasn't right, and as the cold beads of sweat begin forming at her temples and sliding down her cheeks in little balls, she struggled to understand what was going on and why she was so suddenly afraid. Then, there it was, that "ping" again – what should've been an innocuous sound but, instead, filled her with dread.

"Taryn." The voice was beside her, in front of her, behind her, all around her. It was warm, but commanding, and Taryn had no trouble recognizing it as her grandmother. Although she'd been dead for many years, that whiskey-soaked voiced, turned hard by years of chain-smoking, was unmistakably Nora Jean Magill's.

Blinking, Taryn pushed herself up, the afghan sliding to the floor. She moved as if in a daze, half expecting to look down and see her still-sleeping body below her. Her movements were fluid, unlike her normally clumsy nature, and in the cool darkness of night her limbs felt as though they were traveling in slow motion.

She wasn't alone.

While the outline of her grandmother's body might have been gauzy and not quite as solid as Nora had been in real life (Nora's presence had always been solid) she was as real as anything else in the room and standing just a few feet from where Taryn now sat on the cabin's sofa. She wore not the lavender burial dress Taryn had last seen her in but a simple striped polyester shift that hung smartly to her knees and hard-soled brown loafers. Her steel-gray hair was recently set and perched on her head like coils about to spring from a clock; her dentures shown evenly and brightly in the dark room. There was no light shining down on her, no glow emanating from the curves and angles of her body, yet Taryn didn't question her undeniable appearance and her own ability to make out her features. Just as she didn't question the fact she was face-to-face with a departed loved one.

An unyielding ball of sorrow, grief, and excitement rose in Taryn's chest and erupted from her mouth in a mournful "oh" that slipped into the quiet room like an unwelcome intruder. She longed to run to her grandmother's side, throw herself at her feet, and cling to her like a little child. She wanted to raise her face, now wet with unfelt tears, and have it covered with kisses from those dry lips that had once soothed her and offered words of both comfort and criticism, depending on what she needed. She wanted to feel those leathery hands, dry with age, on her skin as they touched her.

Taryn felt like she'd gladly have sold her soul to continue the feeling of relief she felt in her grandmother's presence, but there was an undeniable sense of urgency in the room, and she knew there wasn't much time. Even as she watched, Nora's body wavered, as if unsure of itself. Taryn opened her mouth, tried to speak, but nothing would come out. Nora looked at her with a mixture of love and pity and then raised her left hand, the large rings she'd always worn casting sparkles against the walls and floor. As Taryn watched in confusion, a handful of dry, brittle leaves fell from Nora's hand and floated to the floor where they landed in a small pile at her feet. Then, with a sad smile that still managed to light up her careworn face, she reached her hand out towards Taryn and softly disappeared. She didn't fade out, like a vision might in a movie, but simply ceased to be. Taryn collapsed back down on the couch, drawing the afghan back around her shoulders, and cried. The room still carried her grandmother's scent.

Matt found her curled up on the couch, hours later, when his alarm went off. "Sorry," he apologized as she wiped the sleep from her eyes and glanced at the cup of tea he offered. "You were sleeping so well I didn't want to disturb you. I didn't think you'd sleep through the night."

"I didn't," she muttered. She hated crying herself to sleep. Now she had a sinus headache and her face felt red and puffy. "I got a visitor last night."

As Matt perched on the edge of the couch she quickly relayed her grandmother's visit and what had happened. "I've never seen her before, Matt," she explained, her eyes threatening to fill with tears again. "I kept hoping, and what with the Miss Dixie doing what she does, I thought maybe..."

Matt got up and walked to the center of the room where Taryn had pointed her grandmother's location. "Well, she left behind some presents," he mused as he knelt down and studied the floor.

Wrapping the afghan around her shoulders like a robe, Taryn walked to Matt and knelt down beside him. The small pile of colorful leaves smiled up at them, their edges curled inward and the stems pointing up with glee. In the middle of the pile was something sparkly, something that caught the overhead light and threw a glimmer on the wall over the couch. Taryn poked her fingers into the dry heap and pulled out a large ring–a simple gold band with an ornate sapphire in the middle.

"It's hers all right," she mused, laying it on her flattened palm and studying it with the care of a surgeon. "It even smells like her. If a ring can have a smell."

"I definitely catch a scent," Matt agreed, patting Taryn's knee, although whether he was being truthful or humoring her in comfort was debatable.

"What do you think this means?" Taryn couldn't help but feel waves of excitement in the pit of her stomach. Her grandmother had been with her. Maybe just for a few seconds, but it was closer than she'd been to her in a decade. She wanted to kick herself for not trying to communicate with her more, for not holding onto the moment longer, for not being able to join her... And she'd do anything to be able to repeat the experience.

"I have no idea, Taryn," Matt murmured. "I wish I did."

Taryn's class flew by quickly, and she couldn't remember a single word she'd said. She'd given her students homework at their last meeting and now their sketches were piled up on her desk before her. She thought she might hang around the classroom and look over them before going home. She had the car since Matt had wanted to stay home, do laundry, and pack. The room emptied out in a hurry, like it usually did, and the building was quiet. She could faintly hear the sound of a man lecturing down the hall, but the noise was faraway and had nothing to do with her so she was able to tune it out. Soon, however, she could hear the staccato sounds of footsteps in the hallway and as they grew louder she looked up from the desk and watched as Emma's slight frame filled the doorway.

"Hey," she began with what Taryn thought might be nervousness. "Can I talk to you for a sec?"

"Yeah, sure," Taryn motioned her to a seat. "Have a seat. What's up?"

Emma's red hair was pulled back in a loose bun, a few blazing tendrils falling down in her face becomingly. She wore camel-colored Uggs, leggings, a red infinity scarf, and a dark brown down jacket. Taryn envied her stylish, pulled-together look and felt dowdy and drab in her own ancient jeans, cheap sweater, and ratty hiking boots. Her hair could use a good washing (the water pressure at the cabin was a little lacking so she never felt fully rinsed) and she was developing a pimple on her chin. Or maybe it was a cold sore. Either way, it wasn't nice.

"I know you went to Cheyenne's house a few days ago," Emma began. At Taryn's look of confusion she laughed. "It's not that big of a town, and I'm from here. Cheyenne's kind of my cousin in that southern sort of way."

"Ahh," Taryn nodded in understanding.

"Well, I wanted to help you, if I can," she continued. "And there are others, too, who want to help. Cheyenne's best friend, Ruthie, is my roommate. We live with two other girls and have a house off campus. We've kind of been playing amateur detectives, I guess you could say, and we were wondering if you wanted to come over and hang out, maybe put our notes together or something."

"Like a murder club," Taryn mused and then instantly regretted it. ""Oh my God, I am so sorry. I don't mean to imply Cheyenne was murdered. I just meant..."

Her cheeks flaming with embarrassment, Taryn was mortified, but Emma just laughed and waved it off. "I know you what you meant. You meant like one of those true crime clubs that sits around and discusses cases."

"Yeah, like that."

"Look," Emma leaned forward and lowered her voice to a stage whisper, despite the fact that nobody else was around. "We know we're probably not going to bring Cheyenne back. Whatever happened to her, she's gone. She wouldn't have put her parents through this and, besides, she didn't have a job or anything so it's not like she could've just taken off and started a new life somewhere else."

Taryn bit her bottom lip and studied Emma's young, earnest face. She still wasn't sure what to think about the whole thing. Thelma actually seeking her out to come and help find Cheyenne, the strange dreams she'd had at the cabin, her grandmother visiting her...

"I don't know," she answered at last, thinking more about how it might be a conflict of interest with her teaching job than anything else.

The look of disappointment that crossed Emma's face made Taryn feel bad, and she instantly regretted turning her down. The regret was followed shortly by anger. Why did she have to feel guilty? After all, it wasn't like she was a real university professor–she'd been lured to the college under false pretenses, brought not for her artistic talent or because someone thought she'd be a good fit for the school but because they thought she was some kind of freak show. She'd already given in to the self-pity that morning and broken down to Matt before going to class but now it was creeping back up on her, twisting its spindly little legs into her brain and whispering self-doubt soliloquies to her.

"Yeah, okay," she conceded. Emma's face lit up so brightly that Taryn felt a little embarrassed. "When and where?"

Chapter 11

"I don't know..." Matt grumbled for what must've been the hundredth time.

Taryn, curled up on the couch with a spread over her for warmth, watched him pace back and forth, his hands occasionally raking through his hair. Her grandmother's ring rested on her forefinger, a little big but calming. She hadn't had a bad dream since she put it on.

"You *have* to go," she sighed again. "I'll be fine."

"Something just feels off about this."

Picking at a piece of lint in the Sherpa, Taryn shrugged. "I feel okay here in the house. I actually feel okay out there. Still a little upset about why I'm actually here..."

Squatting in front of her, Matt fished both her hands out from under the throw and engulfed them in his. His fingers were long and narrow, like a piano player's, and they were chilled from the trips he'd taken to the car. "They might have brought you here to help with the search, but they couldn't have offered you the job if you weren't good."

"Money talks. Maybe they paid someone off."

"Maybe," he agreed with a smile. Taryn scrunched her face in mock anger. "But does it matter? You're making money and the students seem to like you."

" Isn't it strange that I'm going to hang out with one of the students outside of class?"

"I don't know. I certainly never hung out with any of my professors, but they were mostly old, nerdy geezers – you know, me in forty years. If I'd had a hot teacher like you, then maybe."

Taryn leaned forward and pressed her face against his until their foreheads met. The curve of her forehead and nose fit perfectly onto his, like they were made for each other. It was a comforting pose for her, sometimes even more thrilling than kissing, and when she did it something always tugged at her – something deep-rooted and primal.

"I think I might even feel better knowing you'll be around people while I'm gone. Just promise me you won't go out to the farmhouse until I get back. Not even with someone else," he added before she could protest.

"I don't think there's anything there," she insisted. "I get something, but nothing definite. I don't think Cheyenne is there."

"It doesn't matter," Matt muttered stubbornly. "I picked up on something too, and, even though my sensitivities aren't anywhere near as strong as yours, I'd just feel better if you stayed away."

The oldies CD Matt had playing changed to Otis Redding and as "These Arms of Mine" filled the room. Matt stopped talking and drew her up until she stood in front of him and wrapped her arms around his neck. Between the feeling of being close and the weight of her grandmother's ring, she felt incredibly safe and protected. Moving in slow circles around the room, she let the sadness of the music and lyrics weigh her down a little, not in a bad way, but in a yearning. Torn between wanting to feel independent, and wanting him to stay, she'd pretended she'd be just fine. But she might not, not really. Taryn's biggest fear might just have been that she couldn't really exist on her own, that the safety of Matt was what kept her heart beating.

The apartment building Taryn parked her car in front of looked exactly like the other ten buildings in the development. A breezeway with four apartments squared around it contained a steep staircase where, at the top, she found the exact same thing. Someone at Emma's apartment had hung a wreath decorated with silk fall flowers and tiny pumpkins. It was a reminder that it would be Thanksgiving soon, and she had no idea what she was going to do this year.

When she knocked on the door, she could hear a flurry of activity inside. Emma, dressed in snug yoga pants and a hoodie, opened the door. Her red hair was piled atop her head and she looked beautiful in the casual way only young women can.

"Hi!" she shouted, and in her southern way engulfed Taryn in a hug before pulling her into the room and shutting the door.

A gathering of young people congregated around a coffee table laden with Domino Pizza boxes. There were six of them in total – two girls counting Emma and four young men. Some of them didn't look old enough to be in college.

"Everyone, this is Taryn!" Emma announced with pride, holding onto Taryn's hand the way a child might. "She's my teacher, and she's here to help us!"

"I'm not really a teacher," Taryn mumbled, feeling embarrassed. "Just an instructor for a little while."

"Oh, but she's great," Emma bubbled. "Here, sit on the couch and have some pizza!'

A young guy in camo pants and a black Guns-n-Roses T-shirt was already piling slices on a plate for her while Taryn settled down on the blue microfiber couch. The springs creaked under her weight, and Emma apologized. "I know, it's a little old, but it was cheap."

"Cheap?" The other girl in the group laughed. "It was *free*! We found it on the sidewalk. Someone set it out," she explained to Taryn.

"Yeah, but we washed the cushions and sprayed it real well. There's nothing wrong with it," Emma said defensively. "Oh, and this is my roommate, Lindy."

Lindy looked eighteen and had shoulder-length blonde hair. She was hard-looking and brown, like someone who spent an equal amount of time at the gym and tanning bed.

Emma went around the room and made the other introductions: Joe, Brad, Eric, and Mike. Taryn knew she'd forget their names by the time she got back to the house but now she nodded and smiled at each one.

"So what do you guys do?" she asked, taking a bite of pizza. Domino's hadn't changed much since her own college days.

"We're trying to find Cheyenne," Eric grunted. He was the oldest looking in the group, although it could've been his red, bushy beard hiding his baby face.

"Did all of you know her?"

"Mike didn't," Emma explained. "He's Brad's roommate, though, and really good with computers so we roped him into this."

"I have nothing better to do," Mike smiled. He was strikingly good looking with a head full of dark, curly hair and an olive complexion that made him look Mediterranean.

"Don't let him fool you," Lindy smirked, giving Mike a punch in the arm. "He's as invested in this as we are."

"I don't know how much help I can be," Taryn interjected. She still wasn't sure *why* she was there, and not in the apartment but in Georgia at all.

"They all know about your, um," Emma faltered, searching for the word.

"Powers?" Brad of the camo pants suggested.

Taryn laughed. "I'm not a superhero! And it's more my camera than me. I've tried taking pictures of the farm, but I'm not really picking up on anything. All I can tell you is I know she was there. And, of course, you know that already."

For some reason she wasn't ready to share anything about her dreams yet, or the scream. Those felt too personal and she thought it best she play things as close to her vest as possible at the moment.

"Well, we can show you what we have," Emma insisted, snapping to attention and suddenly becoming business like. They removed the pizza boxes from the coffee table, which turned out to be a shipping crate, and began putting folders on it. Emma picked the first one up and opened it. A few sheets of paper fluttered out. "This is a time-line. It shows everything Cheyenne was up to in the forty-eight hours leading up to her death. There's also some copies of receipts in here to prove where she was."

"How in the world did you get *those*?" Taryn asked, raising her eyebrows. "Surely the police didn't..."

"Oh, no," Lindy replied. "From Thelma herself. She's given up on the police. They were dragging their feet. She hired a private investigator and a lot of this stuff is things she gave him. We just asked for copies, too."

"What happened to the private investigator?"

Emma shrugged. "He didn't turn up anything new. That's why Thelma let us take a crack at it."

"And brought in you," Mike smiled.

"To be honest, we don't have much to go on," Brad explained.

121

"It's like she just vanished into thin air," Eric quipped, the first thing she'd heard him say.

Taryn glanced over the time-line and receipts but there were no red flags. Cheyenne looked like a typical teenager: McDonald's (quarter pounder with cheese, no pickles), tanning bed, Walmart (Revlon lipstick, a bag of Doritos, and a Keith Urban CD), and a milkshake from Dairy Queen. She'd apparently used her own bank card for all of the transactions.

"Did Cheyenne have a job or anything?" she asked after she'd flipped through everything.

"No," Emma replied. "She worked at a car wash one summer and talked about applying at Walmart after she graduated but..." Emma let her voice trail off as the implication hung in the air. Cheyenne had never gotten around to applying at Walmart because she was gone.

"Her parents gave her money," Brad supplied. "They worried about her and didn't want her to get stranded somewhere."

"Did they have a reason to be worried or was it just your typical parent thing?" Taryn asked. She remembered Thelma saying Cheyenne hadn't gotten along with her step-father.

Emma folder her hands under her chin and propped her elbows on her knees. "Cheyenne wasn't happy at home. That last year was probably the worst. She was hardly ever there. She'd come stay with me for a while, with Lindy a little bit, with an aunt... I mean, she always called home and checked in and all; she just didn't like being there. You know what I mean?"

"Is there any chance she just got too tired of it and left?" Taryn asked gently. In a lot of ways it did look like a runaway case. At least, the armchair detective in her, schooled by episodes of *Law and Order* and *Criminal Minds*, thought.

"No," Emma objected stubbornly. "I could see her doing it for a few days, maybe even a couple of weeks, but never for this long."

"Did they ever find anything of hers from that night? Any clues at all?"

"Her purse," Lindy offered. "It was still by the bonfire. One of the detectives thought when she caught the ride she must have been in a hurry and left her purse behind."

"I don't buy that," Emma frowned. "She always had that damn thing with her. She kept a ton of makeup in there, some emergency cash, her cell phone... no. She wouldn't have gone anywhere without at least her cell."

The group was quiet, lost in collective thought. The silence between them was almost tangible.

"So what else do you have here?" Taryn gestured to the table, breaking the stillness in the air.

Brad and Mike began picking up folders and opening them. "We've got topographical maps of the farm and of the county, a list of people who have been interviewed and who we think need to be interviewed, pictures of her..."

Taryn hadn't planned on being alone in the total darkness as she drove back out to the house. While Emma's apartment was only a twenty minute drive away, the long driveway that separated the house from the rest of the outside world felt like a dark tunnel, channeling Taryn to another realm. The tall pines on either side reached up to the black sky, menacing now, shading the road from the glare of the moon and stars. She drove with her brights on, but still had trouble seeing more than a few feet ahead.

The normally soothing sounds of the Emmylou Harris CD she had pushed into the player now sounded eerie, a forbidding backdrop to the shadowy road and almost perfect stillness. She had to turn the song when "Love Hurts" came on, the almost dragging sound of her voice intertwined around the now-deceased Graham Parsons was just too much. Taryn slowed down to a crawl and poked around in the passenger seat for something else. A collection of Bryan Adams' hits might have been a little cheesy, but it was hard to feel frightened when "Summer of '69" was blaring through the speakers.

"Well, that's better," she mumbled to herself. Taryn had no problems talking to herself when she was alone. One day she'd probably be the crazy cat lady with the lavender-painted house and garden gnomes lining the walkway but for now she figured it was okay.

The night was cold so she'd cranked up the heater. The coldness made her joints hurt worse than usual, and she couldn't help but think about her grandmother; she'd always complained of arthritis in her knees and hips. "I'm getting older every second," Taryn sighed. "Pretty soon I'll be adding Vic's salve and support hose to the shopping cart."

She felt a sigh of relief when the road opened up to the meadow where the house sat, but then rolled her eyes when she realized it was as dark as a dungeon – she'd forgotten to leave a light on. "I'll be damned," she muttered, opening the car door to the wind and cold.

Running in an attempt to hold onto the heat of the car, she bounded onto the porch, trying not to think about the fact that when she got the door opened she'd be stepping foot inside a dark house.

When she placed her hand on the knob, though, and tried to turn it she remembered that she'd locked it behind her when she left. Still muttering to herself, she rummaged through her coat pocket, the cold leaving her fingers stiff and numb.

Taryn had just fished the key out and was inserting it into the slot when the wind unexpectedly died down and the other sound began to build. It was subtle at first, a whisper, but it had her stopping in her tracks, the key left dangling loosely in the door. Then the whimper was all around her, a sound of helplessness. It encircled her like the wind, growing louder and louder. Taryn felt it in her feet, in her hands, prickling at her brain. As it began to build in volume, so it grew in distress. It was no longer a whimper now, but a cry of terror.

Taryn turned in circles on the porch, her hands over her ears trying to block the horrible noise out, but could see nothing. She watched in shock as the keys shook on their chain and the windows rattled in their frames. The black night was a curtain and even the moon had slipped behind a cloud, leaving her completely alone with the horror unfolding around her. Taryn was at the center of a vortex, surrounded by a sound of incalculable fear she'd never felt herself. "Please stop, please stop, please stop," she chanted, but her words were lost, consumed by the night.

And as quickly as it started it stopped. There was nothing; the night air was quiet again, with only the sounds of Taryn's labored breathing breaking up the silence. She kept her hands over her ears, forgetting they were there. The moon and stars reemerged and shone down, illuminating the walkway and part of the porch. She took a tentative step, back towards the door and nothing happened. Now, more quickly, she scurried forward and began turning the key again.

But that was when she felt it.

With every instinct she had she *knew* there was something behind her, maybe only a few feet away. The key was stuck, probably from the rattling. As she began working faster to dislodge it, she could feel whatever it was moving closer and closer to her, an icy arm reaching out for her. A strand of her hair might have moved, tugged on, brushed aside. Drops of dirt fell at her feet. The breathing on her neck was cold, sour, and reminded her of throwing up after one too many cocktails. The scent lingered on Taryn, threatening to sink down into her skin and stay.

Taryn's blood ran cold, her fear mounting as she fumbled with the door and lock. The fear started at the top of her head and quickly moved down to her hands and then feet as the eyes she knew were not far behind bore into her. There was a hitch of someone else's breath and then, finally, with one frantic shove, she opened the door and stumbled into the house, slamming the door to whatever was waiting for her on the porch.

Chapter 12

$\mathcal{M}$att had been gone for four days and Taryn barely slept a wink because of it. It was nearly impossible for her to sleep at night so she'd taken to dozing during the day and then staying up during the night, editing photos and watching infomercials (thank goodness she was currently broke or else she'd been ordering everything she saw). The few times she *had* drifted off she'd gone straight into terrible nightmares, despite the fact she still wore her grandmother's ring. Even awake she listened to every little creak and groan the house made. And it made a lot. The night before she'd been sure she heard laughter upstairs, followed by footsteps in the kitchen. Cellphone in hand, she'd stalked the sources of the sounds and even called out in an attempt to communicate, but received nothing. It had her on edge and was enough to drive anyone insane.

Still, when Matt called she refrained from telling him about what had transpired on the porch; after all, he was working on something important and didn't need to be distracted. She could figure this out on her own.

She'd worked in haunted houses before. Few things would ever be as scary as Windwood Farm, or as troubling as Griffith Tavern. But this felt different. In hindsight, Permelia's ghost at Griffith Tavern was trying to give her clues and point her in a direction. And she wasn't completely certain that what she'd seen, felt, and heard at Windwood was really ghosts at work or just leftover energy. This, though. *This* felt pointed. Whatever was going on outside was being directed at her. It was *aware*. Proactive. And she had no idea what it wanted, although she could take a few guesses.

Despite the warm autumn sun pouring through the windows, Taryn wrapped herself up tighter in her fluffy bathrobe. Matt would be back soon and then at least she'd be able to sleep through the night again. And she'd definitely eat better. Without him there she'd resorted to pasta meals and takeout. And by "pasta meals" she wasn't talking about penne with sun-dried tomatoes and a white wine sauce. It was more along the lines of mac and cheese.

When she wasn't preparing for class, trying to sleep, or editing her photos, she was busy trying to organize her thoughts about Cheyenne's disappearance. She'd made notes, jotted down questions to ask Emma, and gone back over her pictures a dozen times. She didn't feel like she was closer to achieving any answers. But she was almost positive she was being haunted by the missing girl.

It had been so long since Taryn paid for gas inside rather than at the pump that she almost found the act charming. Almost. It would've been more so if sleet hadn't been coming down in angles, stabbing her from all directions. She'd forgotten to fill the rental car up, again, and couldn't make it all the way to the college. Instead, she'd had to stop at the gas station on the outskirts—that one hadn't yet upgraded to "pay at the pump" status but still served biscuits and gravy inside for $2.99.

Before she paid she wandered around and picked up a few essentials for her drive into class and back: a couple of candy bars, a Mountain Dew, and some stomach acid tablets since she was pretty sure she was rotting her lining out with all the junk she'd been eating.

The overweight, frizzy-haired woman at the counter paid her no mind as she bagged up her items. Instead, her face was turned away, her eyes glued to something that was going on outside. "Six dollars and seventy-three cents," she announced vaguely, quickly glancing down at Taryn's card before looking back outside again.

"And thirty in gas?" Taryn supplied helpfully.

"Oh, yeah. My mind's somewhere else," she offered as an apology.

"Is everything okay?"

"Just watching," she murmured.

Now Taryn's eyes were peeled to the window, too. A stocky man with a blond crewcut and goatee was kneeling by his truck pumping air in his rear right tire. Colorful tattoos ran up his arm and disappeared under the sleeve of his white T-shirt. He didn't seem to be doing anything to warrant such careful observation. When he was finished, he jumped back up into his truck and peeled out of the gas station, black smoke billowing behind him.

Taryn was still waiting for her card when the cashier finally gave her a full inspection. "That was Travis Marcum. He doesn't get out much, but I like to keep my eye out for when he does. You just can't trust someone like that."

Wanting to pry so badly, and yet feeling the need for decorum, Taryn walked a tightrope between manners and curiosity. "Is he the guy who..."

The cashier nodded with such vigor that her glasses almost fell off the end of her nose. She used one finger to push them back up and the other to punch in digits on the credit card machine. "Yep, that's him. Everyone knows he killed Cheyenne Willoughby, or at least helped hide the body."

Travis Marcum. Taryn rolled the name around in her mind. That would be the older friend Cheyenne was last seen with.

"So did you know Cheyenne?"

Obviously pleased with the idea of being important enough to share information with, the cashier leaned forward and stage whispered. "Known her since she was a little thing. And one day law enforcement will have everything they need and give that no-good account a ride in the electric chair!"

Dang, Taryn thought, *talk about the night the lights went out in Georgia.* (Although she didn't think Georgia used old sparky anymore.)

"So what's Travis doing now?" she asked, hoping for more information.

"Nothing," the cashier sniffed. "Nobody around here with any sense will hire him. He lost his job driving the fork lift over at the speaker factory, and I reckon his parents keep him up now. He moved back home."

"So you probably know everyone around here," Taryn prodded.

"Yeah, mostly. The town's not the same as it was when I was growing up, that's for sure, but it's still small. Better when the college clears out. A bunch of prissy tree huggers who think they know more than anyone else. Asking for a Starbucks to come in here and complaining there isn't a decent place to buy groceries - like the Wal-Mart isn't good enough for them."

Taryn nodded her head in what she hoped resembled commiseration, despite the fact Matt had also pined for those very same things.

"It's a pretty place, though," Taryn smiled. "I like a small town."

"Yeah, well," she sniffed. "It will be a lot better when certain people are locked up where they belong. At least we'll know the streets are safe again."

"**I** didn't get everything wrapped up here like I thought I would," Matt apologized. His voice was muffled and she suspected he was on the other side of room, shouting back at her. It made her want to shout back.

"It's okay, I'm fine." She hoped she sounded more lighthearted than she felt. "I taught today and have tomorrow off. Then there's the weekend. How's it going?"

"Oh, I got to train a new group of student interns today. They all called me 'Professor' or 'Mister.' (One of those was wrong and the other just made me feel old. You?"

"Not much. Just been working on some things here at the house." Of course, she couldn't possibly tell him she spent most of the daylight hours sleeping because she was too scared when it was dark. He wouldn't have made fun of her, but he probably would've been back on the road and home in time for a midnight snack at the very least.

"Any new break-throughs?"

"No, but I *did* see the guy they said was the last one with her. I mean, I didn't *meet* him or anything. I saw him from a gas station window."

"Oh yeah? What's he like?"

Taryn smirked. "A little bit like Apple Valley's very own Boo Radley. He looked harmless enough, but I think if the cashier

133

could've called the police she would have. You could tell she was looking for a reason."

"Listen, I want you to be really careful," Matt ordered, worry edging his voice. "I didn't like leaving you there alone, and you really don't know what you're getting into."

"Oh, I'm fine," Taryn tried her best to sound casual. "Remember, I've been on my own for a while, and this isn't my first rodeo with the strange and unusual."

"Yeah, but it's different this time. This time around all the key players are still alive. And we don't know what happened to Cheyenne. If someone hurt her, they could very well go after someone else next. Say, a pretty redhead who asks too many questions..."

Although she could hear a smile on Matt's lips, she knew he was anxious to get back. And she also knew he was right. This was the first mystery she'd ever been actively involved in. After all, this one had actually sought her out and brought her there. Some people might not take that lightly.

Emma picked Taryn up at noon, only about thirty minutes after she'd gotten up and thrown some clothes on. Taryn had stayed up late the night before, supposedly working but really watching a *Friends* marathon, and hadn't passed out until after daybreak. She'd nearly forgotten about Emma's email and invitation for lunch.

134

When the maroon Chevy pulled into the driveway Taryn pulled on a Vanderbilt University hoodie, grabbed her knapsack, and pulled the door to behind her. At the last second she decided to lock it. She and Matt didn't normally lock it behind them, but coming back to a house that had remained open all day didn't seem prudent anymore when she was there alone. Of course, it might have come in handy to have it unlocked a few nights ago... ...

Lindy was riding shotgun, a baseball cap perched on her head, her long hair streaming in a ponytail out the back. In contrast to Emma's put-together look of long skirt and leather jacket, Lindy's tight sweatpants and tighter T-shirt made it look as though she'd just come from the gym. Both girls had fresh, young faces that would be pretty, thanks to their ages, even if they weren't particularly attractive. Taryn felt old as she squeezed in beside Lindy.

"I had to get out of the house," Lindy explained sourly as the sped down the gravel road. "My mom is driving me nuts."

"But we have to stop by there because Miss Thang forgot her purse and she doesn't go anywhere without it," Emma added.

Lindy shrugged and studied her fingernails, wrapped in the latest Jamberry special. "It's got my phone and shit in it. It will just take a minute."

"I'm glad to be getting out, too," Taryn admitted. "I've only been getting out of the house to teach and grocery shop. I'm starting to go a little stir crazy back there by myself."

"Don't you get, like, scared or anything?" Lindy asked with interest. Sitting so close to her, Taryn was breathing in her strong scent – a mixture of cigarette smoke and some pop star's perfume.

135

It reminded her of how Matt always said smoking was a dating deal breaker for him, no matter how much he liked the woman, and she was suddenly filled with a longing for his OCD ways.

"I don't always like being by myself," Taryn admitted. "And you know how it is. You start hearing every little noise. I leave the TV on a lot."

"Shit, I couldn't last a night out there," Lindy swore. "Better you than me."

"You couldn't last a night anywhere that was more than a five-minute drive from Taco Bell," Emma teased her and Lindy laughed. "Seriously. We went camping once and after about an hour she was begging Cheyenne to drive her to Walmart . She didn't need anything; she just wanted to walk around."

"I like Walmarting ," Lindy shrugged.

"I didn't think you guys knew her that well," Taryn countered lightly.

"Yeah, well, we were all friends back in middle school and our freshmen and sophomore years. We've only got the one middle and high school here and, like, three elementary schools. So we all knew each other. Technically."

"But we hadn't been friends for a while," Lindy added. "Cheyenne started dating a guy named Stuart when we were sophomores. He was a real asshat. She didn't have much time for friends after that."

"Just too busy dating?"

"Nah. He didn't like us. He said we were too loud and trashy."

"Lindy, he didn't say that," Emma admonished.

"Yeah, well, I'm paraphrasing, okay?"

"He was kind of different," Emma explained. "He was two years older than Cheyenne. Real smart. Took classes at the college when he was still in high school. Made fun of country music because he said it was 'redneck.' Only wanted to watch things like documentaries and serious movies. I think Cheyenne started dating him at first because she was so flattered he liked her. And he had a car."

"So what happened to him?"

Emma sighed. "He went up to Duke on some kind of academic scholarship and broke up with Cheyenne two months later. His parents moved to Virginia the next year and nobody has seen him since."

The double wide they pulled up to was one of the fancy ones, designed to look like a log cabin. The porch boasted a standalone swing, pots of dead flowers, and a menagerie of children's toys. "My mom babysits during the day," Lindy explained as Taryn got out of the truck to let her slide across the seat. "Come on, you can come in. I'll just be a sec, and it's too cold to sit out here."

There was total chaos inside, with a horde of toddlers chasing a red dachshund through the living room. They appeared to be trying to tie a bonnet on his head. When he dove under the couch they began working together as a team to coax him out. At the sound of the door shutting, a tall thin woman with wild, shaggy black hair and what looked like chocolate frosting coating her white T-shirt came out of the kitchen.

"Sorry," she called over the noise. "Didn't hear you guys pull up."

"What?!" Lindy shouted in a decibel level Taryn thought unnecessary.

"Julie!" Lindy's mother raised her own voice. A plump young woman ambled into the living room, a look of frustration on her face. "Take them to the playroom so that I can hear myself think."

Within seconds the kids were rounded up and marched down the hallway, the room almost immediately quiet. "I hired her to help but she don't do a whole lot," she complained as she cleared off a space of toys on the couch and flopped down, the springs creaking under her. "You guys want anything?"

"I'm just here to get my purse," Lindy muttered before stalking off, leaving Taryn and Emma alone.

"I'm Bonnie," she introduced herself at last. "Welcome to the nuthouse."

"It's lively," Taryn bubbled, trying to maintain a smile. Since every other available surface was littered with either toys, baby wipes, or random articles of clothing she perched on an armrest.

"Yeah, well, I get disability but it don't cover shit anymore, not with the price of gas and everything else going up. My water bill was almost forty-five dollars last month. Who can afford to pay that? The babysittin' money's my spending money."

"I hear that," Taryn agreed. "Everything's getting higher." Although her water bill in Nashville averaged around thirty dollars a month, and she lived alone and was rarely ever even there.

"Are you feeling okay, Mrs. Clifton?" Emma asked politely.

"Oh, it's my back mostly. But then sometimes it starts in my legs, too, and that makes it tough to walk around," Bonnie crowed, a sorrowful look immediately creeping over her face. Still, Taryn got the distinct feeling she enjoyed talking about her ailments. "I was in a wreck a few years ago and it messed me up. And now I got this arthritis on top of things," she explained to Taryn.

She didn't think Bonnie looked a day over forty, but she carried herself like someone much older.

When Lindy came back into the room she sported an over-sized Ed Hardy purse and matching cell phone case. "Have those little brats been going through my shit?" she demanded, glowering at her mother.

"I tried to keep them out of there, but I can't be everywhere at once," Bonnie whined.

"I had perfume spilt all over my dresser, and there's something brown and sticky on my comforter," Lindy complained. "And I am not cleaning it up."

"You know," Bonnie began tragically, her eyes looking down at the laminate hardwood floors as she slowly shook her head back and forth. "Your uncle had cancer and died just three months after being diagnosed."

"What the hell does that have to do with anything? It was two years ago," Lindy balked.

"It's just a reminder that some people have bad things going on in their lives and you'd best remember that before you start complaining about little things."

139

"That perfume cost me sixty dollars!" Lindy's screech cut through the room like a knife, and Taryn jumped a little, feeling embarrassed to be subjected to the drama. .

"I read on Facebook today that Janine Evans' daughter was in a car crash last night and is still in ICU," Bonnie continued, like she hadn't heard her daughter.

"Who's Janine Evans?" Lindy's look of confusion almost had Taryn laughing, but she thought better of it.

"You know. I went to high school with her that year my family lived in Atlanta? She sent me a friend request back last spring."

"Oh my God," Lindy muttered. "Let's go." Swinging past Taryn and Emma she was out the door and on the porch before Taryn could even get up.

"It was nice meeting you, and I hope you feel a little better later," Taryn spoke politely to her hostess.

"Oh, I don't know. Seems to get a little worse every day," Bonnie sighed with regret.

Back in the truck Lindy was still complaining about her mother. "She does that too me all the time. Totally interrupts me with random crap about people I don't even know. She refreshes her Facebook news feed every fifteen minutes to keep up with people she hasn't seen in twenty years."

"How bad was the car wreck she was in?" Taryn asked.

"Oh, hell. It was a fender bender. And she was pulling that disabled shit long before," Lindy declared with a sigh.

A crackling fire was roaring in the Cracker Barrel's dining room, and the perky waitress seated them in front of it, much to Taryn's delight. She was freezing, thanks to the lack of heat in Emma's truck, and wished she'd worn something warmer.

"So I've told Lindy about what you do," Emma confided to Taryn after they'd all ordered off the breakfast menu and were sipping on their root beers. "You know, the ghost stuff. She knew about the painting."

"Don't worry, I don't think you're a freak or anything," Lindy laughed. Like a lot of girls her age, she had the talent of being able to text incredibly fast on her iPhone and still manage to remain an active participant in the conversation.

"Well, that's good," Taryn mumbled. She still wasn't real comfortable with people knowing about her and Miss Dixie, although, since working at Griffith Tavern, there had been quite a bit about the stuff that went on there, including her part in it, written online. She couldn't escape it.

"So back to you staying out there by yourself," Emma began. "Have you seen or heard anything scary?"

A little nagging sensation at the corner of her brain kept her from spilling the beans about the noises and what she'd experienced on the porch. So she lied. "No, nothing spooky."

"I think Thelma is hoping you'll pick up on something to do with Cheyenne," Lindy explained. "I'm sure that's why she put you out there instead of at a hotel."

"Or because they own the place and it was free for them," Emma frowned at her friend.

"You think she thinks it because Cheyenne was there that night?" Taryn asked. "I mean, from all accounts, she was also at her friend's house, and that was later in the night."

"I don't know," Lindy shrugged. "She's probably just grasping at straws, you know?"

"I would be, too, if it were *my* daughter," Emma put in softly. "So have you come up with any new ideas you could share with us? You know, about what happened?"

"Not really," Taryn answered honestly. "It all just seems to be all over the place, you know what I mean? Was it drug related? Did she run away? Was it the friend? An accident? A total stranger?"

"Human trafficking," Lindy added.

Emma cocked her head and glared at Lindy like she'd sprouted another mouth. "Really? Here?"

"Hey, it's everywhere now, man," Lindy replied with heat. "I watched a Lifetime movie about it and everything. And we are right off the interstate. It could happen."

"It seems to be a thing now," Taryn agreed. "Even police can't rule it out in missing person's cases anymore. Especially when it's a missing female."

"When we grew up here it was totally safe. I rode my bike everywhere. We walked to each other's houses, played outside after dark," Lindy reported wistfully, her eyes taking on a dreamy look and her face softening until she magically looked even years younger, and Taryn could almost see what she might have looked like as a little girl. The waitress came back, her arms laden with food. She began doling it out in front of the women. "It's not like that anymore."

"Now kids don't even go trick-or-treating like they used to because everyone is so afraid," Emma ranted, getting worked up. "They get a bunch of businesses and line them up downtown and then march the kids through. They get a lot of candy, but there's so many kids they don't even get the chance to say 'trick-or-treat.'"

"That's sad," Taryn murmured, now feeling a little depressed. She'd mostly grown up in a subdivision outside of Nashville and she, too, remembered playing outside after dark and riding her bike down to the corner store to buy pop and candy bars alone.

"It's just not the same world anymore," Lindy complained through a mouthful of hash brown casserole. "You can't trust anyone."

Despite the fact Taryn was having difficulty sleeping in the house alone, when 10 pm rolled around she found herself dragging her tired feet up the stairs and collapsing into the bed. She'd spent nearly all day with the girls, being dragged first from one store to another and then to the movies. They might have been ten years younger than her, but it was the first time she'd really felt like she had girlfriends and the warm, tingling feeling of limited acceptance flooded through her like wine.

"High school would've been so much better if I'd had girlfriends," she muttered as she slid under the covers. Taryn had always been jealous of the girls who had best friends and a close circle of friends – people they could confide in and giggle with and act silly with. Television shows like *Sex and the City* depressed her and even though she couldn't stand Carrie Bradshaw she found herself unable to take her eyes away, not because she liked the romance or tawdriness but because she was jealous of the relationships between the four women. Sure, Matt had always been there for her and was the greatest best friend one could ask for, but at the end of the day he was a dude and there were some things she just couldn't share with him. She'd found that out in high school when she'd confided she'd lost her virginity and he'd refused to talk to her for a month. She now saw that for what it was – jealousy – but at the time all she'd felt was embarrassment and hurt.

Because she spent so much time on the road she didn't have the opportunity to make lasting friendships as an adult. Her first few years after college were spent with Andrew, ensconced in marital bliss. Andrew was likable and friendly, but they didn't have "couple" friends together, just acquaintances they mostly met during jobs. After his accident she'd delved into her work and stayed gone as much as she could. She didn't even know her neighbors back at her Nashville apartment.

As she drifted off to sleep, the sound of the television in the bedroom turned softly to a crime show, she let herself think of the group of kids who'd grown up there in the town. What must it have been like, going all the way through school with the same group of people? To have folks know your name in almost every business you walked into? To have that feeling of being *known* by everyone, even if those people weren't your friends? Was it comforting? Stifling? At the moment, it sounded nice.

Something was in the house. Taryn's eyes flew open at the sound but still she laid in bed, her heart racing in her chest. She didn't move a muscle as she trained her ears to the dark. The television, set to a timer, was off. The low rumbling of the heater was now the only noise pulsating through the air.

Still, she'd heard something.

By turning her head a little to the left she could see the clock on her nightstand. The red numbers flashed 3:15 am. *I should've known*, she thought to herself. Taryn had a tendency to wake up, unprovoked, at the same time on a regular basis.

The air around her was still, almost unnaturally so. Again, she strained her ears to pick up the sound that had awakened her, but all she could hear was the sound of her own labored breathing and the pumping of her heart in her ears. *Calm yourself, calm yourself*, she chanted in her mind. She would not give in to a panic attack. Taking a deep breath she held onto her air for several seconds, hoping to hear something. When she thought she would burst, she let it out. Of course if she tried to hear a sound she would. That didn't mean anything was there.

Angry at herself for getting scared and disgusted with feeling like an idiot, she sat up in bed and stared into the darkness. She could barely see her hand in front of her face, but there would be a lamp on downstairs if she wanted to get up. But something made her stay. The darkness pressed in around her, a wall, and kept her rooted to the bed. Her blankets, bunched around her hips, were a shield and she wasn't ready to let them go. Although the night was silent, and she was certain she'd locked all the doors, every nerve in her body was on fire, all going a million miles a second. If she touched something she expected to see sparks fly.

She might be scared, but she wasn't crazy. Something wasn't right.

Before Taryn could make a move, the noise came again. It was a definite creak, the sound of weight on a floorboard. The movement was hesitant, testing. She knew then, that what she'd heard had been real. She was aware of something downstairs and, whatever it was, it was equally aware of her.

Taryn's overactive imagination immediately went into high gear. The creak was close, at the bottom of the stairs perhaps. A quick-moving figure could be to her in a matter of seconds. She had no gun, no knife, or weapon of any sort. It was so dark in the room she'd fumble grasping for something to use as one. Maybe the lamp? But how could she find it? She didn't know where the plug was. Why had someone come in on her? What did they want? Were they there to kill her? Rape her? Worse? (And what was worse?)

Slowly, holding her breath, Taryn rose to her knees and shed the blanket. It dropped to the floor in a soft thud. Her weight

146

shifted the box springs and as a small groan escaped from them, the creak came again, this time louder. Was it closer? Was it on the stairs?

Suddenly, Matt's face appeared behind her eyes, his dark eyes flashing at her. She wanted to cry out for him, reach for him, but he was far away from her. She was on her own.

And then, as her phone on the nightstand let out a shrill call, she realized she wasn't. Grabbing it in relief she flipped it open to the sound of Matt's voice. "Are you okay?" he asked with urgency. "I-"

"Oh, good!" she cried into the phone. "I thought maybe you'd given up on coming tonight because it was so late!"

With newfound energy, Taryn pounced off the bed and fumbled for the lamp switch. The bedroom was filled with a soft glow. It was quiet downstairs, listening.

"What?"

""So you think about five more minutes?" she asked loudly. "Oh, you can see the driveway? I'll go ahead and get the coffee started." She laughed at herself then, and the fact neither one of them drank coffee. It sounded so absurd.

"Taryn? You want me to call the police?"

"Yes please," she nearly sobbed. "That would be great!"

Moving quickly to her door she pushed it to with an urgency and force she didn't know she possessed and then dragged the small office chair and placed it under the knob. She knew then her activity meant she couldn't possibly hear what was going on beneath her, but she didn't care. She would be safe for a few minutes.

"Calling now," Matt vowed. "Using the land line. Stay on the phone."

"Okay." She cried now, sliding down to the floor at the foot of the bed. "Please hurry."

Matt stayed with her on the line until the blue lights reflected in her bedroom window. "I'll call you back," she promised. "They're here."

"I'm packing now. Be there in a few hours."

There was no way she was going to argue with him.

The pounding on the door below was comforting but even as she flew down the stairs she was scared, scared someone might be behind her or waiting for her at the bottom. She opened the door without any trouble, though, and two middle-aged officers stood waiting for her.

While one sat with her on the couch, the other walked through the house, looking. "I'm going to feel silly if it was my imagination. Or a ghost," she tried to laugh. The serious-looking officer, who introduced himself as Worley, smile grimly.

"Better safe than sorry," he declared. "Especially you being out here by yourself."

It didn't take more than ten minutes for the other officer to scan the interior and exterior of the house. When he came back, Worley stood up to greet him. "Miss Magill here is afraid she might have just heard a ghost," he stated.

"No ghost, ma'am," he muttered. "Unless you have a very active one."

"What do you mean?"

148

"Kitchen window is smashed. That's how they got in. Probably what woke you up. You're lucky you had someone call us when you did. This could've ended very badly for you."

Chapter 13

*O*ther than the broken window, there were no other signs

anyone, besides Taryn, had been in the house. "It was probably a random burglary," someone had told her while she waited in the small police station, wrapped in a warm blanket. She couldn't stop shaking. "That house is usually empty. They were probably surprised to find you there."

"But my car was there," she muttered. Nobody seemed to hear her or care.

After taking her statement, she had an officer drive her to the local Hampton Inn. There was no way she could go back to the cabin. Matt would be there soon and he agreed the motel was the best place for her.

Thelma, beside herself with worry, had wanted Taryn to stay with her. "We have plenty of room, sweetie," she'd moaned, all but wringing her hands together. She blamed herself, even though she'd been miles away and nobody had ever bothered the place before.

"I'll be fine," Taryn assured her. "Besides, it has a hot tub and I could do with a dip."

The false positivity she was emitting was a stark contrast to the terror she felt inside. She'd been confronted by an angry ghost, trapped inside a small room by a confused ghost, subjected to multiple dead bodies, and held at gunpoint. None of those things had prepared her for the helplessness and fear she'd experienced in the house.

Thelma continued to comfort her and engulf her in random, bosomy hugs until she was released and then she drove Taryn to the motel. "My friend will be here soon, and he'll drive me back to the house."

Thelma and her husband insisted on waiting while Taryn checked in and then accompanied her to her room. She hadn't packed anything but her laptop and Miss Dixie so there was nothing to carry. "Don't you worry about a thing, sweetie," Thelma reassured her before they left. "We're fixing that window first thing and installing security tomorrow. And we've paid for three nights here. If you need more, just let us know. You don't have to go back at all if you don't want to."

As exhausted as she was, sleep wouldn't come. The motel had interior corridors and these made her feel safe and secure, but every time she closed her eyes she could still see the darkness of the bedroom, hear the creak of the floorboard. A late-night black and white movie was playing on the standard-sized motel television set and she lost herself in it while she waited for Matt.

The sun was bursting through the sky, streaks of red and purple against white, when Matt knocked on her door. She opened it and fell against him, instantly feeling a mixture of relief and disgust with herself for not being able to hack it on her own. "Well that was fun, wasn't it?" he tried to chuckle but she could feel him tense under her arms.

Gently, he led her back to the bed where he pulled down the covers and tucked her in. She curled her body in towards his as he sank down in beside her and began stroking her hair back from her forehead. "Sweet girl," he murmured. "Go to sleep, and I'll be here when you wake up."

After three days in the hotel she was ready to return to the cabin. "We don't have to go. We can keep staying here," Matt suggested. "You only have a few weeks left."

152

Taryn was restless, though, and feeling silly for all the drama she seemed to have caused. Even her students were walking around her on eggshells, treating her gently. Emma and Lindy had visited her at the hotel twice. They claimed it was to make use of the pool and hot tub, but both had appeared worried to her and Emma even apologized for not offering to stay with her while Matt was gone. "I should've just moved in until he got back," she swore. "What were we thinking, leaving you out there alone?"

"It's okay, really." Taryn was embarrassed not only by the attention but by the fact people didn't seem to think she could take care of herself. "I've been on my own for a long time and have stayed in much more isolated places. I once stayed at a farmhouse in the mountains for almost two months and barely saw a soul."

But, of course, nobody had disappeared on that farm and there was no ongoing investigation that quite possibly included people in the general vicinity.

Since Matt had gone to the cabin to look around and packed her an overnight bag, Taryn hadn't returned since the night of the intrusion. She stood in the front yard now, looking at it against the harsh October sun. It appeared harmless enough, a picturesque log house set amid a forest backdrop. But as soon as she stepped foot on the porch she could remember waking up in the darkness, the blind panic at not knowing what to do next, the rush of adrenalin as she'd pushed the chair in front of the door and then held her breath as she waited for the inevitable sound of her intruder charging up the stairs.

Could she really stay here?

Yes, she could and she would. She wasn't a wimp. A new alarm system was installed and anyone coming in through the doors or windows after they went to bed would set off a shrill and notice that would go straight to the police station. And then there was a tiny part of her invigorated by what happened. There was no way the break-in was random. Someone was trying to scare her, or worse, and that meant she may have been onto something and didn't even know it. She aimed to find out what it might be. Cheyenne deserved it.

Matt didn't feel good about letting her roam around the property without him, but he was too polite to invite himself along. When she'd turned down his offer to accompany her he'd let it go. Still, as she walked across the yard towards the treeline she could see him standing in the kitchen window, pretending to wash dishes.

She felt safe in the daylight. Although she knew it was a false sense of security, hundreds of women were abducted every year in the middle of the day and even in public, she forced herself onward. She had a hankering to visit the old farmhouse again and to put herself back on the site where Cheyenne was last seen.

When the air was crisp and the sunlight shockingly bright against the naked trees and brittle grass it was almost hard to believe something frightening had taken place at the cabin just a few days before. She'd been surprised at just how calm she'd felt inside, sure she'd be plagued by post trauma that would keep her up at night. But Matt's calming presence had helped and his positive energy filled the rooms with light. She was safe near him, protected.

The woods, though thick and quiet, were peaceful. She loved the country, even though she hadn't grown up in it, and found a sweet solace in the soft pine needles under her feet, the burnt smell of autumn, and the closing out of the world around her.

But then she stepped out of the trees and into the meadow where the farmhouse stood and everything changed. Again.

"There's something not right here," she murmured to herself. Miss Dixie slapped against her thigh in agreement. "I wonder why?"

For the longest time, she didn't move and stared in perplexity at the house and fields before her. They were innocuous enough. But she felt safer in the shadows of the trees, just knowing they were only a few feet behind her.

It didn't make sense that's she'd feel such a sense of foreboding there. Cheyenne hadn't disappeared at the farmhouse. Witnesses had seen her leave in a pickup. They'd watched her drive out the gate. Other witnesses placed her in a house miles from here, long after the party ended.

And yet...

If it were Cheyenne's energy she was picking up on, then why the fear? Why the gnawing sensation something was wrong? Cheyenne had been celebrating here; school was over and she had the freedom only youth in summertime could know. A bonfire,

155

drinks, laughter, music... this should have been a happy place for her.

If Taryn closed her eyes and reached out past the corners of her mind she could almost feel the sweet, youthful energy of the eighteen-year-old around her. The mounting excitement of seeing friends, catching a glimpse of a crush, drinking something bitter and distasteful but loving the warmth it provided inside. Cars, trucks, and four-wheelers parked in the damp grass, someone's radio on. Girls gathered around a group of guys by the fire, watching in earnest as they strummed guitars and tapped rhythm on their knees, maybe with dreams of moving up to Nashville or heading out west when they could afford to go.

It had been a long time since Taryn was a teenager, but things didn't change much; people didn't change that much. Girls would always segregate themselves in clumps, whispering and giggling as they talked about other girls and guys they liked. The guys would always fit into two groups – those who came across standoffish and those who came on too strong. Both would be nervous, their confidence shaky.

What had Cheyenne done? Had she sat by the fire, nursing a lukewarm can of beer? Or had she perched on the edge of the farmhouse steps, surrounded by her girlfriends while their laughter and sparkling smiles faded into the ethereal darkness? Had she danced around, her boots scraping the dirt and her dark hair flying behind her, carefree and oblivious to the world around her? Or had she been quiet, timid, and stayed close to her pack, finding safety in numbers?

What happened at the house after she'd left here? Taryn tried to see her, tried to see Cheyenne standing outside in the early morning air, puffing on a cigarette by herself. A car pulls up a few houses down, two men unknown around here. They watch her for a while, marveling at her youth and fragility. One gets out, offers her a joint or a drink. She's not so nervous at first because he's friendly and good looking. But then the other one comes. He's bigger, threatening. He doesn't crack a smile. She starts feeling the first waves of panic and turns to go inside but then feels a large hand crushing her shoulder, dragging her down. Before she can let out a muffled scream she's unconscious, floating away to a car with an unknown destination.

And for what? To be beaten, raped, killed? Sold to a bidder? Would human traffickers come here to feast on naïve country girls?

That scenario didn't set well with Taryn. It relied too much on convenience and coincidence.

But there was another one that sounded right. In this one, Cheyenne is sitting in a basement bedroom, playing PlayStation. . She's woozy and sick from too much to drink and is trying her best to control her hands but they won't stop shaking. She knows the people around her; they went to school together. She remembers them in kindergarten, learning to read. In middle school, playing basketball. She isn't scared. She's as much at home here as she would be in her own house, and maybe even more so. She feels like she's going to be sick, but nothing will come up when she races to the bathroom.

And then someone hands her something else. The white oblong pill is small and weightless in her hand. "It will make you feel better," the faceless voice in Taryn's mind promises. "You need something to bring you down."

With great trust and little trepidation, she takes it. And, at first, she does feel better. But then comes the feeling of pressure in her chest, the sharp pain radiating to her back. The shortness of breath. The dizziness. God, even when she laid down on the floor she had the feeling of falling. She struggles to keep her eyes open, sure if she closes them something bad will happen. The nausea reaches a crescendo and she spits up a little, but not enough. Finally, the effort is too much and she turns her head and closes her eyes, giving in to the darkness.

What happened to Cheyenne?

"Nothing?" Matt was up to his elbows in flour, making bread.

Taryn sat at the kitchen table, going through her emails. She had two job offers, both wanting her start after Christmas. One was in Arizona. The other was in central Kentucky. She wasn't sure she was ready to return to Kentucky after her experience with Windwood Farm, but working at Shaker Village might be too good of an opportunity to pass up.

"Pictures all came back normal," she answered absently. "House and land look exactly the same as they do now. Nothing out of the ordinary."

"I think it's because nothing actually happened there," Matt declared. "Maybe you're picking up on the energy because it's the last place Cheyenne felt good."

"Then why does it feel off?"

Neither had an answer for that.

"I'm going to have to visit the last place she was at. I know they're not going to let me walk around or anything but I need to at least see it, maybe take a picture of the outside."

Wiping his hands on a dishrag, Matt turned around and leaned against the counter. "You want to go for a drive later? You can hang your head out of the car, and I'll drive the getaway vehicle."

"Sounds like a plan," she grinned.

Chapter 14

It would've been a stretch to call Travis Marcum's

neighborhood a subdivision, but the houses were close together
and his street definitely wasn't isolated. In fact, it was just two
miles from Walmart. . His house was at the end, in a cul-de-sac. It
was a newer construction and looked like all the other ones around
it: one-story, brick, with a garage that stuck out from the front like
a sore thumb. The only differences among the houses around his
were the brick shades and which side of the house the garage stuck
out from.

It was mid-afternoon and the street was quiet. A few
houses had cars in the driveway but Travis' was empty. Still, Taryn
felt like a stalker. As they slowly cruised down the street,
pretending to have an actual destination, Taryn kept Miss Dixie

out on her lap, turned on and ready to shoot. "Okay," she said as they drew close. "I'm gonna roll down the window and when you get in front of the house kind of come to a stop and I'll take some as fast as I can."

"You got it, captain."

Just as they pulled in front of the house and Taryn fired off the first round she was sure she saw the living room curtain move slightly, as though someone might be watching them. Feeling like a deer caught in headlights, she quickly pulled Miss Dixie back down in her lap. "Go, go, go!" she hissed. . Matt pushed on the gas and they sped off, Taryn unable to look back behind her.

They were both laughing when they pulled back out onto the main road. "I think someone was home," she giggled. "We'll probably get the police called on us!"

"We can't be the first people to have done that," he smiled.

"No, but I feel guilty. Like we think Travis is guilty, even though he says he had nothing to do with her disappearance."

"Well, take a look at the pictures when we get home. Maybe you caught something that will help his case."

The pictures, however, were one-hundred percent normal. If there were any contradictions between the past and present, they were too minor for either Taryn or Matt to notice.

"Not what I was hoping for," Taryn frowned, closing the top of her laptop.

"And what was that?"

"I don't know," she shrugged. "Maybe I was hoping to see Cheyenne standing outside on their front porch, smoking or something."

Both were quiet, lost in their own thoughts. Taryn was falling behind in her class. She hadn't been overly prepared yet anyway but at least knew what she was going to talk about. Now she was basically winging it. That wasn't fair to her students. She might have been brought in under false pretenses but the students were paying for her knowledge, however limited that might be, and they deserved to get their money's worth.

"I just don't think I can help this family," she worried at last. "I'm really not that good of a detective, and I've hit brick walls everywhere I've turned. Miss Dixie isn't picking up a damn thing and neither am I."

"I don't know about that," Matt replied thoughtfully. "Maybe you're looking at it in the wrong light."

"What do you mean?"

"Maybe you're getting more than you realize. Maybe you just haven't been able to put all the pieces together yet."

"That's a lot of 'maybes,'" Taryn answered doubtfully. "But do you think I am getting in too deep?"

"Yes," Matt smiled. "But I always think that. Do you want me to call Rob?"

Rob Orange was a friend of Matt's and owned a small store called New Age Gifts & More in Lexington, Kentucky. He sold ritual aids and refurbished electronics and was extraordinarily

162

helpful to Taryn when she was working in Vidalia at Windwood Farm.

"It couldn't hurt, I guess."

Before her experiences at Windwood Farm Taryn hadn't known much about the world of the paranormal at all. She certainly hadn't known there was such a business side to it. The first time she'd found herself in Rob's shop she was astounded by the crystals, incense, oils, how-to books, altar cloths, and wands. And the prices, too! Apparently, the paranormal was big business these days. Later, after exploring the chat rooms, blogs, forums, and websites the Internet had to offer she'd found herself overwhelmed even more. Her "gift," if that's what you wanted to call it, scared her a little. It certainly made her nervous. And yet there were certification courses out there you could pay big money for, to increase or unlock your psychic potential. Some of the information was presented in a straightforward, almost scientific manner. Other things were so far out there she'd thought they were jokes.

People could be freaks.

She liked Rob, though, and if he could help then it was worth a try.

Taryn wouldn't have ordinarily gone to bed alone; she would've stayed awake downstairs and waited for Matt. Or she'd have been the one to stay up late and crashed sometime around daylight when she was just unable to keep her eyes open any longer. But the headache plaguing her all day was now being trumped by the horrendous pain in her left hip. She couldn't figure out if it was muscular or nerve-related but it hurt like the dickens and getting comfortable was impossible. Sitting on the couch with her laptop hurt too much and the glare of the screen was making her head throb. She was even feeling a little dizzy.

"I'm getting old," she muttered to herself. The television was on for the noise, but she wasn't watching it. All the activity and colors were making her jittery.

Maybe it was her shoes. She DID buy cheap shoes. Payless wasn't the bargain it used to be – cheaply made shoes that, price-wise, didn't live up to their name. She'd walked around the property a lot that afternoon and maybe the ragged, off-brand tennis shoes just weren't supporting her legs like they should've been. She was thirty now; she wasn't the young whippersnapper she once was. A good bra and proper support on her feet were becoming increasingly important. It was funny: she never bought off-brand ice cream because she didn't think the quality was the same and yet she thought nothing of putting cheap, worthless crap on her feet.

Matt had spent the evening alternating between rubbing her temples and applying heat and pressure to her hip. She'd also popped some Extra Strength Tylenol and taken a long, hot bath – what Matt teased was warm enough to boil a chicken in. But she was still in pain and it was starting to take over not just her body but her mind as well. Irritated, frustrated, and confused, she tossed and turned while the throbbing grew stronger and stronger, making her whimper and moan into her feather pillow. Small tears leaked from her eyes and puddled beneath her cheek, threatening to soak the pillowcase. She could feel her nose start to fill and the new pressure in her face just added to the pain in her head. "Damn it," she cried, sniffing back the tears and willing herself not to be a wuss. She knew from past experience that crying herself to sleep meant she'd spend the rest of the next day dealing with sinus issues; the first year after Andrew died she'd walked around with one sinus infection after another.

She was tossing and turning, considering just getting up and going back downstairs, when the temperature in the room suddenly changed. It was a noticeable difference as the chill blasted her uncovered legs and arms and eradicated all traces of the lovely heat that had been encompassing her just moments before. The arctic blast sent chills down her spine and raised a road of goosebumps along her exposed skin.

Downstairs, she could hear Matt singing in the kitchen. He was probably still wearing his "Kiss the Cook" apron while he washed dishes and wrapped up the leftover lasagna. Her television was set to low and the sound was friendly, chatty. But she was scared. The logical side of her knew nobody could've gotten into the house without either her or Matt knowing but the irrational side tensed, waiting for the other shoe to drop.

As if by instinct, Taryn slowly slid her feet back under the comforter, engulfing them in the heat and safety of the blanket. Like a little kid afraid of the monster under the bed, she eased towards the middle until there was no chance of some horrendous creature being able to reach out and grab onto a dangling limb.

Except for the television, the room was otherwise quiet. But the air was frigid and still, a cold breath from something that was no longer human. Or alive.

"Hello?" Taryn whispered. "What do you want?"

The glare from the television cast shadows on the walls and floor and as she peeked out from under the comforter she could see them dancing in frantic shadows. The bedroom door was partially open and the hall light glowed brightly, a sharp contrast to the darkness. And still, the cold air poked and pulled at her, seeking her warm flesh and covering it with icy fingers.

Tempted to call out for Matt, Taryn sat up in the bed, clutching the cover to her breasts. She balled the thick fabric under her fingers, the feel of it reassuring. Lucille Ball argued with Desi in black and white and a laugh track chuckled on cue. Taryn knew she wasn't alone. She couldn't see anyone in the room, but could feel their presence as though they were standing beside her, breathing down her neck.

Feeling the beginnings of a panic attack coming on, Taryn took slow measured breaths and attempted to control her racing heart. She knew if she opened her mouth to call out her voice would be high-pitched and frantic. She'd worry Matt to death and she didn't want to sound or be helpless. Yet, she was terrified.

"Oh, to hell with it," she muttered, finally tossing the covers back in disgust. She didn't have to sit there on her own and freak herself out; she was going downstairs.

She didn't even have the chance to swing her legs over the side of the bed, though, when she saw it. At first, she thought the shadow in the corner of the bedroom by the closet was merely that

166

– a shadow. Low to the floor and stubby, it looked like a pile of clothes or a suitcase with a wet towel thrown over it. But then it moved. The lumpy shape began to change in front of her eyes and while she wouldn't call it solid, she couldn't exactly see through it, either. As she watched in horror, it languidly stretched itself out until it was long, perhaps five feet in length, and rested couple of feet off the ground. Darkness swirled around it, a kind of grayness that set it apart from the dusk of the room. It slowly shuffled towards the bed, a large animal awkward and unsure of its movements. As she watched in horror, she began making out details–a swatch of inky hair, the separation of joints in the front that resembled fingers, feet dragging behind. It wasn't an animal at all, but a person and it was coming for her in slow motion.

Unable to scream or even move, Taryn was rooted. She couldn't have sat there on the bed for more than a second or two but it felt like an eternity. The length between the figure and her bed was only ten feet or so but it advanced in the night, covering the ground and space in almost a single movement. Taryn edged backwards, pulling the comforter with her. There might have been a scraping sound coming from the floor, or it could have been her own breathing.

And then, it was at the bed. As the long, thin, pale hand touched the sheet and the bony, dirt-splattered fingers clawed at the flannel, Taryn had just enough time to look down and see Cheyenne's pale, lifeless eyes looking back at her before she let out a scream that shook the house. And passed out.

Chapter 15

*T*aryn's students, for the most part, were extremely talented.

What they lacked in technique they made up for in enthusiasm. She'd divided them into two groups: those who were in the class for the art and those who were there for the history. The artists simply loved sketching and drawing; their subject matter didn't necessarily matter. The other group might not have been as talented but had a passion for the history and architecture she talked about. They didn't care that the buildings Taryn had them draw weren't mansions or historically relevant - they were just as happy to sketch a dilapidated farmhouse as they were the governor's mansion. These were the students after Taryn's own heart. Her love of history had come before her love of drawing and painting. She was lusting after ramshackle American four squares and the sad little neglected bungalows in Germantown (they'd held happy, proud families at one time) before she knew anything about shading.

Word had spread about her "other" talent and even though the students were too polite, or too nervous, to ask, she could feel their questions hanging in the air. She wondered how many of them knew she'd been lured to the town for reasons other than to teach. She was faintly embarrassed by the fact, something she'd cried to Matt about. "Hush," he'd scolded her while stroking her hair. "You're a good artist and a good teacher. They're all getting something out of your class. Who cares why you originally came?"

But now she felt like she should address the issue.

"Hey guys," she began once they were all seated. Taryn was wearing a long wool skirt, tall black boots, and a black leather jacket over a red sweater. She'd taken the time to pull herself together and even applied a little bit of blush and mascara. Living with Matt was starting to make her a little sloppy, especially since he seemed to love and want her no matter what she looked like. If she didn't watch it, she'd start buying flannel pajama bottoms at the Dollar General and wearing them out in public with her house shoes. "I need to talk to you all for a second before we get started today. I'm anxious to look at everyone's pictures but I kind of have something to say first."

She had their full attention and felt on the spot as they turned their eyes to her, their inquisitive faces making her blush.

"So I know some of you know that in addition to my job I also, er, work with the paranormal." Make it normal, she thought. Make it sound like just part of the job. "I was asked to help out with a case while I was here and so some of my time is going to be devoted to that. I don't know what you've read or heard but if you have any questions, I just wanted to let you know it's okay to ask me."

It didn't take long before they started flying.

"Are you looking for Cheyenne Willoughby?"

"Have you seen any ghosts while you're here?"

"Can you talk to the ghosts?"

"Have you ever worked as a psychic for the police department?"

"How long have you known you're a psychic?"

Now feeling overwhelmed, Taryn tried to answer them as they came but there were just too many. Holding her hand up, she quieted them down and laughed. "Okay, okay. Let me try something else. First of all, I am not a psychic. I can't see the future, never have. Most of what I do is seen through my camera. Miss Dixie is the one with the real talent, I guess; she can see the past. At first I thought it was just her but now I realize it's me and she's more like the..."

"Conduit?" one of the more vocal guys volunteered.

"Yes, thank you. The conduit. I don't always need her, but she helps me see the bigger picture I guess. And, as some of you know, I am here trying to help with Cheyenne Willoughby's disappearance, although so far I haven't been able to add anything constructive. As for talking to ghosts, I have tried talking to them but haven't had any response back. I still think spirits might be leftover energy and not real entities with the capability of communicating."

"I don't know," a quiet little blonde in the front stammered. "I mean, when my papaw died I saw his ghost about a week later. I spoke to him and told him I loved and missed him. He told me he loved me, too, and then he disappeared."

Although nobody snickered or poked fun at her, she shrank back into her chair as though the laughter would soon follow her confession.

"I've talked to other people who have been able to communicate with spirits," Taryn revealed carefully. "But so far I am not one of those people."

At the risk of turning the class into a paranormal session, she tried to wrap things up. "I guess, the thing is, you might be hearing a little more about me. I hope that doesn't change your impression of me or make you freaked out about being in the class. I promise I'm not a weird-o." The students laughed, a sound that cut the tension. "Okay, well, maybe I am a little bit, but I'm not a freak, and if there's anything you want to talk about, then please find me after class or email me and I'll do the best I can."

As a previous assignment, she'd asked the students to go around the county and take pictures of their favorite old homes and buildings. Each one got a couple of minutes to pull their image up on her laptop so she could show the whole class on the board. They then got the chance to talk about why they'd taken the shot and what drew them to the building.

When everyone was finished, Taryn flipped on the lights and stood in front of the group again. "All right, those were great. Now, your next assignment is to draw one of the buildings you saw today. Only, you are going to have to draw it from memory, the

172

best you can, since you won't have the picture in front of you. I want to test your imaginations, memory, and creativity. Don't worry, there is no right or wrong way to do this," she added when a few groans erupted around the room.

Emma took her time and waited for everyone to leave before approaching Taryn. "Hey," she smiled. Taryn coveted the beautiful white pea coat she wore. She knew she spilled too much and had hips that were too wide to be able to carry off such a thing. "How you holding up?"

"Okay," Taryn shrugged. "Better now that my friend's back in town." There was no way she was going to tell her about the nightly visitor she'd had.

"Good, I'm glad to hear it. Any news on who it might have been?" The concern on Emma's face was touching and Taryn felt warmth at the young woman's compassion.

"Not yet. Probably just someone who thought nobody was there," Taryn answered. Of course, the lamp was on downstairs.

"Or someone looking to score," Emma declared. "The drug problem is getting really bad here. When I was a kid it was all about the booze. Some people smoked pot but most of us couldn't afford it. We were lucky to score a Marlboro. Then it was prescription pills. OxyContin, Percocet's, shit like that."

"What happened?" Taryn asked with interest. "Has it moved on to something else?"

"Yeah," Emma scoffed. "Heroin. Cocaine. Used to be cocaine was just stuff rich people or celebrities did. You know, very 1980s. But then they started cracking down on the prescription pills, making them harder to get. Shut down the pain clinics, made

173

it impossible for doctors to prescribe them, even to people who needed them. My mom? She had a hysterectomy and they sent her home with Tylenol. And not the kind with codeine."

"That's usually the way it happens," Taryn agreed. "The people who need it can't get it and those who don't need it and abuse it still find a way."

"Yeah, well, they didn't find a way to get it; they just moved on to something else," Emma explained. "Now it's heroin and cocaine. They got these drug runners coming up from Florida and down from Detroit. It's not even that much. After school job, allowance? A little money goes a long way now and it don't take much to get you hooked. Some people still do crystal meth, but that shit's scary. Girls around here don't like what it can do to your teeth, to your skin. They think heroin is safer."

"Nothing with a needle is safe," Taryn mumbled. "They're playing Russian roulette with their lives."

"Tell me about it," Emma replied. "We had two heroin deaths last spring and our county hadn't had that in almost twenty years. But I wasn't actually up here to get all depressed and talk drugs. I wanted to invite you to a party," she offered brightly.

"Oh, yeah, when?" It had been a long time since someone invited Taryn to a party. The invitations dropped off after Andrew died. Someone who sat in the corner of the room or parked themselves by the buffet table all night and didn't socialize wasn't a person most people wanted around, especially when booze made her a downer.

"It's going to be at the farm, you know, the one you're staying at? And it's on Halloween night. Should be fun."

A feeling of unease ran down Taryn's spine. What was it her grandmother used to say? A goose walked over her grave. "But I thought Cheyenne's uncle said there wasn't going to be anything else out there?"

"Yeah, well, Eric and I persuaded him. And Thelma said it was okay," she added hurriedly. "We thought a bonfire, a cookout, some costumes, and live music? It's what people need around here. And, of course, we want you to come. And for you to bring your boyfriend."

Taryn didn't correct her about Matt. She didn't know how he'd feel about it. He wasn't into loud parties with alcohol and dancing. Matt was more of a quiet dinner for two and live jazz, twirling her around a dance floor kind of guy. Still... as morbid as it felt to attend a party at the last place Cheyenne was seen, it might not hurt to be around others who knew her.

"Yeah, we'll come," she declared. "In two weeks, right? I guess I need to start looking for a costume."

"**W**hat do you think? Sexy Eve or sexy witch?" Taryn held both costumes in front of Matt but his lack of response had her lowering her arms and rolling her eyes. The dressing room lines were long and she was already agitated. "How about sexy Yoda?"

"What?" he asked, confused. His eyes were glued to his phone. "Sorry. I'm just trying to answer some emails."

"You didn't have to come with me," she reminded him. "You could've stayed back at the house."

"Oh no, it's fine," he insisted. "I like getting out. I'm just really behind."

She knew that, of course, and knew he was behind because of her. Not only had he taken a bunch of time off from work, something he never did, but he'd rushed back when the intruder came in on her and that had thrown him even further off course. "I'm sorry," she apologized, feeling ridiculous for toting around sexy Halloween costumes when, for all Taryn knew, his job could be on the line. He was there to help her work, sort of, and there she was trying to find a slutty costume to keep in line with a bunch of teenagers.

"It's okay. I'm enjoying myself. I don't know about the party, though." His forehead burrowed in concern and he began biting his lower lip – a sure sign he was feeling uncomfortable and didn't know how to vocalize his feelings. "I'm just not into getting out with a bunch of people I don't know and spending the evening with them."

"I'm not either usually," she agreed. "But she asked and it does sound like fun. Besides, I might learn something."

"I guess I could make some chocolates. Or bread. You think they like sourdough?" he asked hopefully.

If the party was anything like the ones she'd heard about in high school, but had never actually attended, then she was certain there'd be more making out and drinking than eating from a buffet. But that was something she'd have to work up to with him

176

gradually. "I think chocolate might be a good idea," she offered. "Or you could do a dip and chips. Everyone likes those."

"Okay," he agreed, a light turning back on in his eyes. "And a bottle of wine?"

Or a box, she muttered to herself.

"We don't have to do too much, okay?" she repeated gently. "These are young adults who probably just want to listen to music and dance. Get into some trouble. We're going to be the old fuddy duddies hanging out because they were too polite to not ask us."

"Are you going to drink?" he asked with honest concern. "You know how alcohol has been affecting you recently. It might make your headaches and joint pain worse."

"I don't get that," she mused. "That glass of wine I had the other night with dinner was nothing compared to what I've done in the past and, yet, I felt like I had a major hangover. Do you think that's why I..."

"Passed out?" he offered. "Maybe. You said you were feeling a little dizzy earlier."

"I was going to say see Cheyenne's ghost but I guess passing out could have been because of the wine, too. Matt, do you think maybe there's something wrong with my brain?" The idea had been troubling her but considering how she was feeling before Cheyenne's spirit, or whatever it was, took a little stroll on all fours to her bed she couldn't discount the notion.

"What do you mean?"

"My brain. The headaches? The dizziness? The tingling I've been feeling in my arms and my pain? Do you think there might be something wrong with my brain and that's why I am the way I am?" Tears pricked at the corner of her eyes and she did her best to fight them back. Breaking down in the middle of the old Wal-Mart that had temporarily been converted into a seasonal Halloween store would not be cool.

"What do you mean 'the way you are'?" he asked gently.

"The ghosts, the feelings. What I see through Miss Dixie. What if I am not sensitive or I'm not seeing or feeling things at all? At least nothing paranormal. What if I just have a brain tumor?"

"Oh, sweetie, my little love,' he patted her affectionately on the cheek. "You do need to get yourself to the doctor. I think there might be something wrong that could easily be fixed. But what you've been going through with the spirits has nothing to do with your physical health. Unless you're bringing me into it by some sort of weird mass hallucination deal."

Taryn felt a wave of relief wash over her, followed by another nagging concern of finding a physician. "But, haven't you noticed things are different here?"

"How so?"

"I'm seeing more, I guess you could say. Or hearing more. It's not just in the photos anymore. I feel like Cheyenne has found me and is trying to talk to me. Or something. Why have things changed?"

"Didn't you know?" he asked nonchalantly, picking at an invisible piece of lint on her black sweater.

"Know what?"

"It's because I'm here."

"Oh Matt," Taryn giggled, giving him a slight push on the shoulder.

"I'm serious," he vowed and she could see he was. Her smile faded. "I've always known we're stronger together, that we can create our own energy. You're my soul mate, Taryn; together, we're a force. The other world knows it, too."

Chapter 16

"*C*helma, at the risk of sounding weird, I want to ask you

something."

Taryn was sitting with Cheyenne's mother in her sun room.
The bright October sun offered warmth through the windows,
although the day was deceivingly cold. The temperature was
hovering around 35 degrees and the weather man had even called
for snow flurries, although nobody thought it was cold enough to
stick.

"What is it, dear?"

Taryn fumbled with her mug of hot chocolate and
delicately wiped at the lipstick smudged she'd left behind. Elvis'
face from the 1968 comeback special smiled at her every time she
took a drink. Thelma, on the other hand, was drinking from a

chipped mug that boasted an image of two cartoon girls with the words "A Sister is a Forever Friend" inscribed on the side.

"Have you ever felt like Cheyenne was trying to communicate with you in some way?" It was a sensitive question because, no matter how Taryn phrased it, it alluded to the idea Thelma's daughter was dead.

Rather than looking upset, however, Thelma cocked her head and studied her drink. Finally, she answered. "There are times when I feel like she is near me. I've prayed to God she would give me a sign, either way, and let me know she's okay. I've seen her in my dreams, I've even heard her voice when I was almost asleep. But nothing concrete. I wish I could. Why, have you?"

She asked this last bit hurriedly, with a dash of hope Taryn found sad and pitiful. She couldn't tell her about the vision in her bedroom; that wasn't the Cheyenne Thelma would want to know about. But maybe she could offer her something.

"I don't know," she replied honestly. "I mean, I don't know how much of it is Cheyenne and how much of it is just my over-active imagination because she's on my mind. But in my first few days here I heard a woman scream. Before I even knew about your daughter. And I've heard it since then, too."

"But Cheyenne's not on the farm," Thelma protested.

"I know. And that's what I don't understand. Maybe I am just picking up on her energy there. I've dreamed about her a lot, too. I can't tell you what that means – if she's trying to communicate with me or I'm just wrapped up in her story. I mean, in her life." Taryn corrected herself since, to Thelma, this was not a story but her daughter's life they were speaking about.

"It would make sense to get a feel for her in the cabin," Thelma agreed. "She loved it there. Used to go with us and stay when it was hunting and fishing season. She'd take her books and read, play with the dogs, just kind of run ragged. Then, when she got older, she didn't care for it as much. You know how teenagers are. She didn't like staying out so far away from her friends. The last couple times we went she stayed with friends."

"I'm enjoying being out there," Taryn assured her. "The break-in excluded, of course."

Thelma leaned forward and, in a conspirator's whisper, confided in Taryn. "I haven't been sleeping real good lately. Been staying up late, sometimes all night. I found this website, see, where they post pictures of people who have been found dead but they don't know who they are? Well, they ain't real pictures; they're artists' renderings of the bodies. I look every night, going over the images and ages and heights of all them girls. They've got 'em from all over the country. I keep thinking I might see her. Maybe she went to another state and someone found her and she's out there, laying in a morgue, and nobody knows who she is."

The awfulness of it struck Taryn cold. The idea that Thelma, was wrapped up in her housecoat, glued to her computer night after night, staring at images of dead bodies, hoping and not hoping one of them might be her daughter was horrible.

Taryn could hear the front door open and what sounded like the stomping of boots on the laminate floor. "My husband's home," Thelma explained. "Jeff. Excuse him. He works foundations and always comes home covered head to toe in mud and concrete."

A few moments later, a middle-aged man with a stubby beard streaked with gray and a paunch belly walked out to the sun room. He'd taken off his boots and his once-white socks were dingy and gray. A big toe poked out on the right side. Like Thelma had said, he was covered from top to bottom in muck, but he was a nice-looking man and had a friendly smile.

"How's it going over there? Any more trouble?"

"No, it's been quiet," Taryn replied.

"Your man back there with you now?"

Taryn reddened at the question, embarrassed. "Yes, he's there with me."

"That's good. You don't need to be staying out there by yourself. Need yourself a gun, too," he grunted, crossing his arms in front of his chest.

Taryn badly wanted to point out that she'd lived by herself for a long time, traveled alone, and had spent more time in the isolated countryside than in the city. And then there was the fact she was more masculine than Matt and could probably kick someone's ass before he could. But that wasn't the point. In his own way, he was showing concern.

"Taryn just asked me if I'd heard or seen Cheyenne's ghost since she disappeared," Thelma explained.

Taryn opened her mouth to protest, since that's not exactly what she'd asked, but Jeff waved her off. "Naw, can't say I have," he said "Wish I did. When she up and left I ain't seen hide nor hair since. Not a trace of her. Like she disappeared off the face of the earth. I still think she's going to come back. I have to, you know."

183

Taryn used her time to try and study the man whom, by some accounts, Cheyenne hadn't particularly liked. He was friendly, likable, but what would it have been like to live with him? Was he really that tough on her? Was there something more? Had she really watched too many episodes of Law and Order?

"You know, some people didn't like the way we handled things," he continued.

"What do you mean?"

Jeff shrugged and a cloud of dust fell from his shoulder. "Some folks thought we ought to be more active, get on that Nancy Grace show or talk to Oprah."

"We tried," Thelma cut in. "We contacted all the big shows. Nobody cared about a girl from the middle of nowhere in Georgia. Never even got any replies."

"We did some TV interviews, but I did the talking. Some folks thought it ought to have been Thelma here pleading for her little girl to come home." He spat this out, disgusted. "Said if there was a kidnapper, the mama would appeal to them more. But like hell I was going to put her in front of the TV like that. When we married I vowed to take care of her. And I meant it. She was in no shape to talk to reporters. I'm the closest thing that girl had to a daddy. She was my responsibility."

"I wasn't doing too good at the time," Thelma confessed, gazing up at Jeff with veneration. "They gave me this medicine that was supposed to take the edge off. Made me feel like a zombie, is what it did. Some people said I was on drugs. And I was! I had to be, just to get through the days. He was doing me a favor by taking over."

"When it's not happening to them, everybody's got an opinion on how you should be handling things," Jeff hissed. "Unless they've been through it themselves they can kiss my ass."

"I know what you mean," Taryn agreed, trying to break the tension. "When my husband died people kept telling me I needed to move on, get out more, do this and that. And that was just a few weeks after it happened. My real grief took months to kick in, almost a year. Before, I was just in shock, a zombie."

Jeff nodded, relief on his face. "Yeah, well, you get it then. You never know how you're gonna act until you're in the situation. And we'd never knowed anyone to lose a child before, at least not like this. We didn't know what to do or how to act."

After he went off to get changed, Thelma turned back to Taryn. "I'm sorry," she apologized. "He gets worked up a little. Some people even think he had something to do with her missing. But I don't believe it. They might not have seen eye to eye regularly but he loved her. He'd never hurt her."

Taryn had no idea what to say. The more she thought about it, the more awful it sounded. There in the sun room, she was surrounded by memories of Cheyenne. Pictures on the wall painted her life, from the row of school photos to the senior portraits of her standing in a field of daisies, her red cowboy boots gleaming in the morning sun. Cheyenne might not have been dead, but Taryn was in her tomb and everyone around her in a wake they hadn't yet left.

Although it was chilly, and growing colder by the minute, Taryn sat on the ground in the middle of the farmhouse's front yard. The grass was dry, but the cold earth below it still managed to numb her bottom and legs. The wind whipped icy fingers around her face and down the back of her neck. Her feet, always cold regardless of temperature, ached from the walk over. Her hands, snug in gloves, were about the only things that still had feeling left.

The old house set stoically behind her, watching her. The air was still and quiet. In just two weeks the sounds of laughter, music, and clinking of glass and plastic would fill the air. It would be a whole lot like what Cheyenne had heard on her last night. Would Miss Dixie pick up on anything then? Would it feel like recreating that fateful party? Taryn didn't know.

If I do have something, she thought to herself, then let me feel it now. She sat cross-legged, her hands on her legs, palms up. Willing herself to be open to any energy surrounding her, she took deep breaths, in and out, tried to clear her mind. Maybe it was true that being with Matt made her stronger but it didn't negate the fact that whatever she saw and felt originated in her. If the trees or grass or house knew anything, they weren't giving up their secrets. The fire pit was dry as a bone, lifeless. The last fire it had seen was a long time ago. The wood pile was stacked and ready to go, waiting for slaughter. There was nothing around her offering any clues for Cheyenne.

"I'm losing it," she finally giggled when nothing happened. "I'm freezing my ass off and losing my damn mind."

Nothing had ever happened to her by sheer will before; she didn't know why she expected this time to be any different. Still, she'd tried.

As she was rising to her feet, the sound of the screen door behind her slapping against the frame with a "bang," startled her. She nearly lost her footing and tripped a little before catching her balance and straightening up. When she turned around, she half-expected to see someone standing on the front porch, watching her. But the porch and doorway were empty; the front door was closed, too. It was only the wind making the screen thrash back and forth.

But then it happened again, only this time, as she watched, the door opened slowly, deliberately. It held itself open for a few seconds before, once again, banging shut with a force. Maybe it was the wind, and maybe it wasn't. Taryn couldn't be sure something was trying to send her a message but since it was the only thing she had to go on, she turned Miss Dixie on and aimed her at the house.

A few clicks later and she was studying her LCD screen, hoping she might have caught something but not holding her breath. She'd taken dozens of pictures of the farmhouse and had so far been unlucky. This time, though, she'd found something.

While it was still daylight now, in the picture it was nighttime. Blaze from a fire cast shadows on the front of the house and she caught these pretty vividly with the camera. The house was dark, except for a faint light glowing from the downstairs left window. A candle, maybe? Flashlight? It wasn't the shadows or the light she focused on, however. Standing in the doorway, peering out at her with the same pale eyes she'd seen at her bedside, was Cheyenne. Only this time she was very much alive.

Chapter 17

*T*aryn was depressed.

She'd ordered a new Allison Moorer CD off Amazon and was excited to see it had arrived in the mail. When she'd taken it inside, though, she'd found Matt blaring Beck and dancing in the kitchen, baking bread. Ordinarily Taryn would've shrugged it off, taken her laptop upstairs, and done her own thing. She'd have been thankful that there was actually someone in the house baking bread.

But for some reason today it just ticked her off.

Except for brief periods in the car when she was on her own, and that wasn't often since Matt usually drove her in, she barely had a minute to herself. He dominated the radio in the car and, because he took charge of the kitchen and cleanup, he also dominated the musical entertainment segment of the show in the house. She hadn't been able to crank up Allison or Tift Merrit or Iris Dement or any of her women in weeks. And she depended on music to keep her going, to be her soundtrack to her work. She might not have possessed a musical bone in her body and couldn't carry a tune in a bucket, but music was important to her. When she did try to listen to hers, Matt would politely put on a pair of earbuds and go about his business. And that pissed her off.

Then there was the matter of the kitchen.

It was no secret: Taryn didn't like to cook. However, just because she didn't like doing it didn't mean she couldn't do it. She was actually pretty good at it. After being on her own for so long, though, she'd just gotten used to eating out. Most boxed items and packaged vegetables were too much for one person and she didn't like to waste.

It sounded whiney to complain, and she loved that Matt cooked for her, but she hated feeling like he thought *she couldn't*. She listened to him ramble on about new recipes and new cookbooks and new things he'd discovered. She even listened to him brag about how his blueberry cobbler was the best he'd ever had and how he could replicate any food he tasted at a restaurant.

Sometimes, she didn't want to eat at home. Sometimes she didn't care that he could make O'Charley's brown bread in his own kitchen. Sometimes she *just wanted to go to O'Charley's!*

It was on the tip of her tongue to storm into the kitchen, announce that she didn't like Sade and her weird music and that she was going to order a pizza. But that was wrong and weird and it would hurt Matt's feelings.

190

It wasn't about him, anyway. It was about her. Taryn craved people and attention like anyone else but she also worked best alone and had gotten used to being on her own. She just didn't know how to deal with always having someone around. Andrew was different. They'd been so much alike in so many different ways. Although he was much more sociable than her, he'd been perfectly content on his, too. They often spent their afternoons in different parts of the house, working on their individual projects, or even in the same room without speaking, alone in their comfortable silence. She figured that eventually she and Matt would be like that, too. They were still trying to find their footing.

Her bedroom balcony was cool and inviting. Now that the morning rain had cleared up she was able to set up her easel. People called her talented when it came to her art, but she didn't feel like it came easily to her; she worked hard at it and had to keep up with it or else she'd lose whatever skills she had.

In one of her college art classes her old professor, regionally acclaimed artist Ron Isaacs, had showered praise on a sketching she did of a live model. It wasn't very good. In fact, she'd started over and changed things so many times that she'd actually made a hole in her sketch pad and had charcoal up to her elbows. Sheila Griggs, the student on the other side of her, was having no such problems. Her sketch was beautifully rendered, had taken her half the time it took Taryn, and was so realistic Taryn thought you could practically balance a glass on the model's perfectly apple-shaped rump.

Still, Dr. Isaacs had praised Taryn's work and not Sheila's. Indeed, he'd even criticized Sheila's work, something that shocked Taryn so much she'd nearly made another hole in her paper.

Later, as she was packing up to leave, she'd overheard Sheila arguing with the wired-hair, quiet professor. "I don't understand," she'd whined, on the verge of tears. Taryn knew a good cry coming on when she heard one. "I worked really hard and my drawing was good. Taryn didn't even finish hers and it has all kinds of mistakes. Why did she get a better grade than me?"

Taryn had to admit, her sympathy for the budding artist dropped a couple of notches after that but, for curiosity's sake, moved slowly. She wanted to hear his reply, too.

"Your rendering is superior," he'd replied in that slow, steady way of his. His bushy eyebrows rose in an arch, the white threads of hair in them shining in the overhead light. He was so frumpy in his wrinkled khakis, oversized sweat shirt, and cheap loafers with a hole in them that the average person would have never thought his last painting sold for five thousand dollars. "But your work, your work was lacking."

"I don't get it. What's the difference?"

Taryn wondered that as well.

"Miss Magill's work shows promise. She is very good, but she has to work at it. Yours is very good and you know that. Therefore, you do not try. In the long run, I have much respect for the person who constantly works to achieve better. To work so hard at capturing the vision in their mind – that is more than technical skill; that is passion."

Taryn still worked hard at what she did and never felt like a painting was completed.

There was a slight breeze outside and it ruffled what few leaves were left on the skeletal trees. She'd been able to hear Sade until she shut the door and then that sound, as well as all the house sounds, dissipated and she was left with the outside noises. Taryn had barely finished setting up her easel, however, when the other music started.

At first, it sounded like the radio. The music was twangy with a distinctive electric guitar. It could've been Dwight Yoakam's "Fast As You" and she found herself humming along with it, even growling to the "Aw, sookie" part. Maybe Matt's changed his mind, Taryn thought to herself as she poured in a tiny bit of linseed oil. If she'd known he was going to put in Dwight (what that man did to a pair of jeans) she might've stayed inside.

The music began fading out, however, and there was a stretch of uncomfortable silence that made Taryn's mind start to wander again. To ward off any negative of unpleasant thoughts she began singing to herself, an old folk song about blackbirds her grandmother used to sing to her. But then the music started up, this time a woman. She would've known Patty Loveless' "Timber I'm Falling in Love" anywhere. Matt must've found a classics station, she mused. The volume was turned up loud, loud enough for Taryn to catch an occasional lyric, and the comforting sound of a familiar song and voice she'd known all her life cut through the chill of the afternoon and warmed her bones.

When she grew a little thirsty, though, and started back inside to grab her a drink she stopped in her tracks. Sade was still blaring below; all traces of Dwight and Patty were gone.

"Well that's weird," she muttered aloud.

In an experiment, she closed the bedroom door and stepped back out onto the balcony. Sade stopped, Patty returned, this time singing "Lonely Too Long."

Shrugging, Taryn went back to work, forgetting about her drink. She figured it must be someone on the other side of the woods, perhaps working outside. Maybe Cheyenne's uncle working at the farm, getting things ready for the party the kids were going to have.

Later, when she saw Matt come out of the house and head to the car to retrieve something, she called down to him. "Can you hear that music?" she yelled.

Startled because he hadn't known she was outside, he jumped a little and then looked up at her and grinned. "What music?" he asked, innocently.

'The music playing outside. I think someone's got a radio on or something. Sounds like Patty Loveless, but I can't make out the song now."

Matt stood still, cocked his head to one side, and listened. "Nope, nothing. Maybe cause you're higher up?"

"Yeah, maybe," she nodded.

He went back in and she returned to her landscape. Her head and joints might be killing her, but at least it appeared her hearing was in good shape.

Something woke her up again and it had Taryn sitting straight up in bed, gasping for breath like she'd been held underwater. Her lungs were full to bursting and she clawed at her throat in the dark, reaching for air her body told her she so desperately needed. In her half-dreaming state she panicked, fighting off an invisible attacker that was keeping her from moving, from breathing. But then she opened her eyes, her movements ceased, and she acclimated herself to the darkness. Once again, she was back in the bedroom with Matt snoring peacefully beside her, nothing out of the ordinary except for her heart trying to beat its way out of her chest.

Still, something had woken her up—something more than a bad dream. It was another sound, a sound that wasn't quite right in the house.

Straining her ears, she listened for a follow-up, fearful of hearing the pounding of heavy shoes on the staircase or the padding of unwanted feet below. The house was quiet, however, and the only thing she could hear was the white noise of the dehumidifier by the bed. Thelma'd installed it a few nights before. With all the rain they'd been having, she was worried about moisture and them getting sick with allergies and sinus problems.

Although her body was still trembling and her mind was racing with horrible thoughts of death and rape, she lowered herself back to the pillow, sneaking her leg over to wrap itself around Matt's. The warmth of his skin was heartening and a gentle reminder that she wasn't alone. Still, she was by herself in her fears and thoughts, and the fact that something had woken her up was unsettling. The numbers on the clock flashed 3:15 am, and she groaned aloud. She never should've watched *The Amityville Horror* as a kid.

She'd nearly dozed back off again, lulled by Matt's gentle breathing and the hum of the machine, when the room suddenly filled with sounds. This time, she was sure of it. The voices were low, conversational, and it sounded as though there were several people speaking at once. While she couldn't make out what they were saying, try as she might to strain her ears, she could pick up on a word here or there.

Puzzled, she listened quietly, rising up on her elbows to hopefully catch more. There was no sense of urgency in their voices, nothing menacing that should have caused her any alarm. And yet the simple fact that a random conversation was going on around here when nobody else should've been in the house was unsettling. .

At first she thought, hoped rather, that the voices were from Thelma and Jeff. Perhaps they'd needed something or were worried about her. But the thought was ludicrous; Thelma would never come into the house in the middle of the night like that. She wouldn't have scared Taryn. Her next thought drifted towards another burglar, or somebody up to no good. But she was very good at reading tone and the conversation going on was light, airy, mild. It didn't sound like people planning a sneak attack on the two sleepers.

Then there was the fact that the voices seemed to be coming from every direction, surrounding her. An echo from outside perhaps?

Softly letting her feet land on the floor, Taryn got out of bed and tiptoed towards the balcony door. It opened quietly and she stepped out onto into the night, gently pulling the door to behind her. The wood was cold under her feet, the October air bitter with a hint of moisture. There were no sounds, however, other than the night ones. She listened for a minute, willing them to start up again, but there was nothing. In something not quite fear, she walked back into the bedroom. The conversation immediately picked up again, the voices maybe just a little bit softer but still there nevertheless.

Now she made herself walk out the bedroom door towards the stairs. Along the way she grabbed her curling iron. It wasn't much but she might be able to beat someone off with it as she called for Matt if she had to, and it was the closest object she could find.

The humming of the dehumidifier trailed off behind her, growing quieter the more distance she put between her and the bedroom. Likewise, the voices diminished, too. Nothing drifted up from downstairs; whatever she was hearing had to be originating from the bedroom.

When she turned around and started back towards the bedroom, Taryn came to a sudden halt. A candle burned in the room and its flame flickered, throwing odd-shaped patterns against the wall. From where she stood, the murky room looked distorted, like a carnival funhouse. Knowing what awaited her inside, her feet refused to move. She just couldn't bring herself to go back in there. The fear of the dark she'd fought as a child was coming back to her now almost regularly and she was tired of it. She was going to be thirty-one soon, for God's sake. She was behaving like a toddler.

Having her back exposed to the staircase, where anything could fly up the length and attack her in the dark, didn't seem much better. Panicked now, she turned in circles and weighed her options. Go downstairs and spend the night on the couch, alone, or enter the bedroom and snuggle in next to Matt? The latter sounded more appealing but would she even be able to sleep?

At last, after giving herself a firm and stern lecture, she gave in and walked back to the bedroom. Matt woke a little when she slid in next to him (okay, maybe it was because she poked him hard in the ribs and tried to wake him up) and his voice was hoarse and thick from sleep. "Everything okay?"

"Do you think you could go downstairs and get my Benadryl?" she asked, embarrassed. "I'm spooked and don't want to go alone."

"Yeah, sure," he answered without any questions. "Be right back."

She flipped on the lamp while he was gone, unable to sit alone in the dark even for a few minutes. When he got back she popped two and then cuddled into the crook of his arm, wrapping her arm around his neck so that she could curl her fingers in his hair. "Matt?" she whispered when his breathing became steady again, a sure sign he was almost out.

"Yeah?"

"Do-do you hear that?" she stammered.

"Hear what?"

"The voices. There's at least three. And they're talking."

Matt listened and then patted her on the head. "I don't hear anything. Must be the dehumidifier."

And somewhere, wherever they were coming from, someone laughed.

Chapter 18

As soon as she heard Rob's voice on the phone, Taryn felt like she was reconnecting with a long-lost friend, despite the fact it had been less than a year since she last spoke to him. Of course, what a year that was!

"Sorry it took me so long to get back to you," Rob apologized. "I actually closed shop for a week and took the lady on vacation to Gatlinburg."

"Oh yeah? That sounds like fun!" It had been a very long time since Taryn had been on an actual vacation, staying in a motel room she didn't have to work in and doing nothing but relaxing and having fun. "What all did you guys do?"

"You know, the usual stuff." Taryn could hear the grin in his voice. He sounded happy. "Go carts, mini golf, crappy buffets. Went through Wonderworks. Some of that shit just blows my mind. She dragged me through the Titanic museum – two hours of my life I'll never get back again. Made me buy her a teacup, supposedly the replica of the exact pattern they had on the ship. She put it on the shelf with the shot glasses from Excalibur in Vegas and seashells she made me pick up off the beach in Daytona."

But he didn't sound like he was complaining. In fact, he sounded excited and proud. Taryn was happy for him. Despite some of the crazy-looking paraphernalia Rob carried in his shop, he was just about one of the straightest guys Taryn had ever met and, outside of Matt, the only other person she felt she could be truly honest about her gift with.

"It sounds like you're really happy, Rob," she said sincerely.

"Yeah, well, I hear you're shacking up with my buddy now. Good for you guys!" Both had trained in engineering; Rob went the alternative route and now sold ritual gear to Wiccans and repaired the occasional iPhone screen.

"Yeah, um, it's going well," Taryn agreed hurriedly. "So listen, I have some questions for you; things I'd like to talk about."

"Shoot. What's up?"

Taryn leaned back against the throw pillows on the couch and propped her feet up. She settled in for comfort – this was probably going to take a while.

"I don't know how much Matt filled you in on," she began.

"Very little. Just that you're in Georgia teaching a class, kudos by the way, and he's staying with you and taking some time off. Said a girl was missing and you were helping with that."

"Yeah, well, I guess that's the gist of it," Taryn agreed. "The problem is, I feel like I am supposed to be here, and yet I can't pick up on anything. A noise here, a flash of something there. One night I was certain I saw her in my bedroom, crawling towards me." Taryn still shuddered at the thought. "It was horrible."

"Are you doubting yourself now?"

"Yes and no. I guess in the clear light of day it's easy to think it might have been in my head, that maybe I was dreaming or seeing things or had one too many Benadryl or something. But at the time..."

"Well, you're a rational, logical-thinking human being," he declared. "It's no wonder you'd question such a thing. But after all that, what makes you think you're not getting anywhere? Sounds like you're getting into a lot."

"True. But I am no closer to giving the parents any answers than I was before. I know she's dead." Even just saying it aloud gave her chills. Cheyenne was dead, and someone had killed her. And maybe even tried to kill Taryn, unless she was being too melodramatic. "I know she's dead," she repeated, "but have no way of figuring out who, where, or why."

"Have you tried a clarity spell?" Rob suggested. "It might help."

As someone who'd never been a church-goer and rarely prayed, much less experimented with alternative religions, Taryn was still a little taken aback by some people's casual attitude towards spells, rituals, and the Craft. "No, no, that's one of the reasons I wanted to talk to you," she smiled.

"I have something that might work," he mused. "But you'll need quite a bit of stuff to do it well."

"I'm more of a kitchen witch," she lamented. "Anything I could do that would just require a little garlic, a little olive oil? Maybe a nice tomato?"

"I'll see what I can come up with," Rob laughed. "In the meantime, I'm sure you've had Miss Dixie out and put her to work?"

"Yes, but only a few things and I don't know how they fit into the big scheme of things." She quickly filled him in on the image of Cheyenne she'd seen on the porch and the other subtle nuances her camera had picked up. Rob was as lost as she was.

"I'm afraid I haven't been much help," he apologized with regret. "I can try to come up with a simpler spell, though, that you might be able to use."

"I'm willing to give anything a shot at this point."

For the next few minutes they talked about the weather, the new season of their favorite zombie post-apocalypse show, and Matt's cooking. Before she hung up, however, she asked him one last question.

"Oh, Rob, there was one more thing I wanted to run by you."

"What's that?"

"You know how you told me that sometimes you hear things that other people can't?" she prodded.

"And things that are far away?" he answered. "Yes, it happens. Why?"

"I think I'm doing it too. Or else I'm going crazy," she added nervously.

"I highly doubt that. I figured the longer you went on, the more your gifts were developed. Interesting that it would happen in this way," he mused. "Tell me about it."

Taryn filled him in on the voices, the music, and the other smaller things that she hadn't even considered until she had him on the phone. When she was finished his end of the line was quiet. "You still there?"

"Yeah," Rob replied, "just forming my thoughts."

"So what do you think?"

"It's called 'clairaudience.' Now, some people interpret it as another way of channeling, like a medium would. It's a way of communicating with spirits, but through sound. It's part of being clairvoyant, only instead of seeing things or feeling things, you actually hear them. You're basically picking up on another frequency that's not accessible to most people."

"I've never heard of such a thing. Why did it start all of a sudden?" Taryn asked. Although she shouldn't have been surprised. Miss Dixie had certainly started picking up on past images out of the blue.

"My guess is you've always had a little bit of it, it just wasn't very developed. Are you a big fan of music? Always have to have it on? Feel depressed when you can't listen?"

"Yeah," Taryn laughed.

"And my guess is that in a car you're constantly changing stations, searching for that perfect song or sound. People might even complain about it..."

Taryn thought of her parents and even Matt who were driven crazy by her radio channel-hopping. "That's me."

"And it's probably easy for you to pick up on other people's voices and tell them apart that way, maybe even better than looking at them," Rob pushed.

"That's so weird," Taryn mused. "I never knew that was a 'thing.'"

"Welcome to the world of clairaudience."

"I notice it most in the bedroom," she stated, remembering the overlapping of voices. "That's where it was the loudest."

"Did you have anything on at the time? A heater? Fan? Snow on television?"

Taryn didn't have to think twice. "Yes, actually. I had the dehumidifier on. It's been raining a lot."

"Well, a lot of people, and highly respected people, think that white noise is a conduit for picking up on other frequencies. And you don't even have to be psychic to hear it," he explained. "I wish I had a better explanation for you but I'd say that coupled with what you get out of pictures and your feelings, this is probably just the next step."

"So what you're saying is that now not only can I see things through my camera but I can communicate with them through my microwave oven?"

"Well, when you put it that way, yeah."

Travis Marcum sat in the booth across from Taryn at the Cracker Barrel. She tried, unconsciously, to watch him as he devoured his stack of pancakes and bowl of grits. They were both alone, and he sat at a table for two, shoved back into a corner by himself. She'd observed that, despite the fact his glass was empty from the minute she sat down, he was never offered a refill. Her server, on the other hand, badgered her almost to the point of annoyance.

It was cold outside and even starting to flurry a little bit – not something she expected to see this far south. They didn't get a lot of snow in Nashville. The last big snow she remembered was when she was a lot younger. But, a few fat courageous flakes slowly drifted down where they were immediately soaked up by the parking lot. The fireplace was going full throttle just a few feet away from her, though, and a grandfather was playing a rousing game of checkers with his little redheaded grandson. All in all, it was a pleasant place to park yourself, even if it was a chain and most of the food probably got delivered frozen.

Still, she couldn't take her eyes off Travis. Like most people probably did, she tried to envision him assaulting Cheyenne. Maybe peeling her jeans off while she kicked frantically at him, or perhaps laid unconscious on a hard floor. Her shirt lifted over her head, her bra ripped open revealing firm, teenage breasts. Had he smacked her? Banged her head on the floor? Did she vomit in the middle of the act, the liquid running into her dark hair and matting it? Had he held onto her while life faded from her eyes? To look at him now, an average-looking guy spreading butter on a biscuit, he looked young, incapable of killing someone. He kept his face down, staring at his food, and seemed oblivious to everyone else.

Emma said he'd lost his job at the factory he worked at, that he was still living at his mother's house, sleeping in the basement. His clothes were clean and fresh; his flannel shirt looked ironed. Someone took care of him. Someone ironed his clothes, washed them, and gave him money to eat lunch out at a restaurant. Somebody loved him.

Taryn had met more than one killer in her life. Since Miss Dixie started doing her tricks it felt like Taryn drew them like flies. She shouldn't be shocked anymore by the secrets people lived with. It felt like everyone had a double life these days.

She didn't think Travis had noticed her but after he flagged his server down (the same one who had been so attentive to her but had completely ignored him) he paused at her table as he was passing by. "I know who you are," he growled through his teeth, barely looking down at her. "You don't have to keep staring at me."

Embarrassed she'd been caught, she began to apologize in haste. "I'm sorry. I know it was rude. It's just that..."

"You just wanted to know what a killer looks like?" he snorted.

Taryn did not think it prudent to point out that she'd met others who'd been accused of similar crimes, and those people had tried to turn their actions on *her*.

"Innocent until proven guilty, right?" she asked faintly. Suddenly, the fire felt just a little too hot, her red sweater a little too snug. She was aware that the people around her had stopped eating and were staring at them.

"Yeah, right. Well, you're the psychic, right? Then you should know the truth. I didn't kill nobody. I never saw Cheyenne after that party. I didn't touch her, didn't even talk to her except when she bummed a smoke off of me around the fire."

There was no pleading in his voice, just a matter of fact-ness that was hard to rebuttal. He stood there in the middle of the restaurant, a young man in work boots and a thick coat, and stared down at the floor, unable to make eye contact. She could feel the frustration rolling off of him in waves.

"You mean she didn't go back to your place after?"

Travis shook his head. "Shit no. I know what they're saying, what they say. And people gonna believe what they want to believe. Look, I don't know where she went or who she went with, but it wasn't me. I didn't touch her," he repeated, his face growing redder with anger.

"Then what happened to her, Travis?" Taryn asked gently.

"I don't know. Isn't that why they hauled your ass here? You figure it out!" And, with that, he marched away from the table, barely missing a server with a heavy tray of breakfast in his path.

"**I**'m missing something, Matt, I know I am. I think I'm going to go back to the farmhouse." Taryn paced back and forth in the living room, nervously chewing on her fingernails. It wasn't even a bad habit of hers; she was just nervous and looking for something to do. The three Cokes she'd already had that morning couldn't be helping matters.

"You've been over there half a dozen times," Matt reminded her. "Don't you think your camera would've picked something up by now?"

"I don't know," Taryn snapped. "How am I supposed to know how this works?"

She immediately felt guilty for yelling at Matt and, in a rare scene of public emotions, sat down on the couch and burst into tears. God, she was such a girl sometimes. Matt, whose inner peace was solid to the core, patiently put down the epic fantasy novel he'd been reading for the fifth time and trudged over to her. His arm slid around her protectively and as he squeezed her shoulders she felt even worse. There she was, being mean to probably the only person in the world she cared about.

"I'm sorry," she blubbered, wishing she was the type of woman who looked pretty when she cried. "I don't even know why I'm on edge."

"You haven't been getting a lot of sleep," Matt reminded her. "And you're pushing yourself really hard on something you just might not be able to fix."

"I know you're right," she sighed, wiping at her eyes with the back of her hand. "But why would Cheyenne be contacting me, and I know it's her, if I couldn't do anything. I feel like the answers are right at my fingertips, and I'm just too dense to figure it out."

"You're not dense," Matt chided. "One of the things I love about you, and the main thing that drives me crazy about you, is that you have very good perception and can read people like a book. Honestly, if I had a mystery to solve you'd be the first person I'd come to because you're so good at cutting through the bullshit. It's no wonder the dead seek you out."

Taryn smiled a little, her mood lifting. "You said 'bullshit.' I think I've only heard you cuss twice in twenty years."

"Yeah, well, I save the foul language for special occasions. I think it shows lack of creativity unless it's used wisely," he grinned.

Taryn, on the other hand, might have been creative when it came to her art but not in language. She cussed like a sailor – all words learned courtesy of her grandmother.

"Their party is in a week. I wanted to have answers by then. We're leaving a few weeks after that and it's not a lot of time. I just feel so... involved," she finished lamely.

"Why do you think that is?"

Taryn turned around so that her feet were propped in Matt's lap. He stretched out on the other end of the couch and, facing each other, they carried on as though she'd never had her little outburst. "I don't know," she replied honestly. "Maybe because we're here, in the middle of it? Maybe because I can feel her a little bit. You know how I've always had an active imagination?"

Matt nodded. When they were little she used to make him pretend that they both had magical unicorns. They'd gallop all over the neighborhood on their adventures until their legs were worn out. She had him so wrapped up in her imagination that he'd even get off his first and help her down since she was so short.

"Yeah, well, it's different this time. I don't need the camera or my dreams or even her spirit. I can see her in my mind. She's as real to me as you are. And maybe it's just my mind playing tricks on me, I don't know," she shrugged with agitation. "But I feel like I'm supposed to be here."

"Well then, you are. If you feel it then you're meant to be. It just means we're going to have to start looking under other rocks. In the meantime," a little gleam formed in Matt's eyes as he tickled the bottom of her feet. "In the meantime we have an hour before you have to leave for class. How about I get under you?"

"Why Matthew," Taryn purred in an exaggerated southern drawl. "That's downright lewd and vulgar of you."

"Yeah well, like I said. I save my foul language for special occasions."

Chapter 19

$\mathcal{T}$aryn and Emma squeezed into a booth at a small, greasy

diner on Main Street. Emma promised her the breakfast was the best in town and she wouldn't find better ice tea.

"That's okay," Taryn waved her hand in the air. "I'm kind of off the stuff. I'll take an apple juice."

Emma raised her eyebrows but didn't press and Taryn didn't volunteer her past experience with her once-favorite drink.

"So, any news?" Taryn asked once they made their orders and settled back into the plastic seats.

"I met with the guys last night. Nothing new," Emma sighed. "I really thought we would've been farther along at this point."

Taryn felt a stab of shame, knowing that several people had hoped her presence would bring some answers. So far, it hadn't. "I'm still working my end," she said, all the same. "I'm not giving up yet."

Emma smiled brightly and pushed a lock of hair behind her ear. Despite the fact there'd been snow flurries just a day or two before, now the sun was out and her car thermometer boasted a whopping sixty-six degrees. Welcome to the south.

"Let's say, for argument's sake, that Travis did kill Cheyenne," Taryn began. "Where's her body?"

"Unfortunately, there are lots of places around here to hide one. Some sinkholes, wells, creeks, the river, a cave or two..." Emma shrugged. "And he would've had several hours to do it in. Nobody even realized she was missing until later the next day."

"What do you know about him?"

"Not much. He's older than most of us. Was in the marines and got injured. Afghanistan? Maybe Iraq. I can't remember. Anyway, he came home and went to work for Sieko, that's the cell phone factory."

"What was someone older, like him, doing at a party that was mainly meant for high school students?" Taryn wondered aloud.

"Oh, well, anyone could go. It was kind of the place to go, if you know what I mean," Emma explained. "There's not much to do around here, not even a theater. So you just kind of hang out until you get married."

"Or go to college?"

"Yeah, well, there's that. But I don't know if you've noticed or not – the town and the college are kind of divided. Like, their own little worlds, you know? The people at the college don't really get out in the community. They all shop at the same craft supply store, eat at the same cafes, and then hang out at the different centers on campus. It's a liberal arts school, but our town is anything but liberal."

"But you go there," Taryn pointed out.

"Yeah, well, I always kind of felt like I didn't belong here," Emma admitted. "You know, I didn't go to church or anything growing up. And that's the thing to do. My parents weren't exactly church-going people and then in high school I got into Wicca and stuff. I did a semester abroad in Rome when I was a junior. Some of these people have barely been out of Georgia. And, I don't know if you've noticed or not, but I am a vegetarian." Emma smiled, and Taryn felt even more connected to her. She knew how it felt to feel disconnected to the world around you.

"So why stay here? Why not go to Atlanta or Memphis or even Chattanooga or Nashville?"

Emma sighed and stared over Taryn's head, out the window that overlooked the quiet little main street. "I don't know. Growing up I couldn't wait to get out of here. It's easy to dream, though. Actually leaving just ended up being too hard. I have a love-hate relationship with the place. Living here I feel stifled, trapped, out of my element. But when I'm away I yearn for it. I guess it doesn't make sense."

It did make sense to Taryn, though. Sometimes she found herself feeling the same way about Matt. When she was with him she questioned what she as doing, if what they were doing was right, what her feelings truly were. "Stifled" was a good word. And then, when they were apart, her heart felt broken.

"I don't know," Emma laughed. "Maybe I'll go soon. Seeing you and what you do and how independent you are, it gives me the motivation to make a change. Maybe now is the time."

"**I** need to get out," Taryn stated. Matt was holed up in his makeshift office, a corner of the dining room, and Taryn burst through the door after her class, adrenalin pumping. "Really, I do. How about we drive to the next county over and eat, see a movie, do something?"

"Yeah, okay," he agreed. "Give me an hour to finish this up and then I'm yours. You okay?"

She began to push her boots off and slip off her jacket, careful to stow them away as she went. Matt was a little OCD about cleanliness. It was starting to rub off. "Yeah, just going a little stir crazy I think. I need some perspective."

He nodded in agreement and sent her an absent smile, already back to his work.

Going a little farther than originally intended, they spent the whole afternoon and evening in Athens, shopping, eating, and watching a movie. Picking out a film was always difficult for them because while Taryn tended to like heavy dramas and horrors, Matt leaned towards romantic comedies and fantasy. When she found a theater showing a revival of "Rosemary's Baby," she was excited but he a little less so. "What's it about?" he asked nervously, eyeing the creepy baby carriage on the poster with suspicion.

"It's about some devil worshippers who impregnate a woman to have the devil's baby," she explained. Matt's face turned a little white and she laughed. "Don't worry. It's a classic. You'll love it."

Afterwards, sitting in an Italian restaurant with soft light and softer music he was still musing over the film, shaking his head. "They couldn't have been witches," he complained for the hundredth time. "Witches don't worship the devil!"

"Leave it to you to feel pity for the cult,' Taryn laughed. "Although, to be fair, Rosemary and Hutch are the only two who ever use the word 'witch.' I still can't believe you never saw that..."

Taryn was excited to find a large craft superstore where she was able to stock up on more canvas, frames, and brushes. Matt was equally impressed with the even bigger bookstore next door and for the next hour they holed up in the coffee shop, each with a stack of books at their side: Matt, a collection of sci-fi and Taryn a collection of physic and dream phenomena. She still had a lot to learn.

By the time they were driving back to the cabin both were delightfully exhausted and rejuvenated. "I needed that," she sighed, stretching out in the car seat. Her joints were a little stiff and her back achy from being out all day. "I like getting out."

"Me too sometimes," he agreed. "And I think we did our part to help boost the Georgian economy."

Taryn considered their backseat full of books and art supplies and laughed. "I'm thinking of making my own body balm and candles. I saw some beeswax there. I might try that next."

"You're not going to get all Pioneer Woman on me, are you?"

"Nah, just trying to find a new hobby, something to keep me busy," she shrugged. "I've felt a little down lately."

She wasn't feeling depressed, exactly, just out of sorts. Maybe she was too invested in Cheyenne and what was going on around her. It would probably be a good thing when her class wound up and she was able to leave, although where she'd go next was still up in the air. Should she return to Florida with Matt? Go back to her apartment in Nashville? It was bound to need a good airing out, if nothing else. She didn't have a new job lined up yet and that was making her antsy. She had bills and stuff.

At some point she and Matt needed to sit down and talk about their relationship. So far she'd been a big wuss and avoided it. There was no way of doing it without it feeling like a confrontation and she hated those. She didn't want him to think she was putting pressure on him for anything but, at thirty, she also couldn't afford to half-ass something, either.

The cabin was dark when they pulled up to it; they'd forgotten to leave a light on in their haste to leave. "Stay here, I'll go in and flip the switch," Matt ordered as he turned off the engine.

Taryn waited all of ten seconds then jumped out of the car. Like hell she was sitting in the dark car, alone. It was a moonless night and the increasing clouds were even blocking out the stars, making it incredibly dark. Pushing herself into a little jog and ignoring the pain in her legs, she caught up with Matt and waited for him to fish out the keys. "I get spooked sitting in dark cars. You know, the urban legend about the hook?" Matt looked at her blankly; of course he didn't know that one.

Within seconds the living room and front porch were flooded with light and Taryn breathed a sigh of relief she didn't realize she'd been holding onto. Matt went in first, leaving her to pull the door close behind her.

The living room was bright and cheerful, everything in place exactly as they'd left it. Both of their laptops were on the dining room table, Miss Dixie waiting patiently on the footstool near the hallways, waiting to be used again. The air was quiet, with only the sounds of their breathing breaking up the stillness. Nothing had changed in their absence.

Still, Taryn stopped in her tracks, looked around, and shuddered. "Matt," she whispered. "Somebody was just in here."

"**A**re you sure you don't want to go to a hotel or anything?" Matt asked with concern. They'd been home for hours and now it was 2 am. Both were snuggled down under the down comforter, an old movie playing on the TV. Matt was drowsy and had nodded off a few times already; Taryn was wide awake and wired.

"I'll be fine," she insisted, nervously glancing at the bedroom door. She wasn't sure if she felt better with it shut, or open so that she could see what was going on in the hallway outside.

Matt had checked all the rooms, peeking into closets and looking under all the beds. There was so sign of anyone other than them having been in the house. It didn't reassure Taryn, however. Her skin still crawled from the electrical air currents that spoke of another, or thing, having invaded their space just moments before they'd entered the room.

"Maybe it was Thelma and Jeff?" Matt suggested. "Come to check on something?"

"No," she replied stubbornly. "It had just happened, right before we walked in. I felt it."

He took her word at that, used to her feelings and sensitivity to things he couldn't always feel or see.

Taryn did her best to get comfortable and settle into the bed, but after another hour of flipping and flopping around, and disturbing Matt, she knew it was useless. There was no reason for both of them to suffer a good night's sleep just because she was freaked.

Slowly letting herself out of the bed so as not to wake him, she tiptoed from the room and made her way downstairs. They'd left nearly every light in the house on, something that felt foolish at the time, but now she was glad. There was another television in the living room and she turned it on and flipped through the channels while her laptop booted up. Miss Dixie gazed forlornly at her from across the room. "Yeah, yeah, I know," she muttered, feeling guilty. "I need to get you back out."

There is a point in the night where the thrill of being up late and working in the stillness loses its luster. Suddenly, the nighttime is no longer another world, another time, but just an extension of the day. Taryn usually started feeling depressed at about that time, as she was reminded of the fact that it was going to be daylight soon and instead of feeling like she'd made the day before longer by not going to bed, she was hit with the realization that she'd made the new day shorter. She'd go to bed around 6 or 7 am and wake up after noon, justifiably having slept half of the day away. In the darker months, when daylight was shorter, there were times in which she'd only see a little bit of daylight at all. She didn't prefer being up at night; she just got tired of fighting her fears in it and gave in to it. She'd taken numerous prescriptions to try and help her sleep, both prescribed and over the counter, but all they did was proceed to make her exhausted so she'd sleep just as long. It was a battle she'd been fighting most of her life.

As scared as she'd been lying in bed, now that she was up and her senses acute, the fear seemed silly, whatever was in the dark beatable. Her courage gathered and fighting back demons felt possible. The idea of being asleep, defenseless in bed was what bothered her the most – the feeling of being out of control. This was one of the reasons why she had no trouble rambling around old, spooky houses in the daytime or even seeking out ghosts and yet felt terrified by the shadows that crept around her bed in the dark.

"**I** hereby call to order this meeting of the Justice Club, okay guys I'm just trying different things out, and party planning meeting," Lindy announced with fake sternness.

Brad rolled his eyes and Eric snorted, but Mike (good looking but he was ten years younger than Taryn so it felt like cradle robbing) managed a mega-watt smile.

It was the first time she'd been back to Emma's apartment, and she'd only decided to show up last minute. Matt was busy working on something she didn't understand and, although he might have been too polite to say so, she was distracting him with his constant interruptions. For some reason Taryn just felt restless and couldn't get it under control.

"'Justice Club'?" Brad smirked. "That's a little lame, Lin."

"Yeah, well, you come up with a better idea," she sniffed.

They'd opted out of pizza tonight and were, instead, all gathered around the coffee table with Chinese. The town might have lacked fine dining options and alcohol sales but they managed to fit in three Chinese and four Mexican restaurants.

"Well, before you all start bickering, any news on the party?" Emma interjected.

"I got my costume," Lindy boasted. She was wearing a bright pink velour track suit that ended just a few inches below her breasts, her tanned stomach a stark contrast to Taryn and Emma's paleness. Her hair was glossy and perfectly styled, as it had been every time Taryn had seen her, and she wore full eye makeup. Taryn found herself wondering how long it took her to get ready every morning and grudgingly admired her dedication. It then struck her that she didn't actually know what Lindy did.

"Lindy," she butted in before anyone else could speak. "What do you do?"

They all turned to look at her and in that instant Taryn felt embarrassed by her bluntness. "Man, I'm sorry. I didn't mean to be rude. I just meant, are you a student, do you work somewhere?"

Flipping her pert ponytail over her shoulder Lindy sent Taryn a brilliant smile. "I'm taking some nursing classes, and I work at AMT. It's a temp agency."

"I just can't see you being a nurse," Brad muttered. "You're terrible around sick people."

"Yeah, well, I like kids," she reasoned. "And I'm no dummy. Nurses are almost guaranteed jobs around here as soon as they graduate. Besides, you're getting a degree in English, and we all know your command of the language isn't going to win you any awards," she added sweetly, batting her eyes.

Brad's face reddened briefly and then he shrugged it off. "I want to teach," he explained to Taryn, "or else maybe go into journalism. My dad runs the local paper, and I'm guaranteed a job

222

there, but I'd like to know what the heck I'm doing with it and not just walk in and take over."

"Well, that's a good idea," Taryn said encouragingly. "And Mike?"

"Nothing declared yet," he shrugged. "Just taking some electives and general ed. Maybe criminal justice."

"He works at the student union," Emma volunteered, flashing Mike a smile. Taryn thought she might have caught a spark pass between the two of them. "That's how he met Brad."

"Work study," Mike added.

"I'm taking a semester off," Eric declared. "I got burnt out last spring and just needed some time. I work at a paint store here in town. The pay's decent, and I don't do much."

"So, back to the party?" Lindy pouted, and they all turned their attention back to her.

"Yeah, well, Chris said no hard liquor, just kegs," Brad warned. "I've got those covered. Emma's coordinating food."

"I've got accelerant and firewood covered," Mike threw in. "My cousin has a tree removal business and said I could take what I could haul off." Taryn remembered seeing the big pile of wood already stacked in front of the house. They probably wouldn't need much more.

"And I've got music and lights," Eric concluded. "So that's everything."

"If it rains we can take it inside, but I don't want anyone on the second floor," Emma warned. "The last thing we need is for someone to wander off or get hurt and have all hell break loose again."

"Which brings us back to Cheyenne," Eric intoned. "Any news?"

They all shook their heads and the room grew quiet, save for the radio softly playing Keith Urban in the background. A lot of his songs ran together for Taryn but this time she was a little grateful for the familiarity of their sound. All of a sudden she was feeling alone and vulnerable in this group of strangers, all younger than her and most likely to forget about her once she was gone. It was funny how music didn't change and traveled with you through the rough times, weird times, and happy times. Like a best friend, almost.

"Do you think Evan's going to come?" Emma asked, breaking the quietness.

"I don't think so," Eric replied. "He's working nightshift at Sieko. I asked him. He said he'd try to get off but he didn't think he could."

"It's not really his scene anyway," Brad proclaimed. "He's been going to church a lot, swore off drinking. Quit smoking or some shit like that. I think he found God."

"Evan's a nice guy," Lindy sniffed, picking at the bright pink polish on her nails. "He can't help it if he doesn't want to slum it with you guys."

"Remember, honey, you're one of us, too." Brad smiled as he spoke but there was a hardness in his eyes that made Taryn inspect him closer.

"Evan and I are friends and have been for a long time," she retorted. "I talk to him all the time."

"Who's Evan?" Taryn asked, hoping it was an innocent question, although Lindy clearly had some interest there. Her normally confident stance was shaken a little and it was visible in the way she continued to pick at the polish, watching it flake way and land on the carpet.

"He's a guy we went to school with," Emma explained. "Nice guy, Lindy's right. She and him went out a little in high school."

"Yeah, but he only had eyes for Cheyenne," Brad laughed.

"That's not true, you asshole," Lindy protested, raising her voice an octave. "We dated for almost six months, and he never even looked at another girl."

Brad shrugged and Mike laughed. "Whatever. I thought they were going to hook up that night at Chris'. I don't know; maybe they did. He told me he was looking for her, but I never saw them together."

"That's because he was with me almost all night," Lindy pouted. Then, with a flounce, she got up and stalked down the small room to the bathroom, slamming the flimsy door to behind her.

"It's a sore point for her," Emma explained. "She's had a crush on Evan off and on her whole life. I think maybe their timing has just never been right."

"It's because all he wants to use her for is to get laid," Eric explained. Emma shot him a dirty look. "Hey, it's true! Tell me he doesn't ever want her except when she's with another guy? They could be going out now, but they're not."

Since nobody spoke up in Evan's defense, Eric continued. "I like him, he's cool. But he's not going to date Lindy. When it comes to relationships he's more into the sweet, soft-spoken, innocent girls. Like Cheyenne. And that bugs the hell out of Lin."

By the time she came back into the room, with slightly puffy cheeks and less lipstick than before, the conversation had rolled into something else, and Evan wasn't mentioned again.

Driving back home in the dark, cranking up Kelly Willis' "Teddy Boys" and singing as loud as she could stand it, Taryn felt a little lighter. Despite the fact that they weren't her friends, it wasn't her party, and this wasn't her town she was starting to feel somewhat accepted. She'd never had a group of friends before; the feeling of being a part of something was intoxicating.

Chapter 20

"Are you sure you want to do this?" Matt looked at Taryn with skepticism, and she nodded with outward confidence. Inside, she was shaking like Jell-O.

"Okay," he signaled towards the front door with his head, since his arms were full. "Let's do it then."

Together, they walked out into the cold, damp evening and started for the woods. Taryn wore a heavy backpack, its weight pulling at her muscles almost immediately and making them sore. She, someone who backpacked Eastern Europe in college, was getting to be such a wimp. An achy back, painful joints, tired all the time... what was she, eighty? Pretty soon she'd be like her grandmother, slathering herself with Icy Hot every night and sleeping curled up next to a hot water bottle with an electric blanket cranked up high in June.

Matt carried a blanket, a bottle of wine, and a flashlight. At 6 pm it was already starting to grow dark and the sky was that murky blue color, not quite day and not quite night. She'd heard it referred to as the "gloaming" but only in books and songs; nobody she knew actually called it that. Too bad, really, because the word itself was pretty.

The woods were thick and dark and she was glad for Matt's flashlight or else she was sure she'd have tripped over a root or random stick and gone sprawling down on her face. It didn't take long to reach the other side and when they entered the field Taryn took over leading the way. She stopped in front of the house, near the wood pile but not too close in case there were snakes. She thought it was probably too cold for them, and too dark, but you never knew. She had images of one doing a sneak-attack on her, ninja style, and flying through the air. (In truth, despite all the places she'd stomped around, she'd only seen a live snake once and it was as scared as her as she was of it. They'd both quickly gone their separate ways, not looking back. But she was still terrified of them.)

"Here?" Matt asked. It was the first thing either one of them had said since leaving the house.

"Yeah, this feels right."

Taryn slipped off her backpack and began pulling out the things she needed while Matt spread the blanket on the ground. Soon, Taryn had set up a makeshift altar with candles, oils, stones, and bundles of herbs. Matt fished the wooden matches, they had to be wooden, out of his pocket and handed them to her. She had to refer to her notes a few times to set up the little altar on the large shoe box she'd fished out of a bedroom closet but it only took her a few tries to get it right. Figuring it must have some energy considering where it had come from, a scarf she'd picked up in Bosnia acted as an altar cloth.

A large white pillar candle set in the middle. Flanking it were candles in various colors-blue, gold, indigo, purple, and silver. The myrrh Rob had sent them was carefully positioned by the white candle, the stones arranged according to the chart he'd drawn for them. Taryn also pulled a hand mirror from her bag. This she placed on the blanket next to her.

"You got everything?" Matt asked, settling in next to her. It wasn't as cold as she'd thought it would be and now she felt stifled and a little claustrophobic in her big, bulky coat.

"Yeah, let's do it."

Matt lit the candles, starting with the pillar. Their flames licked at the night sky, wavering in the slight breeze. Taryn was afraid they might be snuffed out, but the nearby wood pile served to shield them from the worst of it. While Matt busiest himself with the candles, Taryn folded her hands in her lap and began clearing her mind, meditating on the task at hand. Between her knees she balanced a photo of Cheyenne, a print off from an online article about her. She started by focusing on the things around her, the sound of the breeze rustling the few remaining leaves on the nearby trees, the chilly air nipping at her cheeks, the faint rays of warmth on her hands from the candles.

She'd never found it easy to clear her mind – just as soon as she tried to do it, it would be filled with random television show theme songs. With Matt sitting next to her, though, his energy provided a calming sensation that made concentrating much simpler. Sometimes she found the fact that Matt rarely showed emotions irritating. Other times, his stillness was necessary to her often frantic-running mind. She was counting on his energy, and whatever they had between them, to make the task at hand easier. And more successful. Without him and left to her own devices she'd probably accidentally summon a demon and open the gates to hell.

Once he'd lit the candles she could feel him soften besides her, his breathing steady and intentional. Matt didn't have trouble meditating; he did it on a regular basis, saying it was good for the chakras. She wasn't real sure what that meant, but it sounded important.

Once she felt her body relaxing and was fairly sure the Broadway cast of "A Chorus Line" wasn't going to break out into song, Taryn began bringing Cheyenne's image to mind. She let her imagination draw her long black hair, big brown eyes, and her compact body. She could see her there, on the farm, on her last night. Using her imagination Taryn tried to see her standing by the bonfire, talking to friends, drinking... Obviously, they couldn't do this at her last known whereabouts since it was highly unlikely Travis Marcum's parents would let them in ("Hi! Can we come in and cast a spell in your basement? We're just going to summon a spirit; it won't take long!") the farm was the next best thing. And maybe even the better option since Taryn knew it.

Now, feeling slightly silly, Taryn began repeating the chant Rob sent them. She'd never been good at reciting poetry and actually saying a spell out loud made her feel self-conscious, even when she was alone, but when Matt joined in with her it was easier to shake off the uncomfortable vibe. His voice was soft, yet strong, and together they repeated it three times.

At first, nothing happened. Taryn peeked out of one eye, like a kid cheating at hide-n-seek. It had grown darker now, the candles casting eerie shadows around them, but Cheyenne's spirit was not waiting nearby, magically conjured from their words and ritual. Still, Taryn wasn't ready to give up. Again, she closed her eyes and repeated the chant, forcing herself to be loud and strong and to forget about what anyone would think if they found the two of them there.

Suddenly, she felt Matt's hand closing over hers, his skin cool and smooth. The spark of electricity that passed between them was forceful, the shock enough to make her jump a little. She felt the heat of the flame grow stronger and when she opened her eyes she could the candle flames were much higher now, at least five inches, and danced in circles on their wicks. The air around them was a vacuum, sucking Taryn's energy out of her in a slow, steady beat. She could no longer see the woodpile, the house, or the nearby forest. Matt's breathing, something she'd been in tune with, was still. Willing herself not to break concentration, she fought down the fear rising in her stomach, shut out the images of someone sneaking up behind her and hurting her. She'd never felt so exposed and the fact they were out in the open tore at her and made her want to run. But this she pushed down, too, and tried only to think of Cheyenne.

Slowly, with her left hand so as not to let go of Matt, she picked up the mirror. The antique silver was heavy in her hand. Holding it at an angle so that she could see into it but not catch her own reflection, she peered into it and waited. The area behind her was dark, solid. She couldn't see a thing – not even the glare of the moon or stars. It was as though there was a wall behind her, or an abyss.

231

But then, as her eyes strained on the glass, an image began to form. It was blurry at first, a ball of light that could've been a headlight coming onto the field or someone walking towards them with a flashlight. It had no definite shape or lines. As she watched, however, the shape changed and began moving. The light bounced up at a frantic speed, reaching for the sky. It became bigger, fuller. It wasn't a solid color but rather a mixture of reds, yellows, and oranges. Taryn finally realized that what she was looking at was a bonfire. It was solid black around the fire, the way the space around them was now. But then, a figure formed. The red cowboy boots, the inky black hair, the long muscular legs... there was no doubt it was Cheyenne. She didn't look at Taryn through the mirror or make contact with her. Taryn couldn't see her eyes at all. In fact, she couldn't even see her face. How could she when Cheyenne's entire body was stretched out on the ground, engulfed by the flames?

"I feel like I should call Emma and ask more questions," Taryn lamented.

"Honey, I think this is something best kept between the two of us now. We don't know Cheyenne was burnt alive or anything. The fire was searched; you told me that. They would've found remains. Not to mention the fact that it would negate the whole idea of her going to Travis' afterwards for the 'after party,'" Matt pointed out.

Taryn stopped, her spoon of rocky road halfway to her mouth. Ice cream was her comfort food; she could eat it at any time – scared, cold, nervous, in sickness and in health…" Yeah, you're right. On the other hand, Travis keeps insisting he's innocent. Maybe he is."

"Did you get a good feel for him at the restaurant?"

Taryn shrugged and took another bite. "Not a good one. He didn't come across as very likable. But then, would you if you were being accused of murder? Besides, just because he's an asshole doesn't mean he's guilty of murder."

"True. I don't know. I've never met a murderer before," Matt mused.

Taryn snorted, nearly sending ice cream up her nose. "I have. And believe me, they come across a lot more normal than you'd think."

"Yeah, well, I am seriously considering not letting you out of the house again."

They were quiet, lost in companionable silence, the events of the night between them. Taryn still shuddered at the sight of Cheyenne's body in the raging fire. She'd been lying down, lifeless. Maybe it was symbolic. Or maybe it was a different fire. She was sure of one thing, though: she'd seen something she was supposed to.

"Maybe another trip through the house?" she suggested at last. "I know I've been through it a dozen or more times, but I can't help but feel like I'm missing something. Maybe I'm just not looking hard enough."

"I don't know. You're trying awfully hard. Don't stretch yourself too thin," Matt warned her, his eyebrows creased in concern.

"Yeah, yeah. I know."

"Did you see or feel anything?"

Matt stared at the ceiling light. It flickered off and on, a short in it or maybe a bulb trying to burn out. Taryn knew he'd have it fixed by morning. "I didn't see anything, but I felt something. Most of it came from you. I could feel you burning up, like you had a fever. And I couldn't let go. Not that I would," he added hurriedly, "but I don't think I could've even if I'd wanted to."

"I think it was because of you that it happened. I don't know if I could've done it on my own," Taryn admitted.

Matt was right, though. As much as she wanted to talk to someone else about what she'd seen and heard, it was probably best to keep it to herself for now. She'd never been good at playing it close to the vest but there was something off about the whole thing, and she didn't want to end up somewhere she shouldn't be. Again.

Chapter 21

$\mathcal{T}$he Halloween party was in four days. She'd talked Matt into

dressing up; he was going as a superhero. She didn't know which one. In fact, she kind of thought he'd made it up. She'd talked him out of baking up a storm, which was his reaction to getting any kind of invitation. Instead, he'd settled on some kind of hand held chocolate dessert thing and wine.

Taryn's class ended at Thanksgiving break. After the party she'd have four weeks left. She was already itching to move on. She enjoyed teaching a lot more than she thought, but she also enjoyed moving around a lot and seeing new things. The students were all kind of doing their own things now, with her simply supervising. They were going on a field trip the next day – an old antebellum house on the outskirts of town that had partially crumbled from neglect. Most of them were looking forward to getting off campus.

Taryn was also nervous about the fact that she and Matt were settling into the cabin. She had to keep reminding herself that it wasn't their home, that it was as temporary as a hotel room. The confusion surrounding their relationship continued to grow. The night before he'd talked about quitting his job and moving to Nashville, but it had been in jest. At least, she thought it was. There was nothing for him to do there that came even close to his current job, and she didn't want to feel responsible for uprooting him and him possibly being miserable. She wasn't even sure she counted Nashville as her home anymore; she was rarely there.

Then there was the fact that when she looked into the future, she wasn't sure what she saw with him. Kids? She didn't think so. She knew she wanted them, eventually, but Matt was so organized and strict in his routine she didn't know how he'd react to a baby or toddler. He had five-year plans and ten-year plans. She barely knew where she was going to be from one month to the next. He hadn't mentioned marriage at all, although that was understandable considering his ex-fiancée had left him at the altar just two years before.

That morning, at breakfast, they'd gotten into an argument over their vague future. "I don't know where this is going," Taryn complained. It was hard to complain when the person you were directing your annoyance at had just cooked your breakfast, but she managed all the same.

"Why does it have to go anywhere?" he'd asked gently. "Can't we just have a good time and enjoy where we're at now?"

But Taryn wasn't sure she could. She liked knowing where things were going and what the future held, despite the fact she generally worked in the past.

"When we leave here," she pressed, "I'll go back to my apartment, and you'll go back to Florida."

"And it will make me sad to be apart from you when I'm used to having you around," he agreed.

Yet he offered no alternative and she didn't feel like his suggestion of moving to Nashville to work in a bakery, when he was currently making six figures, legit.

"Have you thought about getting married? Maybe making this permanent?" But as soon as it was out of her mouth she regretted it. Now he'd think she was pushing it and he might want to do it, for no other reason but that she'd suggested it. And she certainly didn't want that.

"I just don't know if I am ready to go through all that again," he explained. "I tried it once before, and it didn't work out."

"But that wasn't me," she'd sputtered. "And I've always been around." Well, except for those few years when they'd parted ways, angry at one another. But she would've gone to him at the drop of a hat if he'd needed her.

"I don't know. I'll think about it."

So Taryn had stomped off, angry and frustrated. He'd "think" about it? Like he had complete control over the relationship and got to make the decisions? But what did she even want anyway? With Andrew it was much simpler. They'd met, dated briefly, and both decided to get married simultaneously, laughing as they drove to the jewelry store where he'd picked out a ring after careful deliberation and proposed on the very same day. They were married four months later without much fanfare in a ceremony that was sweet and fun. There'd been no hesitation, no qualms, no cold feet, and no questions. She'd never doubted what she wanted to do and how she felt.

With Matt, she questioned it every day. Half of her wanted to say "this is it" and devote the rest of her life to him, the other half was disappointed in the fact that she didn't feel the bells and whistles and certainty she expected. But maybe she was just expecting too much. It happened.

With the day off, Taryn was making her last trip to the farmhouse. At least, the last trip to carry out any "research." She'd be back for the party and it was a nice walk, unrealistic to think she might not wander over there again over the course of the next few weeks. Miss Dixie was charged with a new SIM card. She was ready; Taryn made sure of it by giving her a strong pep talk before they left.

'I haven't been very successful at this, old girl. You're going to have to work a little harder, I'm afraid," she apologized to her camera before setting out. "But you can do it. If there's anything there, you'll find it!"

Miss Dixie had presented her with her usual droll expression, giving nothing away.

Matt was out on a supply run. In addition to the groceries and toiletries she'd asked him to pick up some more Tylenol for her. He was concerned that she'd already gone through the box of sixty he'd bought a week before. So was she, for that matter. The pain in her hips and legs was stronger; the pain in her head was sometimes unbearable. And she was uncharacteristically grumpy, probably from the lack of sleep she'd been getting.

Luckily, it was a pleasant day, almost sixty-five degrees, and the sun was high in the sky. The farmhouse looked inviting, the spot where they'd tried their ritual was unmarked. If anything horrible had truly taken place on the grounds, there were no visible signs of it now.

Feeling achy, but enthusiastic, she marched towards the front porch, Miss Dixie out and on and ready for action. Taryn aimed to walk through every room, snapping her photos in every single corner. She'd cover the entire house, twice if she had to, if it meant picking up on something she hadn't found before.

The front door opened immediately into a long hallway. A winding staircase rose up in front of her, with rooms on either side of the hall. A kitchen was at the end. She started with the foyer, snapping pictures the length of it and even poking her head inside the coat closet – full of spider webs and dust bunnies but little else.

The living room was large, with wide hardwood floors and a wood burning stove. The floors were stained and scuffed, but appeared sturdy enough. An old sofa, most likely a leftover from the eightiess, sagged up against a wall. A couple of foldout chairs were scattered in front of it. The floor was littered with beer cans and paper plates that wild animals had cleaned off a long time ago. It was a sad sight, but it didn't appear as though the room had been vandalized. Taryn stood in the middle and slowly turned in a circle, snapping pictures as she moved, focusing on the sofa and chairs. If Cheyenne had come inside at all, there was a very good chance she'd been in that room.

The room on the other side of the hall was a bedroom. With the windows boarded up, it was dark and difficult to see, the only light being a few pale rays streaking in from the windows in the foyer. It was entirely devoid of furnishings, although there was some garbage in the middle of the floor. It looked like someone had taken the trouble to bag it up, but animals had gotten into it and ripped the bag open, scattering the contents. Miss Dixie's flash illuminated the room with each click, momentarily igniting it like a strobe light.

She closed her eyes, trying to let herself pick up on any negative energy in the room but felt nothing. It was just an empty room.

Moving on upstairs, she stopped at the top in the small landing and took some more shots. The floorboards up there were painted a murky ivory. Maybe they'd been white at some point. It

240

was a nice little area and she could imagine a small bookcase, an easy chair in front of the window, a little library of sorts. The house wasn't in that bad of shape and could probably be fixed. Of course, Taryn thought every place could be fixed.

There were only three other rooms on the second level – two bedrooms and an unfinished attic space. The bedrooms were small with low ceilings, the floorboards had large spaces between them thick with grime and dust. One room was painted a bizarre neon green, the other a very dark brown. The brown room contained a dilapidated mattress, stained and threadbare. There were candles set up around it, their wax melted in puddles on the floor. She couldn't imagine some girl giving in to a guy and actually fooling around on the thing, but hormones would be hormones she guessed. Now that she'd turned thirty, she wasn't as adventurous as she used to be. Even the couch was pushing it.

Feeling a little queasy and hoping Miss Dixie didn't pick up on any kinky action she'd have to look at later, Taryn headed back down the stairs. A sound had her stopping in her tracks and she hesitated, one foot inches from the second stair. Holding her breath, she listened, waiting to hear it again. The house was silent, though, with nothing but her own breathing filling the empty space. Had she really heard laughter? The tinkling of a female's voice floating through the downstairs rooms? She thought she had, but perhaps her mind was just playing tricks on her.

There were two rooms left downstairs, an extremely long kitchen and bathroom. She'd seen nastier things in her life, she was sure, but it was hard to remember them after peering into the bathroom. The old claw foot tub was stained and cracked, the toilet caked with a dark substance she hoped was mud and rust and not excrement. It was hard to imagine someone ever bathing their children in this room, using the peeling mirror to get ready for a party, or the old wallpaper ever being new and fresh–and Taryn had a pretty good imagination. If anything horrendous had occurred on the property, she truly hoped it wasn't in that particular room. Nobody deserved that.

Standing back in the foyer, Taryn took a deep breath and gazed at the interior of the house once again. It was an old, simple farmhouse. There was nothing unique or interesting about it. She didn't feel any bad vibes or terror in the walls. But, yet, when she looked outside into the yard, something still felt off.

What *was* she missing?

Chapter 22

$\mathcal{A}$ll in all, Taryn had taken over one hundred fifty photos inside the old house. She hadn't realized she'd gotten so trigger happy in there. It took her more than two hours to sort through all the pictures on her laptop and, by the time she was finished, her lap was burning from the heat of the machine.

"Hey, those are pretty good," Matt remarked, peering over her shoulder. "Seriously. You should consider doing something with your photography."

"That's all the world needs, another person with a camera who thinks they're a professional photographer just because they can point and shoot," she grumbled. Taryn was a stickler for education; she reckoned it came from her parents who had both been academics. Although she had natural talent as an artist, she'd attended college and honed her skills and believed in higher education to cultivate whatever it was you had. These days it felt like a lot of people just wanted to take the easy route and go straight to millionaire or professional without putting in the legwork.

But she was thrilled, of course, that he liked her pictures. "Anything?"

"Yes and no," she replied, going back to a folder she'd created with the images that bore a second look. "Pull up a seat, and I'll show you."

Matt scooched in next to her on the couch and peered into the computer screen. "Yeah, okay, I see what you mean about that one. Looks like it could be a girl there?"

The photo in question was taken in the living room, the angle pointed at the old sofa. Although it was very faint, there did appear to be an outline of a person lying flat on the sofa, gazing up at the ceiling. At first glance it could've been male or female and any age. The longer and harder you looked, though, the clearer the long strands of hair and swell of breasts became.

"Looks like it could be Cheyenne," Taryn agreed. "But it's hard to tell if she's okay. Her eyes are closed, but she could've been resting. Or it could mean nothing."

"What about the others?"

"Well, here's another one I took upstairs in the bedroom with the mattress. You can't see anybody or anything suspicious, but the candles are lit which leads me to think that has something to do with Cheyenne."

Sure enough, when she clicked on the image, the bedroom was illuminated by the flashing of the flames. The candles were newly lit and much taller than they'd been when Taryn saw them, leading her to suspect that they'd been taken to the house for that occasion and not items left over from a previous party.

"I don't know why she would've laid on that filthy thing, but there you go…"

"Maybe she didn't," Matt pointed out. "Maybe that's why she's not in the picture."

"Yeah, that's a good point. And here's the last one."

The last shot was taken in the living room again. There was nothing unusual about it to someone who had recently been in the house. Nothing was out of place, no ghostly bodies writhed in the middle of the floor, no puddles of blood seeped through the cracks in the boards, and no murder weapons were carelessly left behind. It was a wide shot of the room, taken from the foyer, and all you could see were the five chairs and the sofa.

"You're going to have to help me out here," Matt said after a minute of staring hard. "I don't know what I'm supposed to be looking at."

"Yeah, neither did I at first but I kept coming back to this one because something was bugging me. And then I figured it out." Using her finger, she pointed at each of the chairs. "See these? One, two, three, four, five. There are five chairs here."

"Yeah?"

"Well, in real life now there are only four. One is missing," she quipped smugly.

"Huh. Well, maybe someone brought their own and took it home afterwards? Just trying to play devil's advocate."

"I don't think so. See how the chairs all look alike? You have four regular matching dining room chairs and then this oddball here. The oddball is still there in the house. It's one of the matching ones that's gone. I mean, it's possible that it got broken or someone stole it. But I think there's a significance there. If there's one thing I've learned from Miss Dixie's pictures it's that she tends to show me things I am supposed to see, even if I don't understand it at the time."

"So you leaning towards any theories yet?"

"Maybe," Taryn contemplated. "Maybe. But I have to talk to a few people first."

"I never hooked up with anyone at a party," Emma insisted.

"Oh, okay. Is that what happened in the farmhouse?" Taryn asked, feeling like the older, pushy sister.

"Yeah, we called it the 'hookup house.' I never had a reason to go in there. I mean I've been, but just to kind of step in and look for someone. I didn't go in there that night," Emma explained.

Lindy was in class so it was just the two of them on Emma's reclaimed couch. Emma had a litter of papers scattered around her, homework. She said she was preparing for an exam, and Taryn was sorry for disturbing her. She didn't plan on staying long but the female companionship was nice.

Emma had George Strait playing again, a nice change from the songs Taryn kept picking up on the radio. Although, in an earlier conversation when Lindy and Emma had asked Taryn what her favorite music was and she'd replied "country," they were confused when she began naming artists they'd never heard of. She'd spent fifteen minutes explaining her "holy trinity of female artists" (Tift Merritt, Allison Moorer, and Kelly Willis). The division between the radio artists and the alt-country artists seemed to be getting stronger.

"So how's college life treating you," Taryn asked, changing the subject from Cheyenne.

"Good I guess," Emma shrugged. "I think the second semester is easier. It's funny because I've lived here all my life but haven't had much to do with the college. They don't really have things for the community to be a part of."

"Have you met other people or do you mostly hang out with the kids you went to high school with?"

"I've met a few. I went out with some girls the other night. We had to go over to Jasper, you know, because our county is dry. I didn't get home until four in the morning," she giggled.

Taryn couldn't remember the last time she went out with "the girls," much less returned home at four in the morning. In college she'd done nothing but study and work.

It was on the tip of her tongue to blurt out the missing chair and burnt-out candles she'd seen, but something held her back. Emma acted as though Taryn's gift was not only okay but fabulous, but it still made her nervous to talk about it.

"Brad went in to talk to the detective in charge of the case," Emma said at last.

"Yeah, why?"

"He follows Travis on the social media stuff. Apparently Travis has been going on about how stupid local law enforcement is and some of his posts sound like he's bragging about a crime. Brad just thought the police should know."

"Yeah, that's probably a good idea," Taryn agreed. "Why would he do that, though? That's incredibly stupid."

"Yeah, well, welcome to our world," Emma laughed.

Driving back to the house, Taryn popped in her Bruce Springsteen CD and cranked up "I'm on Fire," as she sped down the town's small, quiet Main Street, past the county's single high school, and the abandoned cinema. She tried to imagine a thriving community, with people walking out on the sidewalks, teenagers lined up to buy tickets and popcorn, businesses with busy storefront windows instead of dusty "for sale" signs. It was difficult to see it.

The urgency of the music and pull of the desire made her drive faster, back to Matt. She really did feel like her skin was on fire, a pulsing in her head began to throb, whether from the headache she'd been having earlier or the thought of just seeing someone who knew her and loved her. For reasons she didn't understand, she felt desperate, frantic.

By the time she'd pulled into the long driveway and the Boss had long since moved on to "Dancin' in the Dark" she didn't feel like herself at all. There was a tingling in her arms, a weakness in her legs, and she felt like she was being lifted out of her body. Concentrating on the gravel in front of her, she willed herself to stay rooted to her seat, half-heartedly singing along with the music in an attempt to stay grounded to her body.

When, at last, she pulled up to the house she let out a tremendous sigh of relief. Matt was out on the porch, halfway down the stairs before she was even out of the car. The look of happiness on his face was immediately replaced by something she'd never seen on him before. But before she could open her mouth, or even take a step, the whole world turned black in front of her, and she could feel nothing but the continuous feeling of falling into total darkness.

Chapter 23

*T*here was no way anyone could sleep in a hospital. Between the noise in the hallway and the fact that someone was always coming in to adjust something, check on her, or take her blood pressure and temperature it was like living in the middle of Grand Central Station.

"I'm ready to go home," Taryn grumbled.

Matt looked up from his laptop and sighed. "You are the worst patient ever."

"Yeah, well, I feel better. And this IV hurts," she complained. "All this fluid they keep pumping into me just keeps making me want to pee."

She'd been there for twenty-four hours and in that time they'd run a brain MRI, abdominal CT scan, and taken so much blood she suspected they might just be vampires masquerading as nurses. So far, nobody had come back with any results other than the fact that her heart rate bad been extremely high, but her blood pressure very low.

"Can't I just go home and let them call me when they know something?" she asked for the millionth time.

"No," Matt replied without looking up. "There might be something seriously wrong and, if there is, this is the best place for you."

Thelma had already been in to see her and brought a vase of flowers. Taryn wasn't sure what they were, but they were an unnatural shade of purple and smelled like honey. Both Emma and Lindy had texted her. Since it was impossible to sleep she'd watched every single trashy reality show she could find on television. Normally, that would make her happy. But since she was confined to a bed by wires and unable to even go to the bathroom without help it just pissed her off.

Finally, the doctor she'd seen the day before entered the room, two nurses or residents or whatever, scampering behind him. He was young, probably fresh out of med school, and carried a clipboard. It didn't look like it had anything on it, making her wonder if he just carried it to look official.

"So am I going to live?" she joked.

"It looks like it," he frowned. "We got your results back and, for the most part, they're okay."

"Well, I like the 'okay' part but the other is a little concerning. What's up?" Suddenly, she felt a feeling of dread form in her stomach. What if she did have something awful, like brain cancer? What if she were dying?

"Your blood work looks fine. A little low on potassium but we pumped that into you," he smiled.

Taryn frowned. The potassium bit had burned. She hadn't liked that at all. Her arm was still sore.

"And your vitals look good now, although they were all over the place when the paramedics brought you in."

Taryn had no recollection of being carried off in the ambulance. The first thing she remembered was flying down the

251

hallway on a stretcher, her first thought, "Wee! This is fun!" followed shortly by, "What the hell is going on?"

"You do have something called an aortic aneurism in your abdomen," he continued without expression.

"Well, I don't like the word 'aneurism,'" she said. "What does it mean?"

"There's no sign of rupture or that it's doing anything at the moment," he replied, again with an expressionless face. "I'm going to give you an information sheet about it, with signs to watch for. If it does rupture, it's very serious," he stressed at last. "As in life or death. So you'll need to get to a hospital immediately."

"Well, hell," Taryn snapped. "How long have I had this thing?"

"It's hard to say," he answered. "You probably haven't even noticed it, except for the occasional feeling like your heart is beating in your stomach."

"Yeah, I get that sometimes," she conceded. "So is that the bad news?"

"The CT scan included your chest, and we did an echo when you first came in. Has anyone ever told you that you have mitral valve prolapse?"

"No, what's that?"

The doctor briefly went over the condition, explaining that it could account for her dizziness, fatigue, and other symptoms she'd been experiencing.

Sighing, Taryn leaned back in her bed. "Well, that's something then."

"There's still something else," the doctor murmured. "The women on either side of him were stoic, motionless.

"What?" In frustration, Taryn began popping her knuckles, a nervous habit she'd had seen she was a child. "Now you're going to tell me about the brain cancer?"

"No, but..." he trailed off, watching her hands. "Do that again."

"Do what?" she asked.

"Your hands. Let me see you bend your fingers like that."

Taryn laughed. "You mean this?" With ease, she bent her pinkie backwards until it was touching her wrist. "It's my party trick." One of the women cringed slightly.

Setting his clipboard down, he walked over to her. "Can you do that with any other fingers?"

"Sure." While he watched, she bent her other pinkie back and then her thumbs.

"Let me see your legs," he commanded.

Taryn uncovered them and watched as he lifted one, bent it, and then maneuvered the other one in the same way. He then, to her surprise, came closer and gently rubbed his hand down her forearm, studying it intently. "Can you open your mouth real wide now?" he asked, pulling out a little flashlight.

Having no idea where this was going, Taryn opened her mouth and let out a long "ahhh" while he searched for whatever it was he was looking for.

Finished now, the doctor stepped back and studied her. "Have you been having any other symptoms? I mean, other than the ones that brought you in here?"

"Well, my hips and legs hurt a lot, and I get this tingling in my arms sometimes," she admitted. "But I just figured that's because I'm out of shape and getting older."

"Would you call it joint pain?"

"Yeah, maybe," she shrugged. "Sometimes it's my joints that hurt; other times it feels like the bone–like my shin. But then things will hurt and no matter how Matt rubs it we can't really find the source."

"I'm not one-hundred percent positive," the doctor began slowly, "but you exhibit signs of something called Ehlers-Danlos Syndrome. Has anyone ever brought that up to you?"

"Um, no, not that I can remember. What is it?"

"It's a connective tissue disorder," he explained, "that has to do with the way your body creates collagen. It can cause a lot of the issues you're having, including the pain and tingling. You have characteristics of the hypermobility type, , what with you being extremely flexible, having soft skin, and a high palate."

"Yeah, my skin has always been pretty soft," Taryn agree proudly. "So this syndrome, is it serious?"

"Yes and no," he replied. "Some patients experience early onset osteoarthritis and rheumatoid arthritis. Others, like you, have seemingly unexplainable pain. It can also cause brain fog, digestive issues, vision trouble, hearing loss..."

He continued talking but Taryn tuned him out. Brain fog? As in, there might be something weird going on inside her brain to cause it to malfunction?

"With your flexibility, I would venture to say that you have the hypermobility type," he finished. "That's the most common.

However, with the aneurism I am slightly worried about the vascular form."

"What's wrong with it?" Taryn asked, trying not to completely freak out.

"That can cause a whole host of problems, including ruptures of major blood vessels and organs. You'll need to see a geneticist to completely rule that out, although even with the hypermobility type you can still have crossover symptoms of vascular. In the meantime, I can write you a prescription to help you with the pain. That can greatly improve your quality of life. And when you get home you should check in with your primary care doctor to get that referral to the geneticist. It wouldn't hurt to get a good cardiologist on your team, too."

Once he was gone, Taryn turned to Matt, feeling defeated. "Well," she sighed. "That sucked."

"Are you okay?" There was concern written all over his face.

"Did you hear him say 'brain fog'?"

Matt nodded.

"Matt?" Taryn bit her lip and started up at the mindless television show she'd muted. "What if the things I see, the stuff I pick up on..."

"Yeah?"

"What if it's not really there? What if it's just my brain short-circuiting and I'm not really seeing anything at all?"

Matt was quiet. Not even he had an answer for that.

Taryn couldn't bring herself to open her laptop and check any of her emails or even check her social media pages, something she was usually obsessive about. She could feel the tinglings of depression, despite the fact that everyone swore the narcotics she was now taking offered a euphoric high like nothing else. So far, all they'd done was make her sick to her stomach, although her pain level was better than it had been in years.

"You okay?" Matt asked for the fifth time in an hour.

"Yeah, fine." She was pretending to read a book, but the truth was she'd read the same page at least a dozen times and still had no idea what it said.

"You need to make that appointment with your doctor in Nashville," he lectured her. Matt, ever organized and on the ball.

"Yeah."

Little by little it was all making sense – the headaches she'd had off and on for years, the body pain she'd chalked up to poor posture and laziness, even the pain she had after eating. She never realized they were all connected. After a long search on the Internet, though, she'd walked away with more information than she'd wanted. It seemed there was no "cure" or even a standard treatment procedure. The few online support groups she'd found listed the number one complaint as being finding a doctor who actually understood it – it was that rare.

"Taryn, I don't think your medical condition is what's causing your sightings, or what you're hearing," Matt said gently. "I don't. If it were, then how would I be able to see things in your pictures?"

What he said made logical sense to her, but she was still uncertain. The noises she heard at night? What if those were simply her ears playing tricks on her? Some EDS patients, she'd read, had hearing problems, including tinnitus. And when she saw things? Maybe it was vision issues or even a mini seizure? So many of her issues, like fatigue, she'd blamed on working too hard, on her grief. And that was even okay because it meant one day it would get better – when her grief improved, when she learned to handle her workload better, she wouldn't sleep as much. It was a temporary problem. But now that it was tied to an actual medical condition, it was possible she might be like that for the rest of her life – never having the energy or stamina to do the things she truly wanted to do. And then, of course, there was the fact that she could *die*.

Taryn was depressed.

"You want to go out somewhere? Go to the movies?"

"You think I feel like going out?" Taryn shouted. "I feel like I can't even get up from this damn chair without passing out."

She immediately burst into tears.

Matt, who'd likely been expecting that anyway, sprinted over to her and picked her up like she was a baby. "Oh, sweetie, it's okay. We'll figure this out. I've been researching, too, and if we have to fly to Baltimore or Chicago we'll find you the best doctor out there. We're going to get through this together."

But they couldn't, not really. He could lend her moral support but she was completely on her own in the way she felt.

Hours later, while she was dozing on the couch and staring at the television, the phone rang. It was Thelma.

"How ya' doin, honey?" she cooed into the phone, concern in her voice.

"Hanging in there, you know?" Taryn replied, not feeling too bad now. The pain meds seemed to be doing their job at least.

"Listen, I know you don't feel up to it, but there's someone I'd like you to meet, to talk to," Thelma said hesitantly. "She was a friend of Cheyenne's. I, I didn't mention her before because, well, I don't exactly *like her*," Thelma said these last two words in a whisper, like God himself might overhear her.

"Yeah? Why not?" Taryn's curiosity was piqued now and despite the fact she didn't feel like getting off the couch to do anything but pee, she briefly forgot about her earlier meltdown.

"She's a little loose, a little rough," Thelma explained. "Her mother works at a questionable establishment, a place no honorable person would step foot in."

"Oh, she's a stripper?" Taryn asked.

"Yes," Thelma explained. "Hooters."

Taryn smiled wryly.

"Why do you want me to talk to her now?"

"Well..." Thelma hemmed and hawed, "I don't think anyone has. And given my history with her family, I don't think I should. But she might know something."

"Give me her name and I'll check her out," Taryn relented. "But I can't promise much."

"I know, I know. But it may give us more than we had."

Amber Lockley lived in a single-wide trailer that had seen better days. The plastic trim around the bottom was made to look like stones and appeared fairly new, but the siding was flapping in places and the steps to the front door were nothing but a few concrete blocks. The yard was littered with over-full trash cans and plastic children's toys that had been outside for so long the sun had bleached them.

Taryn, with a renewed sense of enthusiasm, had found the girl on a social media site. Instead of blowing Taryn off, like she'd imagined, Amber had been more than willing to meet with her. Matt, of course, drove her. She was still woozy and on medication. She didn't trust herself to drive. She barely trusted herself to walk down the hallway straight.

"Just look at it this way," Matt teased her. "You'll fit in with the majority of the population. Isn't the news always talking about the drug problem of the rural south?"

Taryn shot him a dirty look.

So far, she still didn't feel the euphoria of the medication, although once it kicked in she did sometimes find herself unreasonably chatty.

Matt waited in the car while Taryn precariously balanced herself on one of the concrete blocks and knocked on the flimsy door. It was opened by a heavyset girl with frizzy blonde hair and acne. Behind her, Taryn could hear the blare of the television and the rattling of pots and pans. "Hi, I'm Taryn," she introduced herself.

"Hey," she sniffed, sizing Taryn up. Her face was guarded and she nervously tapped her manicured nails against the door frame.

"You wanna come in or something?"

"Yeah, that'd be nice. It's a little cold out here."

Amber peered at Matt in the car, but when she saw that he was reading she shrugged, her interest in him apparently fading.

Amber's trailer was an oven. The small space was heated to high heaven, warm enough to walk around in short sleeves and shorts. The little living room was cramped and stuffy, filled with over-stuffed furniture that was too big for the space. Despite the trailer's outside appearance, there was a fifty-inch television on a cheap console and the newest game console plugged into it. When Amber sat down on the couch she immediately pulled out her iPhone and began texting frantically.

Taryn wasn't sure what she was supposed to do – interrupt her and start talking or wait until she was finished?

Amber broke the silence by muting the television and putting down her phone.

"So you want to talk about Cheyenne?"

A crash from the kitchen had Taryn startled. A tall thin woman with bleached-blonde hair and a deep tan was rooting around in a cabinet. She was attractive in a hard kind of way and looked way too young to be Amber's mother.

"That's my mom," Amber explained anyway. "She's trying to cook before she goes to work, but cooking always makes her nervous. She wouldn't be doing it but she's on this new diet and trying to be healthier."

Amber's mother ignored them and went on with her business, a cigarette perched precariously against her bottom lip.

"Were you friends with Cheyenne?" Taryn asked. "Close friends?"

"Yeah, we hung out. Some of Cheyenne's friends were real bitches, you know? Thought their shit didn't stink," Amber spat.

Taryn wondered if she was talking about Emma and Lindy.

"Cheyenne, though, she was okay," Amber shrugged. "I'd known her since she was a kid, you know? And we were friends then. Then she got to middle school, started running with a different crowd. Got to high school and was a cheerleader and all that shit. I dropped out after freshman year."

"How did you get back up with her?"

"We went to the same party about three years ago. She got mad at somebody, I can't remember who now, and was off sulking in a corner. It just wasn't my scene, you know? But my ride wasn't able to leave and I was too fucked up to drive. I knew that, thank God. Anyway, we ended up talking. She was cool." Amber showed little emotion in her face when she talked, but her voice was animated.

"And after that?"

"Sometimes she would leave home for a few days. She'd come stay with me. I don't think her mom ever knew who she was with. She'd text her, telling her she was fine, but that was it. She'd

261

come stay here, hang out. Mama didn't care and I kinda liked having her around," Amber explained.

"What did you guys do when she was here?"

"Mostly just hung out here at the house. She'd usually get a ride with someone to drop her off. I didn't drive. I was on some heavy shit at the time and out of it a lot. But with her here, it wasn't too bad, you know? I didn't feel like using as much. We'd goof off, staying up all night, watching TV, baking brownies and shit. She'd leave, I'd get messed up again. It was dumb."

"What were you using, if you don't mind my asking?" Taryn had never talked to anyone who was so frank about her drug use, and she wasn't quite sure how to approach it.

"A lot of shit," Amber laughed loudly, showing off several decayed teeth. "Started with prescription pills. You know, Lortabs and stuff. Then the doctors cracked down on that. Tried mary jane for a while but folks can smell it on you. I got arrested for possession. Didn't do it again. Then I tried heroin. Scared out of my mind at first, but the high was so smooth and so pure. Coming down could be a bitch, but it was worth it."

"But isn't heroin really expensive?" Not to mention incredibly dangerous, Taryn added to herself. She could never imagine doing it.

"This ain't the eighties anymore," Amber snorted. "It's been discounted."

"What about Cheyenne? Did she do anything?"

"Oh, hell no," Amber exclaimed emphatically. "Cheyenne didn't touch nothing, except for the occasional smoke. She was clean as a whistle. Didn't believe in that stuff. Tried to talk me out of it. And did, in a way, when she disappeared. I checked myself into the hospital detox program, let them bring me down. Haven't had a damn thing since."

"Well, that's great," Taryn said with real feeling.

"Yeah, well, not so great. Now I'm depressed as hell. Can't find a job, never see anybody no more, don't have a car," Amber sniffed. "Thinking about getting my GED. At least that would be something."

"Do you have any idea what might have happened to Cheyenne that last night?" Taryn pressed. She was afraid if she didn't change the subject they might not get back round to it.

"No, not really. I was there, though. I was there all night. Drunk and high off my ass, but I remember it well enough. Cheyenne was dancing around the fire, standing on a stool or chair or something. Had a drink in her hand. I can remember that because I kept thinking how pretty she was, how she didn't fit in with everyone else around her," Amber sighed nostalgically.

"Anything else?"

"Yeah. She had this thing for this guy named Evan. He was there. They talked, hung out a little. Maybe he gave her something to drink. She wasn't drunk, but you could tell she'd had something. She was real friendly-like, you know? Happy. They didn't go off anywhere together, far as I can remember. Just sat around the fire, drinking and talking. He plays guitar and sang a little bit. You know that song by Eric Paslay? 'She Don't Love You?'"

Taryn nodded, although she didn't.

"He played that. Was real good, too. I remember it."

"Do you remember when she left?"

"Naw," Amber sighed. "Wish I did. I left before her. She was still there, talking to Evan. Maybe her other friends, too."

"What about Travis Marcum?"

Amber's face hardened a little and she pursed her lips. "I don't know about that. It seems weird, you know? I mean, he was there. You couldn't miss him with his loud mouth. Kept shouting weird shit and acting all tough."

"Was it weird that, with him being older, he was there with you teenagers?"

"No, not really. We grew up with him, too. In case you haven't noticed, there's not much to do around here," Amber laughed.

"Do you think she left with him?"

Amber studied Taryn for a moment before answering. "I can't really say. I do know this, though. Before that night I'd never seen her talking to him or heard her even mention him. I don't think Travis was ever on Cheyenne's radar."

Chapter 24

*C*here was a heaviness on Taryn's chest, an unyielding

pressure that made her gasp. Struggling to sit up, she found herself unable to move. The room around her was mostly dark, peppered by small rays of lights. *Fairy lights*, she giggled to herself, momentarily forgetting about the pressure. *The fairies have finally come to see me.*

There were voices, too, but they were far away. She suddenly felt the need to vomit and turned her head, sour sickness spewing from her mouth and onto the surface beneath her. The pressure released, just a tiny bit, but was replaced by a horrible dizziness that made her body spin around and around in circles.

Then, she was being lifted up into the air. She could feel her soul separate from her physical body, a string from the center of her stomach pulling her upwards towards the ceiling and then out into the night air. *I can astral project*, she thought gleefully to herself as she flew through the trees, reaching out to touch the leaves. *It really is true, and I've mastered it!*

But then she was abruptly lowered back to her body, the harshness and impact of the act soul-crushing. There was no lightness now, only pain that wanted to consume her. The fairies were gone but there were shadows near her, even *on* her.

Trying to scream, she opened her mouth but nothing would come out. A moment of panic had her wanting to claw right out of her skin, to escape the hell coursing through her veins. Then, closing her eyes, she was able to let herself go. Now, again, she was lifting herself out of her body, shooting for the sky. She wouldn't let herself come back this time.

"It was a dream, but it wasn't," Taryn explained to Matt.

He studied her over his tea, worry etched on his face. There was a lot of worry from him these days. "It could be medication-related," he said slowly. "Between that beta blocker they put you on and the pain medication your brain chemistry could be doing some weird things."

"Yeah, maybe," Taryn conceded, "but I *felt* it. I think it was Cheyenne."

"So what do you think it means? That you were reliving something that happened to her?" Matt asked.

But before Taryn could answer, the bedroom door slammed violently, shaking the walls.

"I would take that as a yes," she smirked.

Matt's eyes were wide, but he didn't reply.

"Maybe it's the way she died," she mused. "Something really awful happened to her. She was drugged or had a health problem that made her sick. Or someone attacked her."

"Or maybe she took something, drank too much," Matt put in gently. "She may not be completely innocent here. It could've been an accident."

"No, no, I don't think so. Everyone I talked to said she wasn't into that. And that she wasn't drunk that night. Amber said she never touched dope," Taryn argued.

"Yeah, but you're taking the word of a girl who appeared to be enamored of Cheyenne, or at least what she represented. How do you know her memory isn't tainted a little?" he suggested.

"I don't," she shook her head. "I don't. What I *do* know is that we're going to this party tonight, and I am going to get some answers if I have to grill everyone there."

"Are you sure you feel up to it?" he asked.

Actually, she did. Pain-wise, she felt better than she had in years. She'd taken a walk around the property and even though she'd returned a little tired, there was no throbbing in her hips and legs. She only needed a catnap, too, instead of wasting away the whole afternoon on sleep.

"I feel fine. I'm not going to take anymore medicine today, though, because I'd like to have a drink tonight," she smiled.

The worry was back on Matt's face but he remained quiet, staring at his tea.

The night was mild, a welcome relief from the frigid cold days they'd had scattered around them. Taryn dressed in her snug Catwoman costume, chosen because it covered everything and would provide some warmth. She applied heavy makeup, enjoying the chance to do something different. Her long hair hung freely down on her back so that the mask would fit securely.

Matt came in and whistled. Snatching her from around the waist, he nuzzled her neck, his hand sliding down the leather. "What do you say we just stay in tonight and you keep wearing that?"

Taryn laughed. "I feel a little bloated. I'm not as svelte as I used to be."

"You look great."

And so did he, she reflected. His superhero costume reminded her a little bit of Thor, Matt's longish black hair swept from his face revealing his dark eyes and strong facial features. When had he gotten so handsome? His mixed heritage of Mexican/Native American/Italian gave him the best of all the features and somehow he'd grown from an awkward, skinny kid into a gorgeous well-built man. Maybe they really *should* stay in!

"No, I have to go to this. It's important."

"Yeah, well, how about you just keep that on afterwards? That would be okay, too," he smiled.

They could hear the music before they were halfway through the woods. It was pumping something that sounded like the Allman Brothers or Charlie Daniels. It was hard to make out the lyrics, but it was loud.

Taryn knew Matt was nervous. He didn't really "do" parties or big groups of people and was only coming to support her. She held onto his hand and gave it a little squeeze as they walked along the narrow path, her flashlight leading the way.

The music grew louder as they entered the field and had changed to Alabama, "Dixieland Delight." This crowd apparently enjoyed the classics. There were at least twenty-five people there already, ranging from high kids to those in their early twenties. Taryn and Matt would be, by far, the oldest there. That made her feel awkward, but she tried to ignore it.

Emma was the first to spot them and came squealing over, throwing her arms around Taryn's waist. "I'm so glad you're okay!" she shrieked. "We were all worried."

Emma was dressed like the devil with a small red, flouncy skirt that barely covered her behind, a red bikini top, horns, and fishnet stockings. Matt stared and Taryn poked him teasingly in the ribs.

"Here, we came bearing gifts," she explained, pointing to the bundle in Matt's arm.

Emma took the bag and led them to a table full of finger foods. The bottom end was nothing but booze. As she busied herself taking out the food and wine Matt brought, she chattered on about the people who were coming, her last exam, and the fight she'd had with Lindy. "She's real moody," she explained. "I don't know what she has up her ass this time."

Taryn noticed there were pale lights in the farmhouse and a few people trickled in and out of it, red plastic cups in their hands. "There's no electricity in there, right?"

"No, just candles and kerosene lamps they take in," Emma laughed. "It's a wonder the whole place hasn't burned to the ground yet."

Taryn thought the same thing.

Once she and Matt had loaded up on food, Emma led them over to the fire where fold-up chairs had been gathered around in a circle surrounding it. The three of them sat down, safely away from the flames but close enough to feel the heat.

"By the way, Emma, I don't think you've met Matt," Taryn said. "Sorry about that."

"I haven't, no, but I've heard a lot about him. I'm Emma," she smiled. "And she didn't tell me how gorgeous you are."

Matt's blush was apparent even in the glow of the flames, and he fumbled with his plate. Still, he managed to flirt back. "And she didn't tell me how beautiful you are."

Something rancid and hot formed in Taryn's stomach and then raced to her head. Jealousy? That was just Matt's personality, she reasoned. But she couldn't say she liked it.

People continued to arrive, most in costumes and some in jeans, heavy boots, and jackets. They arrived in pairs, or in groups, the girls either giggling or acting nonchalant, as though they'd been there and seen it all before. Once they got to the fireside, they clumped off in even smaller groups, sometimes pairing up with a guy or squeezing together and whispering, pointing, checking out others without trying to be obvious. Some of the guys stood to the side, drinking, gazing at the fire and the girls. They pretended to be talking to their friends about sports, school, and cars while all the time contemplating their next move on the girl of their choice.

Taryn felt like she was back in high school.

A few people looked at her and Matt questionably, but being with Emma seemed to give them some credibility and in their costumes they looked as young as anyone else. She figured most of them probably knew who she was anyway.

"Is Evan here?" Taryn asked, looking around.

"Well, that's him walking across the field right now," Emma shouted over the music.

Taryn turned around and saw a tall, thin young man sauntering through the grass. He had a guitar slung over his shoulder and a brunette by his side. She was wearing a Little Red Riding Hood costume that dipped low in the front and revealed a long slither of leg on one side. He was classically good looking and built like a basketball player. As he drew nearer, others approached him and shook his hand, clasped him on the back in one-armed hugs. Girls waved.

"People like Evan," Emma explained. "Hey!" she shouted. "Come here!"

Motioning him over, Evan came nearer, the girl at his side shyly hanging back a few feet. "Evan, this is Taryn. She's my teacher," Emma introduced them. "And she's been looking into Cheyenne's disappearance."

"That part of your job, too?" he smiled.

"No, just a hobby," Taryn replied lightly. "You going to play?"

"Maybe," he shrugged.

"We just found out that Evan's moving up to Nashville next week," Emma said. "He's going to become a big country star and forget all of us. Oh, hey, Evan. Taryn lives in Nashville."

Now his face relaxed into something friendlier and he smiled. "Yeah? Maybe we could talk later."

"Sure, that would be great," Taryn said honestly, glad to have a ticket in.

The two wandered off in the direction of the food table and Taryn turned back to Emma. "Who's the chick?"

"No idea," Emma shrugged. "Lindy's going to freak, though. She had it in her head that tonight was the night she was going to make her move on him."

"Where is Lindy?" Taryn peered around, trying to focus in on the shadowy people.

"In the farmhouse. Not getting busy or anything, just talking."

Emma eventually left Taryn and Matt alone, going off to play hostess and making sure nobody was getting into trouble. "You okay?" she asked Matt.

"Yeah, I'm okay. It's not so bad, sitting here by the fire and eating. I don't mind the music. But how long do we have to stay?"

"Not long," she promised. "I just want to talk to Evan, maybe get a better feel for things. And then we'll go."

Several people approached them, introducing themselves. Apparently Emma had spread the word about Taryn and her "gift" and lots of kids wanted to ask her about ghosts or share their own ghost stories. She heard about dead grandmothers coming back for one last visit, demon screams from attics, red eyes peering into bathroom windows, and possessions. Taryn listened to all the tales politely, making the right interested noises.

Finally, when the last one left, she excused herself from Matt. Evan was sitting down on the other side of the fire, fishing his guitar out of the case, and there was an empty seat on the other side of him. "I'll be right back," she pledged.

He was tuning it when she sat down. "Hey, I know this is going to sound like it's coming out of the blue but can I ask you a few questions about Cheyenne?"

Evan turned to face her, bright blue eyes set against a pale face. He smiled, revealing perfectly white, straightened teeth.

"Yeah, sure, it's cool. If you don't mind me picking your brain about Nashville."

"I can tell you what I know," she promised.

"Same here."

"That last night, the party, do you remember it?"

Evan nodded, serious. "I remember. It was kind of a wild one, you know? Just kept getting louder and louder. I couldn't take it. Spent a lot of time sitting right here with Cheyenne, just talking."

"Were you drinking? Doing anything else?" she pressed lightly.

"A little beer, but that's all. I was driving," he explained, "and I had a curfew. Cheyenne had a drink or two. She was relaxed, you know, but not wasted."

"Were you guys dating or..." she let her voice trail off, hoping he'd take it up.

"No, not really. I mean I liked Cheyenne. She was cool, definitely hot, you know? But I'd just gotten out of a relationship. I'd had a crush on her since eighth grade, but she always seemed to be dating someone else. To tell you the truth, I'd hoped that night would be the night we hooked up."

"And did you?"

"Kind of. We made out a little," he admitted. "And then I offered to drive her home."

Taryn straightened up, her ears tuned in. "And what did she say?"

"She said yeah, she'd ride with me but that she had to go tell her friends. She walked away, and I played a little bit. I saw her a little while later, drinking again, and I tried to wave her over. She waved back, like she was coming. But when I turned back around later, she was gone. I had to be home by midnight and couldn't wait for her, so I left."

Taryn narrowed her eyes. "And you never saw her again?"

"Nope," he replied softly, staring at the ground. "Never again. I thought maybe she'd changed her mind, that she'd found someone else. My pride was hurt, you know? So I didn't look for her. I regret that now."

He changed the subject then and began asking her about Nashville, about the clubs he could try to get into. They talked for another fifteen minutes and then she excused herself, going back to Matt.

"Learn anything?" he asked.

"Maybe. Evan claims he offered to give her a ride but that she disappeared. He apparently had a curfew and couldn't wait for her."

"And you don't believe him?"

She shook her head. "He seems okay, pretty straight. But still...Something's not adding up, that's for sure."

"Any vibes about the place yet? Anything coming to you?"

"No," Taryn confessed. "But it's about time to whip out Miss Dixie."

The drink in her hand was fresh, the second Taryn had had so far.

The Coke and whiskey was settling nicely in her stomach, giving her a warm, fuzzy feeling. She hadn't drank anything but wine in so long that the whiskey was working faster than it used to. She was already feeling a little lightheaded, but it was nice.

The warmth of the fire made her feel cozy, fluid. A group of young people had pulled their chairs in closer to her and Matt and even he was engaged in a conversation with a college-aged guy, an engineer major. They were deep in conversation, their heads bent together, while Taryn occasionally added to the discussion beside her – something about the latest reality dating show. The drinks were making her looser, happier. It was the buzz she'd thought she'd get from the pain meds but didn't. The feeling of being part of a group, even a group she didn't belong in, was almost as seductive as the alcohol.

Brantley Gilbert began playing on the speakers, "Bottoms Up" filling the air with its pulsating, steady rhythm. Several of the girls beside Taryn stood up and began dancing, moving their bodies back and forth and dipping low to the ground. One reached down and pulled Taryn up with them and suddenly she was with a flock of girls, dancing around the fire without a care in the world. Matt stopped talking and watched her, as did several of the other guys around the fire. She might have been thirty, but she could still move. After all, she was the MTV generation. Forgetting that anyone was watching, she let the alcohol give her false courage and danced, the heat of the fire urging her on, the music filling her and making her forget how much she despised most of the music on country radio. In this setting, it made sense. Then, breaking free of the other girls she turned to Matt and swayed in front of him before finally dropping into his lap, his arms immediately going around her and holding her steady. She laughed then and kissed him squarely on the mouth, expecting him to pull away in embarrassment. He seemed to forget his avoidance of PDA and kissed her back, hard. They stayed entangled in one another until the song ended and the air grew quiet, peppered only by bits of conversation.

Taryn pulled back and started to get up, but Matt held onto her. Evan had picked up his guitar and began strumming, humming along with it. The Hank Williams Sr. song he went into was unexpected but his baritone voice filled the night with "Cold, Cold Heart" and everyone listened. He truly was good at what he did; maybe he *would* make it in Nashville.

Taryn closed her eyes, feeling dizzy, and was glad for the comfort of Matt's arms and lap.

Then Amber was beside her, talking. "I guess they were afraid the house would burn down," she remarked.

Remembering Emma's earlier comment about the candles and kerosene lamps in the farmhouse, Taryn nodded without opening her eyes. "All it takes is for someone to knock one of those things over. Those floors are old and dry."

"Huh??" Amber's voice had Taryn peering at her.

"The farmhouse, right?"

"No," Amber laughed. "The fire. It's usually over there, where that wood pile is. But I guess they thought it was too close to the house."

Taryn straightened, slid out of Matt's lap, and stood up. A thought was slowly forming in her mind, but it was jumbled, confused by the liquor. She struggled to unwind it. "Amber, where was the fire the night Cheyenne disappeared?"

"Over there, where the wood is," she stated again, looking agitated.

Her photo of the front of the house, Taryn thought. She could see the flames reflected off the front door. That's what had been off with the picture. Where the fire was now, it would've been impossible. So the fire was moved but...

Slowly, Taryn reached down and picked up Miss Dixie. Evan had moved on to Dierks Bentley's "Tip it On Back" and several guys sang along with him, their voices rising. Taryn gazed into the viewfinder, ready to click, but found she didn't need to. The fire was now where it was meant to be, in front of the house. The flames burned brightly, the people gathered around some of the same ones who were there now, but in different clothes and in different places. Slowly, slowly, realization dawning on her, Taryn turned the camera to the fire glowing in front of her. Although she could still feel the heat, through the viewfinder it was gone. In its place was a regular patch of earth, unmarked by flames. The dirt was upturned, though, recently disturbed. And then, as she watched in horror, a long slender arm protruded from it, clawing at the earth and reaching for the sky.

Lowering Miss Dixie, Taryn gazed into the flames, sickness forming in her stomach. She stepped back once, twice, her mouth opened wide. People had stopped talking and were looking at her, although Evan continued to play on, possibly even louder than before.

The air around her became a cyclone then, she a lone vessel in the middle. It spun around and around, faster and faster, while she held on to her balance, her arms outstretched and touching the wind. She felt a surge of energy, of power, and although it frightened her, it also empowered her and she threw her head back, opening her mouth and tried to swallow as much of it as she could.

And then, she could see.

Cheyenne, taking one last drink before leaving with Evan, her crush.

Cheyenne, being led willingly into the farmhouse, urged by a promise.

Cheyenne, on the dirty mattress, unable to move, the candle flames glowing around her. *The fairies have finally come to see me.*

Cheyenne, being ravaged by not one, but two people, her eyes glazed and vacant while someone else stood off to the side, a crimson smile on their face.

Cheyenne, being tossed into a hole, dirt tossed on her like garbage, a spurt of breath still escaping her body.

She'd never left the farm.

The wind stopped, Taryn lowered her arms and shook her head. Lindy stood before her, her brown skin darkened even more by the angel costume that clung to her small hips and tight stomach. Her hair fell around her shoulders, the firelight dancing off it. There was a glazed look in her eyes, like she'd just woken up from a sweet dream. The polished steel of the handgun was pointed straight at Taryn.

Chapter 25

"You set her up," Taryn accused, her voice steady. The people around her began to scatter, some screaming, some tripping over themselves. She could see somebody dialing on their cell phone out of the corner of her eye, the small square of light bright in the darkness.

"Cheyenne was a *whore*," Lindy spat, her voice shaky. She'd been drinking. If Taryn hadn't been able to smell it rolling off her in waves, she'd have been able to hear it in her voice. Her red lipstick was smeared a little across her cheek, like she'd wiped her mouth with the back of her hand and forgotten. And yet, somehow, she'd never looked more attractive.

"How so?" Taryn asked conversationally, trying to keep her voice light, all the while thinking, *how in* hell *does this keep happening to me?*

"She wanted everything that was mine. I made cheerleader, she made captain. I was nominated for homecoming court, she made queen."

The definition of "whore" has really changed since I was a teenager, Taryn thought to herself. But, aloud, she tried to reason. "Being jealous was no reason to kill her," she pointed out, not taking her eyes off the gun. She didn't think Lindy would actually shoot her with half the town as a witness, but you could never really tell about people and it didn't make her want to stop shaking any more.

"Jealous!? You think I was *jealous*," Lindy snorted, the gun waving back and forth as she laughed. "Get real. I was *better* than her. That night was supposed to be *my* chance with Evan. But there she went, straight after him. She knew how I felt, she *knew* I liked him."

"No, she didn't, Lindy," Amber called, her voice high and brittle.

"Shut *up*, Amber," Lindy yelled, firing the gun into the sky. The sound was almost swallowed by the openness of the field, but was still loud enough for Taryn to feel it in her feet, causing her to jump a little. "You're as skanky as she was. Shouldn't you have

282

AIDS or something by now?" Lindy giggled then, amused by her own perceived wit. The quietness that now hung in the air was broken only by the hiss and crackle of the fire.

"So what did you do, Lindy? Did you kill her? Where is Cheyenne now?" Keep her talking, keep her talking, Taryn chanted. Someone had called the police, she was sure of it. Others were stealthily taking pictures and videos with their phones. But that didn't mean Lindy wouldn't take someone down with her – that someone most likely being Taryn.

"Gawd! What kind of person do you think I am, bitch?" Lindy snarled at this, revealing lipstick stains on her teeth. "You think this is some kind of Lifetime movie? I didn't kill her. When she came to tell us she was leaving, we helped her out a little bit. Gave her some extra courage. You know, like friends."

"What did you give her?" Taryn asked reasonably.

"Does it matter?" she waved the gun around in the air again. For a second Taryn thought she was going to drop it and visibly cringed, expecting it to land and go off, but then Lindy appeared to regain control. "Really? She was too good for the rest of us. Bitch needed to be brought down off her high horse. Right? Right!?"

At first Taryn thought she was speaking to the general crowd, a group that continued to watch her, a one-woman freak show, but then Brad and Mike appeared behind her, Emma at their side. The guys' expressions were hard to read in the shadows, but Emma's look of horror shone through clear as day. "Put down the damn gun, Lindy. What the hell do you think you're doing?" Her voice cracked, full of bewilderment. Maybe she thought Lindy was playing, the gun a prop, but when the little blonde turned and faced her, the gun now pointed at her head, Emma shrank back.

"Oh, shut up," Lindy hissed. "You always took her side." She sounded hurt, wounded. For a second her shoulders slumped and, despite the weapon in her hand, looked less menacing then before.

"What did you *do*?" Emma wailed, grief outweighing the fear. "She was our friend! And now you're going to kill Taryn, too? Or blow somebody else's damn head off?"

"You didn't know?" Taryn asked Emma, genuinely curious.

"No, I–I was outside the whole time. I never went into that house. I never trusted the things that went on in there. Lindy told me Cheyenne left, left with Travis," Emma sputtered.

"Yeah, well," Lindy shrugged. "He's a dumb fuck and has a temper. He'd tried to grope me earlier in the night. Other people saw it," she whined with a sniff. "And he cut me off. I had to crawl through his truck window just to score what I had that evening. And then wasted perfectly good shit on Cheyenne."

Evan stood up, drew closer to Emma, but Matt urged him back with a single motion of his hand. Matt was standing now, just a few feet to Lindy's side. She hadn't noticed him, a lanky shadow that moved as softly as a whisper. Taryn could feel his eyes on her, never letting her go from his sight. Fear for Matt now crept into her heart, anxious Lindy would turn on him and fire, if for no reason than her space was being intruded on. It was all Taryn could do not to hurl herself forward, tackling Lindy to the ground and ripping her hair out for what she was afraid she might do if she caught Matt too close. Her thin ray of hope held onto the fact

284

that, since Lindy had never met Matt, she might not know who he was – and who he was to Taryn.

"Lindy," Taryn began with desperation, "let's just go someplace and talk. Just the two of us. Tell me what happened. I want to hear your side. There's no reason to bring these other people into it. We're friends, right?"

Tears streaming down her face, leaving deep rivets in her thick foundation, Lindy vehemently shook her head. "No! You don't know what it's like, to grow up with someone your whole life, to be unable to get away from them. Everywhere you go, everyone you know... there's never any escape. It's a trap! This whole place is a trap," she wailed wildly, the gun waving once more.

Emma sobbed a little, a sound that died in her throat. "What did you *do* to her Lindy?" she demanded again.

"*Me*? I just gave her a drink," Lindy retorted sweetly, the desperation still clinging to the edge of her voice. "Ask Brad and Eric what *they* did," she added harshly without looking back at them.

Taryn could feel the tightness in her chest, the pain, see the shadows around her once again. They'd raped her, both of them, while she was mostly unconscious. And then they'd thrown her in that hole, maybe while she was still alive.

"It wasn't anything she didn't want to do," Eric mumbled defensively, but they began slowly backing away from Lindy, panicked looks on their faces.

"Dumbass there," Lindy momentarily took her eyes off Taryn and looked back at Eric, "buried her right there in the yard. Of course you could see the spot. Anyone could have. Any idiot who's watched a crime show knows the first thing they look for is disturbed ground."

"Jesus, Lindy," Brad whispered, his voice coarse. "Shut the fuck up."

"So you covered up the original fire spot with the wood pile and built another one on top of the grave, burned it awhile," Taryn offered, some pieces falling resoundingly into place. "And nobody figured that out?"

"Why would they?" Lindy reasoned. "The police came out and looked and saw the fire pit. It was used. Cheyenne left the party. There were *wit*nesses."

Yeah, some witnesses, Taryn thought. *The ones who killed her!*

"We didn't know she'd overdose," Eric shook his head with vigor. The crowd of people, who had been backing away, now appeared to collectively regain courage, seemingly forgetting the fact that Lindy still had the gun. The monstrosity of Lindy & Company's actions was dawning on them, each person wearing a sickened and horrified expression. They'd literally been walking around Cheyenne's grave all night, dancing, laughing, and singing atop her brittle bones.

"She got sick, she started shaking. I gave her mouth to mouth. It sucked ass," Brad whimpered piteously, "but I *tried*."

Eric nodded his head feverishly, begging those around them to understand. It was too late, of course. "You're leaving out the rest, Lindy," he cried. "Tell her what *you* did!"

Lindy rolled her eyes but the gun dropped a fraction of an inch and she wavered. With the flick of a finger, Taryn turned Miss

Dixie on and then aimed it at the woodpile. The flash of light that filled the sky had Lindy blinking, but didn't distract her enough to drop the gun. The image that appeared on the screen, though, was enough for Taryn to truly see the extent of the young woman's craziness. A crumpled body lay near the fire, a slender arm shielding a face covered by long, black hair. Lindy stood above the figure, her leg raised in the air, ready to come down in a stomp. Just another inch and the body would be in the fire.

"You threw her in the fire, didn't you?" Taryn asked in wonder. "They brought her out here to bury her and you just rolled her into the flames?"

"Oh, please. She was probably already dead by then," Lindy scoffed, but she looked scared.

"Maybe not," Eric admitted. "We don't know. We pulled her body out and it was still moving a little. You shouldn't have done that, Lindy. She might not have been dead."

"It's *your* fault," Lindy shouted now at Taryn, the gun steadier than it had been. "If *you* hadn't talked to Amber, to Evan, to Thelma. Why did you have to come here? Why were you taking Emma from me? Why do you have to take *every*thing! Why couldn't you just have stayed away!"

Lindy let out a terrible wail then, or did it come from someplace else, someplace deep inside the flames that suddenly shot up into the sky? The sound was at once familiar, what'd she'd heard on the cabin's porch, and inhuman. Before either she or Lindy could react, the flash of movement took Taryn off guard and she was suddenly pushed away, to the side, where she hit the ground and landed on her back, her Catwoman costume ripping on a root.

Now Matt stood in front of Lindy, just inches away, his own gun raised in front of him. Whereas Lindy's hand was still wavering, however, his was rock-steady. "Put it down," he commanded softly, a mixture of steel and honey in his voice. "Put the gun down, or I'll shoot."

She opened her mouth, an ugly red slash, to protest but before she could speak he cut her off. "Do it," he barked, a tone Taryn had never heard him use.

Lindy cackled, her bright red lips black in the firelight. "If you shoot me you'll go to jail." Her voice was weak, though, uncertain. Taryn knew, then, that she was crumbling and fast. She'd lost and for an instant looked like the little girl she must've once been.

"No, I won't. Put it down now." Matt fired then, but at the ground near her feet. The noise caused her to panic, to jump. The gun fell from her hand and in one movement Matt caught it, put on the safety, kicked it out of the way, and grabbed onto her in a tight vise. She barely struggled against him as he placed his own gun in the waist band of his pants, her frame lost against his. She collapsed against him then, and clung to his chest. Matt being Matt, though he gripped her with all his strength, he gently stroked her hair in a tender gesture that caused her to sob.

Taryn picked up the gun and held it gingerly out in front of her. As the sounds of sirens began to fill the air, both Eric and Brad began to make a run for it. Evan was too quick for Eric, however, and threw to him to ground, just as someone else made a beeline for Brad. Neither put up much of a struggle.

Emma, pale and shaking, fell to the ground in a ragdoll heap.

Epilogue

"You still want to finish out the semester?" Matt asked.

Taryn looked up from her laptop and smiled. "Yes, yes I do. I feel better now. Cheyenne is at rest. Everyone who should be in jail is. Emma's at home with her parents. And I keep getting emails from students begging me not to leave. I have no idea *why*, because I think I'm a pretty crappy teacher, but oh well."

"You were worried that the EDS was what was causing your visions," Matt reminded her. He sat in the corner of the bedroom in the rocking chair, his feet propped up on the footstool. They'd barely touched since the party, both of them for different reasons.

"Yeah?"

"It *can't* be. I *saw* what you saw. I felt that energy around you. So did others. You're sick, but you're not crazy."

"Oh, I don't know about that," Taryn chuckled.

"I'm sorry about your costume," he apologized again. "I hope I didn't hurt you too badly."

"Oh, please. I like it a little rough, remember?" she tried to joke but it fell flat. Matt hadn't laughed a lot since that night. His unshakable world had been rocked, and he was still having difficulty acclimating himself to a world where someone admitted to setting up a rape and death and held a gun on Taryn. "And anyway, where the hell did you get a gun?"

"After your job at Windwood Farm. I promised myself I'd protect you, however I could. And I will. I don't like guns, but if that's what it takes then I'll do it. I took lessons and everything."

Of course Matt would.

"The club they formed, the one to supposedly solve Cheyenne's disappearance? It was Lindy's idea. A way to keep up with the investigation, to know what was going on. Maybe throw people off track. Emma and Mike didn't know," Taryn shook her head sadly.

"And the guy who supposedly drove her home?"

"Innocent bystander," Taryn said. "Well, maybe not so innocent. He was supplying the party favors. Jesus, Matt. These kids, and they were kids, were into hard stuff. This isn't the marijuana and beer of our youth. Okay, the beer and marijuana of my youth," she added when he scowled, "this was heroin, cocaine, meth. When the hell did that happen? When did the country kids give up skinny-dipping, horseback riding, and Alan Jackson and trade it in for needles and gang rape? I mean, my God!"

"It's an interstate town. Easy access for these kids. Bad people looking to make a profit. Times have changed, Taryn," he said sadly and both nodded their heads in bewilderment.

"I have felt like I was born into the wrong time period for a long time. I just didn't realize how out of touch I am," Taryn said.

"I was always a future-looking kind of guy," he agreed. "But I think I'm starting to fall over onto your side of the line. Are we getting that old? I feel a little sorry for all of them."

"Yeah, well, I feel a little sorry for the house," she admitted.

Matt laughed and then realized she was serious. "How? Why?"

Taryn shrugged, feeling self-conscious. "I don't know. I guess because it was built in a more innocent time, probably had happy memories of seeing a family live there, kids grow up there. And now it's a crime scene, a witness to something horrible it doesn't understand. That's just as much a part of its memory now as the sad stuff."

"Yeah, well, look on the bright side," he snorted. "Maybe something just as bad happened in it fifty years ago. You don't know!"

292

She laughed then, the first good laugh she'd had in a week.

"I don't get it," Matt confided at last. "I mean, they were graduating. High school was over. They could move on with their lives. Go in different directions. It sounds like this girl just got jealous and offed her competition in some drama."

"Yeah, maybe," Taryn conceded, "but I think there's more to it. Lindy said she was trapped. This town has held her in for so long – all her life. She was even enrolled in college in the same place. Cheyenne represented that sameness, that entrapment. Everything she hated about here."

"Then why not just leave?" Matt suggested. "Go to Atlanta, Chattanooga, Knoxville? There *are* other places."

"I don't think some people can," Taryn said slowly. "When a place is all you know you get comfortable, feel safe. Leaving is hard. You hate it, but it's got its arms wrapped around you so tightly you don't know how to wriggle out. It's hard to admit that the things that are holding you back are in your mind. Sometimes you need to something to blame, something external. And everyone talks about getting out, moving on, seeing the world. But actually loading up on the bus, that's a different story."

"Well, and then there's the fact that everyone involved had to have a few loose screws," Matt sighed.

"And then there's that."

They were quiet now, and Taryn leaned back on the bed, her legs stretched out in front of her. She'd made an appointment with her doctor in Nashville. She'd see him around the first of December. She'd signed up on a few online support groups and was shocked to find that little things she'd dismissed for years were actually a part of the EDS. But not the ghosts. Those were not in her head. Those were real.

It was no wonder Cheyenne's spirit had been so agitated, so hell-bent on scaring the wits out of Taryn. She'd been a teenage girl, raging with hormones, killed in a violent act. Hopefully, though, her spirit was at rest now. Taryn hadn't seen anything since the burial.

Something had changed in Thelma's and Jeff's faces. There had been an almost transparent veil of grayness covering them before; now they were brighter, more vibrant. Taryn herself recognized that veil as one she'd worn herself, a veil of grief, of yearning, of torture. "We can try to move forward now," Thelma whispered at the funeral. "I don't know how, but at least we know now. At least we know."

The town was shocked, rocked to the core. They'd been prepared to accept Travis as a kidnapper, or a killer. But never Lindy, and never the boys. Eric had been in ROTC, Brad a football player who had taken the team to regionals. Travis had kept quiet during the storm that followed. As far as Taryn knew, nobody had reached out to him. She doubted they would. If she knew how things worked, she'd bet that the people in the community would carry on and pretend like nothing happened, slowly bringing him back into the fold until it was all just a bad memory.

"Did you decide anything about that job?" Matt asked, breaking her thoughts.

"The one back in Kentucky?" She shook her head to clear her mind. She felt herself drifting a lot these days, getting lost in her own mind. "I think I'm going to take it. They said I can start after Christmas. Should take about two months. I'm doing all the buildings they're wanting to rebuild and renovate."

"I'll have to go back to work soon," Matt said carefully.

"Yes, I know."

Something passed between them then, something indescribable. Matt walked over to her and knelt down at her side. He smelled of Ivory soap and mint-scented shaving cream.

"She didn't have to do what she did," he said softly. "She had a way out. She could've left."

Then he reached out and touched her cheek, a feather against her skin. And somewhere in the whirring of the dehumidifier, she heard music, the saddest song she'd ever heard. She could almost sing along with the words.

Acknowledgements

Although I did quite a bit of research on missing persons' cases for Dark Hollow Road, the story is from my own imagination. Still, there are several stories that stuck with me, especially the cases of Brookelyn Farthing and Brittanee Drexel– two young women who are still missing.

My own young son passed away in 2010 so I felt a connection with these parents who are still hanging in limbo, not knowing for sure what happened to their children. And I can say, in all honesty, some of their stories have kept me up at night.

Special thanks to my husband for reading over the first drafts and listening to me talk incessantly about the story; to my beta readers for their feedback, and to the Ehlers-Danlos community for their continued support. For more information, visit:

Help Find Brittannee Drexel:

http://helpfindbrittaneedrexel.com/

Missing: Brookelyn Farthing:

https://www.facebook.com/MissingBrookelynFarthing

The Charley Project: Rachel Cooke:

http://www.charleyproject.org/cases/c/cooke_rachel.html

The Ehlers-Danlos National Foundation:

About the Author

Rebecca Patrick-Howard is the author of several books including the first book in her paranormal mystery trilogy *Windwood Farm.* She lives in eastern Kentucky with her husband and two children.

Rebecca's other books include:

Windwood Farm (Book 1 in Taryn's Camera)
Griffith Tavern (Book 2 in Taryn's Camera)
A Summer of Fear
Four Months of Terror
Haunted Estill County
More Tales from Haunted Estill County
Coping with Grief: The Anti-Guide to Infant Loss

Visit her website at www.rebeccaphoward.net and sign up for her newsletter to receive free books, special offers, and news.

Sneak Peek at *Shaker Town*, Book 4 in *Taryn's Camera*

Prologue

The water below was brown and muddy, swollen from the rain the night before. It rose above the creek bank and lapped at the poplar and spruce trees, threatening to drag them down to its murky depths. Off in the distance the bees buzzed furiously, awake and busy after a long winter. Clusters of daffodils grew in the sunny spots, their bright, yellow faces peeping up from the brown, neglected clumps of dirt.

The sobs that escaped from parched lips were dry now, beaten. Most of the tears were long gone and what were left were raspy and slid down tender cheeks, red and chapped from the salt and wind. It was difficult to believe a person could have anything left, after spending most of the night in sorrow.

Loose branches had torn at clothes, leaving then hanging from the body in shreds in some places. A small puddle of blood pooled on the ground and dried, staining the earth with its vulgar shade of red.

They would be coming soon; someone would be there to coax the lost soul back. There would be murmuring, praying, but very little nurturing. What happened when the person was beyond redemption? Beyond saving?

There, caught in the spring breeze, was the light trickle of voices – mostly men. They would be irritated to leave their work, to search for someone who didn't want to be found. But it was their duty and they'd see to it.

There wasn't much time now.

The rocks in hand were heavy and caused tired hands to ache. But they weren't as heavy as the stones in the pocket. Those were the important ones.

Up on the ridge, in the tree line, the voices grew closer. Now the outline of bodies were visible. They'd be there soon, just as soon as they caught the quick flash of fabric in the naked tree branches.

Before another voice could call out, the world disappeared in a flurry and there was nothing but the feeling of soaring through the air, like the bird who sought a taste of freedom. And then, the pull of the water—sweet, dark, and cold.

Available Summer 2015

Shaker Village of Pleasant Hill

Made in the USA
Monee, IL
16 January 2023